Dirty Developments

ANNA & JOEL

THE ONE NIGHT STAND CLUB
BOOK THREE

CARISSA KNIGHT

eBook ISBN: 978-1-953304-24-7
Paperback ISBN: 978-1-953304-23-0

Tonight, I'm committing the ultimate betrayal. Stepping out on Valentine's Day.

Ugh, I think I just threw up in my mouth a little.

To be fair, it's not for romance—*God, no*—but for music. It's a weakness very few know about, but of course I had to open my stupid mouth once around Lily and now she knows. And as soon as Lily knows something, she never lets it die. Especially if it means she can find some way to connect with you over it. It's disgustingly sweet and impossible to say no to.

Ever since she found her soulmate, or whatever, in her childhood BFF London, she's made it her mission to spread the cheer to everyone else like some sort of lust-for-life fairy godmother. Insert eye roll.

"Anna, you need to get out of the house. Come with London and me—just for an hour or two. I promise, it will be fun," Lily had said, wielding her damn empathetic eyes like weapons of mass guilt.

Fun for her, *maybe*.

For me? Missing an evening of coding brilliance, spicy chips, and snarky banter with Alexa feels like sacrilege.

And yet... here I am, God help me.

When I step inside the café, I'm immediately hit with the heady aroma of overpriced coffee and misplaced dreams.

The place is *annoyingly* charming, like it was designed by someone with a Pinterest addiction and a trust fund. Strings of fairy lights crisscross the ceiling, their warm glow pooling over mismatched chairs and tables that look like they've been rescued from various garage sales. The walls are covered in vintage posters of bands no one listens to anymore, and there's a chalkboard menu that's trying a little too hard to be quirky.

The clientele? Oh, it's a hipster's paradise.

I count at least three ironic beanies and four acoustic guitars before I even make it past the doorway. Someone in the corner is wearing a corduroy jacket that probably has its own Instagram account.

I sigh and adjust my glasses, stepping aside to let Lily sweep in like she owns the place. She's practically glowing with enthusiasm, while I'm already calculating the number of polite nods I'll need to fake before I can make a quick and silent escape.

"Isn't it *cute*?" Lily gushes, spinning around like we've stumbled into a romcom set.

"Adorable," I deadpan, shifting my belt bag to tuck it under my left arm.

She shoots me a look but doesn't argue. She knows better. Instead, she grabs my arm and steers me toward the counter. I let her do the ordering because I'm too busy plotting my exit strategy. A dirty chai latte ends up in my hand before I can protest, and Lily's already scanning the room.

"There's London. Come on," she points to the front like she's just found buried treasure. I guess for her, that could be true.

"Have fun," I mutter, veering in the opposite direction.

I can hear Lily's sigh before she flits off to the front like a caffeinated hummingbird, leaving me alone with my drink, my phone, and my scorn.

The back corner calls to me like a sanctuary, far from the stage and the too-loud laughter of people who probably journal their dreams in bullet points. I slump into a chair and take a sip of my drink, reveling in the spices and caffeine.

Gotta admit, the chai's not bad, I'll give it that, but the rest of the evening already feels like a waste of time.

I tap open a game on my phone, but my ears betray me, catching snippets of the first act.

It's a duo—*of course it's a duo*—one strumming a guitar while the other sways like they're channeling the spirit of Woodstock. Their harmonies are... *ambitious*, let's call it that.

A soft snort escapes me as the lyrics hit a cringeworthy crescendo. Another romantic confession masquerading as art. Groundbreaking. *Gag.*

I take another sip of my chai, resisting the urge to check the time. It's going to be a long night but at least I can do it in peace.

The duo finishes their set to polite applause, and the hum of conversation resumes. I exhale in relief, my nervous system dropping into a low hum.

One down, who knows how many to go? Maybe I'll slip out after the next act. Lily will be too absorbed in her lovebird bubble to notice my absence.

The emcee steps onto the stage, a wiry guy with a man bun and a blazer two sizes too small. "Next up, we've got someone special for you. You may have seen him on much larger stages, but our man is back to his hometown, and we managed to snag him for tonight. Give it up for *Joel Price.*"

My chai nearly slips out of my hand.

No.

Not possible.

But then I see him.

Joel strides onto the stage with the kind of effortless confidence that makes you want to trip him. The dim lights catch the slight wave in his dark hair, falling into his eyes just enough to make it look intentional. He's wearing a leather jacket over a plain black tee, fitted just enough to hint at the muscles beneath.

He looks good. *Annoyingly* good. Like the universe is playing a cruel joke on me.

I sink deeper into my chair, my pulse quickening despite my best efforts to stay detached.

He adjusts the strap of his guitar, his movements unhurried but deliberate, like he owns the room—or maybe just doesn't care if he doesn't. Honestly, that's worse.

"Thank you for coming out tonight," Joel says into the mic, his voice smooth and confident, drawing the room's focus effortlessly. He adjusts the guitar strap on his shoulder and leans into the stand, his green eyes scanning the crowd with practiced ease. "It's good to be back in Duluth. It's been too long."

The crowd murmurs their agreement.

Meanwhile, I sink lower into my chair, silently willing the dim lighting to work some kind of miracle and render me invisible. No such luck. As his gaze sweeps the room, it catches on me.

Fuck.

His eyes widen slightly—just enough for me to notice.

Oh yeah, he's surprised to see me. *Good.* That makes two of us, you sanctimonious troglodyte.

I arch a brow, lifting my chai in a mock toast. "Congratulations, you have eyes," I mutter under my breath, the words drowned out by the hum of the café.

For a moment, he looks like he's debating something, his fingers gripping the neck of his guitar just a bit tighter. Then he clears his throat, recovering fast, and shifts back into Mr. Perfect Performer.

"And since it's Valentine's Day," he says, his voice

back to that annoyingly smooth tone, "this one's for the lovebirds out there."

The room lets out a collective *aww* as Joel strums the first chord. Couples lean into each other, their hands brushing over tabletops, their heads tilting just so.

I resist the urge to gag. *Barely.*

But then the melody kicks in, and my stomach flips.

No. Not *this.*

The song pulls at memories I've spent years trying to bury. My chest tightens as the opening notes wash over me, and I clutch my chai cup like it's a stress ball.

Joel starts singing, and the weight in the room shifts. His voice, raw and deliberate, wraps around every corner of the café.

It's too much. *Too familiar.*

And then it happens—his eyes find mine again.

Oh, for the love of—*seriously?*

His gaze lingers, steady and deliberate, like he's trying to say something. Like this whole damn performance is some kind of message meant for me.

Absolutely the fuck not.

The air between us feels heavier, charged with something I refuse to acknowledge. My heart thunders as I sit frozen in place, his voice pushing and pulling at emotions I don't want to feel.

Nope. Nope. *A thousand times nope.*

The scrape of my chair echoes through the café as I shove it back and stand, breaking whatever connection he thinks we're having. A few heads turn, but I don't care. My only goal is *out.*

I adjust my bag over my shoulder and make a beeline for the door, my boots clunking against the floor like punctuation marks to my exit. I'm sure a few people noticed me leave—maybe even whispered about it—but I don't care. Not about their opinions, not about the song, not about him.

I'll apologize to Lily later, but right now, I don't even care about her.

The cold hits me the second I push through the café door, sharp and bracing. It pricks at my cheeks, but it's not enough to cool the heat of frustration simmering beneath my skin. I pull my coat tighter around me and pick up my pace, the muffled sound of Joel's song trailing behind me like a phantom.

I'm halfway across the parking lot when the music stops abruptly. The sound cuts out mid-verse, leaving an echo in its place.

I pause, frowning, and glance over my shoulder. The stage is out of sight, but the café door swings open, spilling warm light and a murmur of confused voices into the cold night air.

My blood runs cold and for some stupid reason, I turn on my heel, racing for my Subaru.

And then I hear him.

"Anna!"

His voice is sharp, insistent, and closer than I expected.

I whirl around to find Joel jogging toward me, his leather jacket catching the glow of the streetlamp above. His breath fogs in the icy air, and he's clutching something in his hand—a crumpled envelope.

"What the hell, Joel?" I snap, my pulse hammering in my ears. "Did you seriously stop your set to chase me?"

He slows as he approaches, his expression unreadable but tinged with something I can't place. "I had to," he says, his voice quieter now. "You were leaving."

"Yeah, no kidding. I'm *still* leaving." I jab a thumb toward my car. "You didn't have to make a scene about it."

Joel exhales sharply, his breath visible in the cold, and holds out the envelope. "This is for you," he says, ignoring my tone.

I glance at it, then back at him. My defenses flare up instantly. "What is it?"

"Just... take it," he says, his voice steady but softer now. *"Please."*

I hesitate, every instinct screaming at me to walk away. But my curiosity wins out, and I step forward, snatching the envelope from his hand. The paper crinkles under my fingers, heavier than it should be.

"What is this supposed to be?" I ask, my voice sharp. "Some kind of apology?"

Joel doesn't flinch, but his jaw tightens. "You'll figure it out," he whispers.

I don't miss the flicker of something in his eyes— something raw, unguarded. It throws me off for a second, but I recover quickly.

"Thanks for the mystery," I say flatly, stuffing the

envelope into my back pocket. "Now, if you'll excuse me—"

"Anna," he says again, his voice low, almost pleading.

But I don't let him finish. Turning sharply, I march the rest of the way to my vehicle, yanking the door open and sliding inside before he can say another word.

The envelope presses against my backside, an unwelcome reminder of whatever Joel thinks he's doing. I grip the steering wheel and take a shaky breath, staring at the frost-edged windshield.

Whatever this is, I'm not ready to deal with it.

Not tonight.

I knew I should have stayed home.

CHAPTER 1

Anna

I f there's one thing I hate more than Valentine's Day, it's uninvited memories of Valentine's Day.

Unfortunately, both seem to be making a comeback, despite my best efforts to ignore them.

Case in point: the unopened envelope in my desk drawer.

It's been eighteen months, and it still sits there, quietly mocking me every time I open *that* drawer.

I should have tossed it. Burned it. Turned it into an origami crane and set it afloat on Lake Superior.

But *no*. Like the masochist I am, I kept it.

So, naturally, my brother Ethan needs a damn phone charger. And, of course, the only spare I have is tucked away in *that* fucking drawer.

I yank it open with an exaggerated sigh, my annoyance amplified by the sound of Ethan rummaging in my kitchen like a raccoon. The envelope is right there, lying in wait like it knows I've been trying to forget about it.

"Find anything?" Ethan calls out, his voice muffled, probably because his face is buried in my leftover dumplings now.

"Working on it," I snap, shoving aside a tangle of USB cords, sticky notes, and a half-empty pack of gum. My hand brushes against the envelope, and my stomach twists.

It feels heavier than it should—like it's stuffed with bad decisions and unresolved feelings instead of paper or God knows what else. It could be filled with the tears of children, for all I know.

Ethan appears in the doorway, a dumpling poised halfway to his mouth. "Why do I feel like you're having a meltdown over something that's not a charger?"

"I'm not having a meltdown," I say, pulling out the charger and slamming the drawer shut before the envelope can suck me into its vortex of regret.

He leans casually against the doorframe, smirking. "That your *'I'm lying'* voice?"

"It's my *'shut up and take this stupid charger'* voice, jerk," I snap, tossing it at him a little harder than necessary. "Get your own damn charger, too. That one stays here."

Ethan catches it easily, his smirk deepening. "You're touchy today."

"You're *annoying* today," I shoot back.

He shrugs, unbothered, and heads back to the kitchen.

I collapse into my chair, glaring at the closed drawer like it's the embodiment of all my unresolved life choices.

"Thanks for the charger," Ethan says, wandering back into the kitchen to scavenge the rest of my leftovers by the sound of it. When he returns, he nods toward my desk. "You know, you could really stand to organize that drawer. It's a disaster."

"It's organized chaos," I mutter, not wanting to get into it.

He laughs as he pops another dumpling into his mouth. "Sure it is. Anyway, it's nice to be out of the house. Do you know how loud a newborn is? It's like she's trying to win an Olympic gold in screaming."

I snort. "What did you expect? Babies cry, Ethan. She's not going to come out quoting Aristotle."

"Yeah, well, nobody warned me it would be *this* constant," he says, leaning against the counter. "At one point, I swear Mina screamed for three hours straight. Three. Hours. Tess kept looking at me like I could fix it, and I'm just standing there wondering if I've aged ten years overnight."

"Welcome to parenthood," I say dryly, spinning my chair halfway toward him. "You signed up for this, remember?"

"Don't remind me," he groans. "Mom's been calling non-stop too, trying to set up some big Korean family celebration to introduce the baby. I'm like, can we not? We don't need to do a doljanchi."

I chuckle, shaking my head. "Let me guess—she

wants the full hanbok treatment, right? All the cousins, a table full of food nobody eats?"

Ethan's laugh is full of exasperation. "You know it. She's already talking about renting out the church basement."

"Classic Mom," I say, grinning despite myself. "Did she at least call it a 'suggestion' to make it seem like you had a choice?"

"Of course she did," Ethan says, rolling his eyes. "I'm not falling for that again. You'd think after thirty years, I'd have figured out how to say no to her."

"Good luck with that," I say, leaning back in my chair. "She's probably already ordered the catering."

We laugh, the easy banter briefly cutting through the tension I've been carrying all morning.

"So," Ethan says, casually shifting topics as he finishes his last dumpling, "Joel's back in town."

I freeze, the humor draining from my face. "Yeah, I know," I say tightly.

Ethan blinks, clearly surprised by my reaction. "You do?"

"It's not exactly a secret," I snap. "It's all over the internet. Every other post is 'Joel Price Returns to Duluth!' like it's some kind of headline-worthy event."

"I mean, some people think it's pretty awesome. Just because you—"

I shoot him a glare that could cap a rhino at the knees.

Ethan raises his hands in mock surrender. "Okay,

okay. I just thought I'd mention it, in case you hadn't heard."

"Well, I have," I say, crossing my arms. "And before you even start—no, I'm not going to see him."

Ethan sighs, leaning against the door frame. "Anna, it's not like he came back to mess with you. He's got a gig at Club Nocté. That's it. I don't understand why you have such a problem with him."

I narrow my eyes at him, my fingers drumming against the arm of my chair. "You don't understand? Really? You're standing there, eating *my* dumplings, in *my* house, and you think this is the time to question why I have a problem with Joel fucking Price?"

Ethan shrugs, like he's genuinely baffled. "He's my best friend and practically family. He's a good guy."

"Oh, sure," I say, the sarcasm dripping off my words. "Saint Joel. Paragon of moral integrity. How could I possibly have a problem with him?"

"You're being dramatic."

"And you're being oblivious." I push out of my chair, pacing to the window and staring out at the quiet street. It's a perfect late September day—crisp air, golden leaves swirling lazily in the breeze. The kind of day that shouldn't be wasted thinking about Joel Price.

Ethan sighs again, that big-brother-patient kind of sigh that makes me want to throw something. "He's not the same guy he was as kids, you know. People change, Anna."

"Oh, please," I say, spinning back to face him. "This isn't about *people*. This is about Joel. And Joel doesn't change. He just gets better at pretending he's not a self-absorbed—"

"Stop," Ethan says quickly, cutting me off before I can finish. "I get it. You don't like him. But you can't avoid him forever."

"Watch me," I mutter, crossing my arms again.

Ethan shakes his head, a faint smile tugging at the corners of his mouth. "You're ridiculous, you know that?"

"And yet, you keep coming over," I snap back, though there's no real heat in it.

He chuckles, pushing off the doorframe. "Alright, I'll drop it. Just... don't make things weird when you run into him. Because you will run into him if Mom's scheming comes to fruition."

"I'm not the one who makes things weird," I say, sitting back down and flipping open my laptop. "Joel's got that covered all by himself."

Ethan snorts, but he doesn't argue. Instead, he shakes his head. "Well, I suppose I better head back. Wish me luck."

"Tell Tess I said hi," I call after him, rolling my chair to the doorway. "And leave the charger here!"

"Yeah, yeah," he says, putting his jacket on and pulling the front door open. He pauses, looking back at me with a thoughtful expression. "You know, you might want to open that envelope someday. Just saying."

I glare at him as the door closes behind him.

For a long moment, I sit there, the room silent except for the faint hum of my laptop. My eyes drift to the desk drawer, where the stupid envelope is no doubt sitting smugly, waiting for its moment to ruin my life.

Why did Ethan have to bring it up? And why does it sound like he knows something? Maybe Joel told him. Or worse—maybe Joel told *Mom*.

If she's using the hanbok parade as some kind of Trojan horse to force me and Joel into the same room, I might actually lose it. I mean, I love Mina, but introducing her to the world doesn't have to come with a side of *family drama*.

I groan, letting my head thunk back against the chair. Ethan's probably right about one thing: I won't be able to avoid Joel forever. Duluth isn't big enough, especially with Mom's enthusiasm for a guest list that always includes people we're *totally* not still mad at.

I glance at the drawer again, half-expecting the envelope to wiggle out on its own, like it's taunting me. "Just open me, Anna. What's the worst that could happen?"

Oh, I don't know. *Everything*.

I shove the thought aside and spin my chair toward my laptop, resolutely ignoring the drawer. Joel Price can have his stupid homecoming, his stupid guitar, and whatever he stuffed into that envelope.

Me? I'll be over here, pretending I don't care.

Because denial? Denial is a perfectly valid coping strategy.

CHAPTER 2

Joel

T he Twin Ports haven't changed much.

Superior still feels like the scrappy underdog to Duluth's polished charm, but there's something comforting about that. The streets are a little quieter here, the buildings a little rougher around the edges. It feels more real—less like it's trying to impress you.

Which is good, because I've had enough of trying to impress people.

I park my Jeep outside Club Nocté and kill the engine, staring up at the venue like it holds the answers to questions I'm too scared to ask. It's a good spot, though. A regular stop for touring acts who are in the know— intimate but not claustrophobic. It's the kind of place that could give you momentum if you play it right.

But let's be honest—I didn't come back just to play it right.

I came back for Anna.

That thought lands like a punch to the gut, but it's

the truth. Eighteen months since I last saw her, and I still haven't figured out how to fix things with her.

The envelope didn't help. That much is obvious. If it had, I wouldn't be here, trying to convince myself that proximity might be the key to earning her forgiveness.

I run a hand through my hair and sigh, leaning back against the headrest.

Knowing her, she's probably still furious. And I can't even blame her. I was stupid and thoughtless. But if I'm going to make this right, I can't keep avoiding her—or the consequences of what I did.

My phone buzzes in the cupholder, Ethan's name lighting up the screen.

> Dinner. My place. 7 PM. You're coming. I need adult conversation.

I snort, shaking my head. Classic Ethan. He's never been big on subtlety.

Fine, I type back, hitting send before I can overthink it.

Hopping out, I shove my phone into my back pocket and grab my guitar case from the backseat. The cool September air hits me the second I step out of the Jeep, sharp and bracing like a wake-up call I didn't ask for. The sign above Club Nocté's door flickers faintly in the twilight, its neon casting a deep red glow on the cracked pavement beneath my boots.

This place is the kind of venue that makes you work for it, where the magic isn't handed to you—you have to earn it.

I shoulder my guitar case and step inside Club Nocté, the steel door closing behind me with a heavy clang that echoes in the dimly lit space. The hum of the place is almost palpable—low conversations, the muted thrum of a soundcheck in progress, and the faint clink of glassware from the bar. The energy here is grounded, intimate, and alive in a way that makes you feel like you're part of something bigger the second you walk in.

At the far end of the bar, a man I assume is London St. James looks up from a laptop. His sharp features are illuminated by the glow of the screen, and the easy confidence in his posture tells me he's in charge.

"Ah, Joel Price," he says, his voice smooth but with an unmistakable edge of enthusiasm. He closes the laptop and strides toward me, extending a hand. "London St. James. Good to finally meet you."

"Likewise," I reply, shaking his hand.

"I've heard a lot about you," London says, nodding toward the guitar case slung over my shoulder. "She won't admit it, but Myles wouldn't shut up about getting you on our stage. I'm glad it worked out."

"Me too," I say, glancing around the space. "This place has a good vibe."

"Appreciate it," London replies, his smirk widening. "We work hard to keep it that way. Nocté's about creating moments to remember, not just music."

Before I can respond, the door to the back room swings open, and a woman with bright purple hair cropped on one side and longer on the other strides out, clipboard in hand. She's dressed in a fitted black tee, cargo pants, and combat boots, her sharp gaze locking onto me immediately.

"Myles," London says, gesturing toward her, "meet Joel Price."

Myles narrows her eyes at London before turning her attention to me. She steps closer, her movements quick and deliberate, like she's always in control. If I didn't know London was the manager, I would have pegged her for the gig instead.

"So, you're the guy Tess wouldn't stop raving about," Myles says, leaning against the bar with her arms crossed. Her multicolored eyes flick over me, sharp and calculating, but there's the faintest glimmer of something else—approval, maybe. "She says you're good. Guess we'll find out."

"I'll try not to disappoint," I reply evenly, matching her gaze.

She raises an eyebrow, a small smirk tugging at her lips. "Oh, you won't. If Tess is right—and she usually is —you'll kill it. But I've got a reputation to uphold, so I've got to give you the whole *don't screw it up* speech anyway."

I chuckle, relaxing a fraction. "Consider me properly warned."

"Good," she says, straightening up and grabbing a rag to wipe down the bar. "Saint doesn't take risks on people unless I nudge him, so don't make me regret it. Not that I think you will."

She says it casually, but the confidence in her tone carries weight. It's not every day someone with her presence lets slip they already believe in you.

"Saint?" I ask, confused.

Myles tips her head at London and keeps wiping.

"Ah."

London, who's been watching the exchange with a faintly amused expression, steps in. "Myles likes to put people in their place, but trust me—she doesn't waste her time on people she doesn't think can deliver."

"Noted," I say, nodding toward her. "Thanks for sticking your neck out."

Myles shrugs, tossing the rag over her shoulder. "Thank Tess. She wouldn't shut up about you. Said you've been looking for the right places to get back into the scene here."

I nod, the mention of Tessa sending a flicker of gratitude through me. She's the one who suggested Nocté in the first place, her knack for connecting people kicking in like clockwork. We've been texting on and off for weeks—her recommending venues, me explaining what I was looking for. That's all she knows, as far as I'm aware.

But Tessa's not just a helpful busybody—she's a strategist. She puts people where they need to be. And whether or not she realizes how deep things run with Anna, I can't help but wonder if she had a bigger picture in mind when she pushed me toward Nocté.

London's voice pulls me back to the present. "Mark's already at the soundboard. Let's get you set up so you're ready for tomorrow."

I nod, following after him.

The stage is cozy—intimate, even—but it's got a presence that makes you feel like every note you play is going to matter. As I unpack my guitar, Mark glances up from the soundboard and gives me a nod.

"Joel Price, right?" he says, his voice calm and professional.

"That's me," I reply, tuning my guitar.

"Cool. Been looking forward to hearing you play."

"Been looking forward to it, as well," I reply, strumming a quick chord that rings out across the room.

Mark smirks and adjusts a few knobs. "Let's start with the acoustic and work our way up."

We run through the setup smoothly, Mark balancing the sound with the precision of someone who's been doing this for years. By the time we're done, the room feels alive, humming with potential even though it's empty.

I pack up my gear and sling the guitar case over my shoulder, stepping off the stage as London meets me near the bar.

"You're set," he says, nodding approvingly. "Tomorrow night, just give them the real stuff. Nocté's crowd doesn't want gimmicks—they want heart."

"I can do that," I say, shaking his hand.

As I head for the door, I catch Myles's eye from across the bar. She leans against the counter, a drink in hand, watching me with that same sharp gaze.

"Don't make me regret it, Price," she says, lifting her glass in a mock toast.

"I won't," I say, casting a wave as I head for the door.

❧

By the time I pull into Ethan's driveway, the sun's low on the horizon, spilling gold and orange across the trees. The crisp air bites at my skin as I step out of the Jeep and grab my guitar case from the back.

"About time," Ethan says, grinning as he opens the door. "I was starting to think you got lost on the way here."

"I'd have to try pretty hard to get lost in Duluth," I reply, stepping inside and shrugging off my jacket.

Ethan laughs, clapping me on the shoulder as he leads me into the kitchen. It's a familiar space, warm and cluttered with the kind of chaos that comes from having a newborn in the house.

"Grab a beer," Ethan says, gesturing to the fridge. "Tess is upstairs with Mina, so it's just us for now. Anna should be here soon."

My hand freezes halfway to the fridge handle. "Anna's coming?"

Ethan looks at me like I've just asked if water's wet. "Uh, yeah. She's my sister. You knew that, right?"

Of course I knew that. I just didn't think she'd be *here*.

Freaking Korean families. They always make a big deal about things. I'm surprised he didn't invite his parent's too, come to think of it.

"Right," I say, grabbing a beer and twisting off the cap. "Got it."

Ethan smirks, clearly enjoying my discomfort.

"Relax, man. It's just dinner. You two can manage a meal without killing each other, can't you?"

Before I can respond, the sound of the front door opening cuts through the room.

"Ethan!" Anna's voice is sharp, followed by the unmistakable sound of boots thudding against the hardwood. "Where is that adorable baby. I need some Mina time."

I don't even have time to brace myself before she rounds the corner, her hair piled into a messy bun and her leather jacket slung casually over one arm. She stops short when she sees me, her eyes narrowing like I'm something she scraped off her shoe.

"Joel."

"Anna," I reply, keeping my tone as casual as I can manage.

She crosses her arms, shifting her weight onto one hip. "What the hell are you doing here?"

"It's called *dinner*," Ethan says from behind me, his tone infuriatingly calm as he slowly pronounces dinner.

Her glare shifts to him, then back to me. "You invited him to dinner without telling me?"

Ethan shrugs, clearly unbothered. "Seemed like a good idea at the time."

"Unbelievable," Anna mutters, shaking her head. "Fine. Whatever. I'm starving and you ate all of my dumplings." Then she slowly and deliberately turns to me, locking her cold gaze on me. "Just don't expect me to play nice."

I raise my beer in a mock toast, a smirk tugging at the

corner of my mouth, despite my heart hammering in my chest. "Wouldn't dream of it."

Her eyes narrow even further, but she doesn't take the bait. Instead, she grabs a plate from the counter and mutters something about regretting every life choice that brought her here.

Ethan just grins, cracking open his own beer. "This is going to be fun."

Fun. Right.

If this is how the night's starting, I'm going to need another beer—and probably a miracle if I'm ever going to fix this mess.

CHAPTER 3

Anna

I should've known Ethan's dinner invite came with strings attached.

But I was too busy debugging a project that refused to cooperate—and too irritated with him for raiding my fridge yet again—to question it. When he said, *Dinner's on me,* I figured it was his way of making up for eating the last of my dumplings.

Turns out, I should've asked a few more questions. Like who else was on the guest list.

Now Joel freaking Price is sitting across from me, smirking like he owns the place, and I'm two seconds away from shoving my chopsticks up his nose.

"So, Anna," Joel says, his tone casual and infuriatingly smug. "Still coding your life away, or did you finally decide to join the rest of us in the real world?"

I stab at my rice, glaring at him over the rim of my bowl. "Still coding," I say tightly. "Some of us like to use our brains for a living."

Joel leans back in his chair, unfazed. "Hey, I use my brain. It takes real effort to deal with people who think they're superior to everyone else."

I blink, caught off guard for half a second before snapping back. "Funny. I didn't realize playing guitar for drunk twenty-somethings required critical thinking skills."

Ethan laughs into his beer, clearly enjoying this way too much. "Alright, alright. Let's keep it civil, kids. Anna, pass the kimchi."

I shove the dish toward him with more force than necessary, the plate scraping against the table.

"You two haven't changed a bit," Tessa says from her seat beside Ethan, her tone light and teasing. "It's almost nostalgic."

"Not the word I'd use," I mutter, earning a low chuckle from Joel.

Tessa shifts her focus to Mina, who's babbling happily in her highchair, her tiny hands smacking against the tray as she grins at nothing in particular.

Mina's laugh breaks through my annoyance like a little ray of sunshine, and I can't help but soften as I reach over to tickle her chubby hand. "Hey, Mina Bean. Are you causing trouble for your mom and dad yet?"

Mina squeals in response, kicking her legs and flashing a gummy smile that makes my heart melt despite my sour mood. She grabs my finger with surprising strength, her tiny fingers curling tightly around it.

"She's practicing her villain laugh," Ethan says,

nudging Tessa with his elbow. "Pretty sure she's plotting something."

"She gets that from you, Anna" Tessa shoots back with a smirk, wiping some sweet potato puree from Mina's cheek. "Pretty sure she's planning on waking up at two in the morning again."

"Smart girl," I say, smiling at Mina as she gurgles something unintelligible, then lets out another squeal. I tap her nose gently, earning a delighted giggle that makes the corner of my mouth twitch upward despite the company.

"See?" Tessa says, tilting her head at me. "Mina loves you. You can't be mad when she's around."

I narrow my eyes at her. "Mina is a delight. Don't think that means I'm giving anyone else a free pass."

Joel snorts softly, drawing my attention back to him. "Glad to know I'm not even competing with the baby."

"You'd lose," I shoot back, the warmth I felt with Mina quickly replaced by irritation.

Joel raises his glass, clearly enjoying himself, which is annoying. "Wouldn't dream of trying."

Mina babbles again, kicking her legs as if to emphasize the point. I glance back at her, my finger still captured in her little hand, and decide she's the only reason I'm still sitting at this table.

"So," Joel says, setting his chopsticks down with deliberate ease, "where's a guy supposed to stay in town these days? Mina took over my old crash pad, and I'm running out of options."

Panic flashes across Tessa's face, just for a second, before her gaze locks on mine.

"No," I say immediately, furiously shaking my head. "Don't even—"

But Tessa's already smiling, that too-sweet look that means trouble. "Anna has a spare room she never uses. It's perfect."

Joel's eyebrows lift, and he turns to me, his eyes wide. At least he has the good sense to show a little panic, too.

"Tessa," I snap, my voice tight with warning.

"What?" she says, shrugging innocently. "You're always saying how quiet it is living alone. A little company might be nice."

"Company?" I repeat, incredulous. "We're talking about *that*, not a lost puppy."

"Hey," Joel says, raising his hands in mock offense. "I'm right here, you know."

I mimic playing a violin.

Ethan, who's been suspiciously quiet, finally chimes in. "Actually, that's not a bad idea. Joel's practically family, and you've got the space."

"Practically family?" I glare at him. "Last I checked, we weren't related."

"Close enough," Ethan says with a shrug. "And you know how Mom and Dad raised us. Family helps family."

I groan, rubbing my temples. "This isn't a family emergency, Ethan. It's Joel being Joel. Besides, he can find a hotel. There's plenty of them in Duluth."

"Come on, Anna," Tessa says, her tone dripping with

false innocence. "It's just for a little while. He's not staying in Duluth forever. Right, Joel?"

"Right," Joel says smoothly, leaning forward to rest his elbows on the table. "I wouldn't want to overstay my welcome. And I can pay—you know, rent."

"You're not staying at all!" I snap, my chopsticks frozen midair.

What is his deal, anyway? He has to know this will be uncomfortable for both of us, but there he is, grinning like he's just won the lottery. Is he *trying* to make me miserable, or is he really out of options?

Knowing Joel, it's probably both.

"Why not?" Ethan asks, giving me that annoyingly reasonable big-brother look. "Like Tess said, it's not like you're using the room."

"Because," I say, scrambling for an excuse, "he'll ruin the vibe!"

Joel raises an eyebrow, his grin bordering on wicked. "Ruin the vibe? That's harsh, even for you, Chang."

"I'm serious," I hiss. "You're not staying with me."

Ethan sighs dramatically, leaning back in his chair. "Anna, you're being ridiculous. Where's your sense of hospitality? Do I have to call Mom?"

"I don't think hospitality applies to freeloaders," I snap, shooting a pointed glare at Joel. "And you wouldn't dare bring Mom into this."

Ethan makes a face that dares me to question him, and I clench my fists under the table.

"Anna," Tessa says, her voice calm but firm, "you're not being fair. Joel's just asking for a little help, and you're acting like it's the end of the world." She pauses, glancing at Mina with a knowing smile. "It's not like he's asking you to share your dumplings."

Joel snorts, his grin widening, and I narrow my eyes at him.

"Don't encourage him," I mutter, stabbing my chopsticks into my rice.

Joel raises his hands, the picture of faux innocence. "Hey, I said I'd pay rent. That's hardly freeloading."

"You couldn't pay me enough to deal with you," I fire back, the heat in my voice rising.

"Come on, Anna," Tessa cuts in, her tone infuriatingly calm. "It's just for a couple of weeks. You're always saying how quiet it is living alone. It might actually be nice to have someone around."

I whip my head toward her, my jaw dropping. "Did you just say Joel would be *nice* to have around? Have you met him?"

Joel smirks, leaning forward on his elbows. "Careful, Ace. That almost sounded like a compliment."

"It wasn't," I snap, glaring at him. "And don't call me that."

Mina lets out a happy squeal, slapping the tray of her highchair with both hands. The noise breaks the tension for a brief moment, and I look at her, desperate for a distraction.

"You see?" Ethan says, gesturing toward Mina with a grin. "Even the baby thinks it's a good idea."

"Do *not* drag Mina into this," I spit back.

"Anna, seriously," Tessa says, leaning forward with

that annoyingly reasonable look she always gets when she's about to corner me. "You're making this a bigger deal than it needs to be."

"It'll feel like forever," I groan, looking at the ceiling as I feel my resolve slipping. I'm fighting a losing battle and I know it.

Joel tilts his head, his grin softening just enough to throw me off. "Look, I get it. I'm not exactly your favorite person. But I'll stay out of your way. Promise."

I snort. "That's rich, coming from the guy who can't go five minutes without making a snarky comment."

"Who, me?" Joel asks, his eyes wide with mock innocence.

"Yes, you," I snap.

"I think you might have us confused," Joel says, scrunching his face slightly.

I raise my chopsticks and point them at him like a knife.

Ethan cuts in, his tone turning more serious. "Anna. Be reasonable. You know what Mom and Dad would say."

I groan, dragging a hand down my face. "I hate when you do that."

"It's true, though," Ethan says, his grin returning. "Besides, you're great at laying down rules. Just give him a list of things he's not allowed to do, and you'll be fine."

"A list?" Joel says, his tone bordering on amused disbelief. "What am I, a five-year-old?"

"You'd be lucky to qualify as a five-year-old," I mutter.

Tessa smiles, her voice softening just enough to drive the knife deeper. "Anna, you can totally handle him. We believe in you."

I stare at both of them, my frustration simmering just under the surface. They've got me boxed in, and they know it. If I say no, I'm the unreasonable one—the bad sibling who can't even spare a room for *"family."*

But if I say yes…

I look at Joel, who's watching me with that infuriating mix of amusement and challenge, like he knows exactly what's going through my head.

The problem isn't just that Joel is smug, or that he has a knack for irritating me like no one else. The problem is that letting him stay means no escaping him —not his voice, not his smirk, and definitely not the memories I've been working so hard to bury.

"Fine," I snap, slamming my chopsticks onto the table. "But there *will be* rules."

Joel raises an eyebrow. "Rules? I'm shocked."

"Yes, *rules*," I say, my voice sharp. "No loud music, no touching my stuff, and no bringing random people over. Got it?"

"Crystal clear," Joel says, his grin widening. "Anything else, boss?"

"Yeah," I say, pointing a finger at him. "Don't talk to me unless it's absolutely necessary."

"Got it," Joel says, raising his beer in a mock toast. "This is going to be fun."

"Fun isn't the word I'd use," I mutter, glaring at him.

Across the table, Ethan and Tessa exchange a look,

their expressions equal parts amused and triumphant. I resist the urge to throw my rice at them. Though I do imagine it a few times for good measure.

Joel leans back in his chair, looking far too comfortable for my liking. "Thanks for the hospitality, Ace. I'll try not to ruin the vibe."

"You're already ruining it," I snap, stabbing at my rice with unnecessary force. "And don't call me *that*." I repeat.

Mina lets out another happy squeal, breaking the tension just enough for everyone to laugh. Everyone except me.

I shove another bite of rice into my mouth, chewing harder than necessary to keep from saying something that'll start World War III. Joel sits there, grinning like he's always been part of this family—like he belongs here more than I do.

And maybe that's the worst part. It's not just that Joel's easy confidence gets under my skin—it's that he makes me feel like I don't fit in my own family. Like somehow, he's the better version of belonging, and I'm the one trying too hard.

It's *infuriating*.

A small, traitorous voice whispers that maybe I *am* being unreasonable. That maybe Ethan's right, and I should just get over myself. It's just a couple of weeks.

But no. *I'm* not the problem here. Joel's the one who walked back into my life, all charm and smirks, like he doesn't have a history of fucking me over.

And now I have to spend the next few weeks

pretending it doesn't bother me that the enemy is living in my damn house.

Joel raises his beer in another mock toast, and my glare sharpens. For a second, his grin flickers—so fast I'm not sure if I imagined it. But the moment passes, and Joel raises his beer like he's already won.

This is going to be a disaster. For *him*.

CHAPTER 4

Joel

I f Anna's glare could kill, I'd be six feet under by now.

I lean against the doorframe of her apartment, my guitar case in one hand and a duffel bag slung over my shoulder. She's standing in the middle of the living room, arms crossed and lips pressed so tightly together I'm surprised they haven't vanished entirely.

"Well," I say, breaking the silence, "home sweet home, huh?."

Her eyes narrow, and I'm pretty sure she's mentally picturing my head on a spike.

"Spare room's that way," she says, jerking her chin toward the hallway. "Don't touch anything, don't make noise, and don't even think about staying longer than absolutely necessary."

"Got it," I reply, giving her my best attempt at a neutral smile. "Anything else? Should I sign a behavior contract? Swear an oath of silence?"

"Don't tempt me." Her eyes narrow. "If you think this is a joke, you're in for a rough two weeks, Price."

"Noted," I say, dropping my duffel bag just enough to flex my shoulder. "So...what's the curfew? Midnight? Or should I be in bed by ten?"

Anna doesn't crack. Not even a twitch of her lips. "As long as I don't see or hear you, I don't care where you are or when."

"Wow," I say, raising an eyebrow. "You really know how to make a guy feel at home."

Her lips press tighter, but there's a flicker of annoyance in her eyes. "Home? Let's get one thing straight right the fuck now. This isn't your home. You're a temporary inconvenience. That's all."

"Harsh," I say, stepping into the living room and closing the front door. "What happened to all that *family helps family* talk from Ethan?"

"That's Ethan's rule, not mine," she snaps, crossing her arms again. "If it were up to me—"

"You'd have thrown me to the wolves," I finish, cutting her off with a grin. "Don't worry, Anna. I'll stay out of your way. Mostly."

"Good," she says, her voice cold. "Because if you don't, you'll regret it."

"Got it," I say, nodding toward the hallway. "Anything else? House rules about toothpaste caps or toilet seats?"

She exhales sharply, clearly done with the conversation. "I'm not your babysitter, Joel. Just... don't be an asshole. Think you can handle that?"

She spins on her heel before I can respond, disappearing into her room and slamming the door behind her.

Off to a great start.

The apartment falls silent after Anna disappears, leaving me alone in her space. I shift my weight awkwardly, my duffel bag heavy on my shoulder and my guitar case pulling on my other hand. The air feels charged, like it's holding its breath. Or maybe that's just me. I exhale, rolling my head from side to side.

I glance around the large open floor plan, taking in my new surroundings. It's not what I expected—not that I'd spent much time imagining what Anna Chang's life looked like these days. But still, it catches me off guard.

The kitchen, dining room, and living room are all one big open space, which is pretty unusual in these old Victorian Duluth homes.

It's neat but not obsessively so. To be honest, that's the most surprising part. She's so uptight, I half expected for her to label her silverware drawer. Just to be sure, I open the kitchen drawers to check. Everything seems pretty normal.

The shelves lining the walls are packed with books and little knickknacks—some practical, like a small jade plant sitting in a ceramic pot, and some sentimental, like a framed photo of her and Ethan at a park that looks like it's from when they were kids.

The furniture is functional, not flashy. A gray couch with a throw blanket draped over the back, a coffee table stacked with what looks like tech manuals, and a simple rug that ties the space together without trying too hard.

The space feels warm—not literally, because she keeps it just this side of freezing—but in the way it's lived in.

Personal.

Like Anna carved this space out of the world for herself, piece by piece.

My gaze drifts back to the kitchen. There's a bowl of oranges on the counter, next to a set of knives that look sharper than her glare. The fridge is covered in magnets—mostly from tech conferences, but one is shaped like a dinosaur. It's bright green and slightly crooked, as if it doesn't quite belong but refuses to be ignored. I kinda like it.

A faint smile tugs at my lips before I catch myself. Anna Chang has always been full of contradictions. Sharp edges and soft moments. The same girl who could argue her way into winning any fight could also spend hours quietly writing lyrics that could make your insides flop around or melt into a puddle.

I shake my head, dragging myself out of my thoughts and back to the task at hand—dropping my stuff in my new room for the next couple of weeks.

The hallway creaks under my boots as I make my way to the spare room she pointed out. The door is already open, and I step inside, taking in the bare-bones setup. A twin bed pushed against one wall, a small dresser, and a rickety desk that looks like it might collapse if I so much as breathe near it. The walls are painted a neutral off-white, and there's a single window with plain blinds drawn shut.

I drop my duffel bag on the bed and lean my guitar case against the wall, letting out a slow breath as I take it all in.

The room is fine. It's not like I need much—just a place to crash. But the silence of the apartment feels heavy, like the place is holding secrets it doesn't want to share.

Come on, Joel. Don't be so dramatic. This is what I wanted, right? Proximity. A chance to fix things.

But the cold shoulder Anna's giving me makes it clear this is going to be a hell of a lot harder than I thought.

After unpacking just enough to keep my clothes from wrinkling into oblivion, I find myself back in the living room. The apartment is still eerily quiet. I can hear the faint sound of her typing from behind the closed door of what I assume is her office, but otherwise, it's just me.

I sit on the couch and glance at the coffee table. A book on the rise of AI sits on top of a stack of programming books, the cover worn and dog-eared. I flip it open, skimming the underlined passages and notes in the margins. Anna's handwriting is precise, almost too neat, but there's a certain energy to it, like the thoughts couldn't stay contained.

A soft laugh escapes me. She used to scribble notes in

the same frantic style when we were kids, always chasing after some big idea or impossible problem. I remember teasing her about it once, and she told me, "If you don't keep up with your thoughts, someone else will."

She was thirteen.

That always amazed me. The depth of her thoughts and emotions for someone so young. I was fifteen and could barely think beyond which Wii game I wanted to play that day.

God, the quiet is suffocating, pressing in from all sides. I glance at the stack of books on the coffee table, then at the framed photo on the shelf. Nothing feels safe to touch, like even breathing too loud might set her off.

Finally, I give in, making my way back to the spare room.

I pick up my guitar, strumming softly to fill the emptiness. The melody comes to me before I even realize what I'm playing.

Her song.

The one I swore I'd never sing again.

My fingers move before I realize it, the notes spilling out in a quiet rhythm. It was the first song we wrote together, back when everything felt simple. Her with the lyrics, me with the melody. Back when I didn't know how much damage I was capable of doing. The music carries memories I've spent years trying to overcome. And yet, it's the one song I can't seem to forget.

The notes drift through the air, soft and familiar, and for a moment, I forget where I am. It's become a part of what I'm known for and it's burned into my fingers—into the part of me that refuses to let go.

It's not until her voice slices through the haze that I realize I'm not alone.

"Are you fucking kidding me?"

I look up, startled. Anna's standing in the doorway, her expression a mix of fury and something else—something raw and unguarded.

"What?" I ask, setting the guitar down carefully, like it's a bomb about to go off.

"One night. You can't even go *one* fucking night," she snaps, her arms crossing tightly over her chest. "Do *not* play that song."

"Anna, I didn't—"

The words catch in my throat as I think about the envelope. Did she open it?

That envelope was everything I couldn't say in person. Every apology, every explanation, every damn regret wrapped up in a few sheets of paper. And if she hadn't opened it? If it's been collecting dust this whole time?

"I mean it, Joel," she cuts me off, her voice sharper now. "You don't get to play that song. Not here. Not ever."

Her words hit me like a punch to the gut. This isn't just anger—it's something deeper. Something I can't fix with an apology.

"I wasn't trying to upset you," I say softly, my hands still hovering over the guitar strings.

"Well, congratulations," she says, her voice trembling. "You did."

As she turns, the question slips out before I can stop it. "Anna—did you even open it?"

She freezes mid-step, her back to me, her fists clenched at her sides.

For a second, I think she's going to answer. But then she turns her head just enough to glare at me over her shoulder. "Don't," she says, her voice low and dangerous.

Her shoulders rise and fall with a sharp breath, and for a moment, she looks like she's holding something back—something bigger than just anger. But the mask snaps back into place, cold and unyielding, and she turns away before I can say anything else.

And then she's gone, leaving the question hanging in the air like smoke.

I drop back on the bed, staring at the ceiling.

You don't get to play that song. Not here. Not ever.

Her words echo in my head, louder than the quiet of the apartment.

I get where she's coming from, I do. But damn, if this is how we're starting, I'm not sure how I'm supposed to fix anything.

I came here for a second chance—to make things right.

I thought being close to her would help, that maybe just being here would start to thaw the ice. But now? Now it feels like I might be making it worse just by existing in her space.

Maybe I was kidding myself.

If she didn't even open the envelope, I don't know what fixing this looks like anymore.

Apologizing? Leaving her alone?

I came here to prove I'm not the same guy who screwed everything up.

But maybe I am.

CHAPTER 5

Anna

Dirty Books smells like paper and ambition—the kind that's scribbled into notebooks, stuffed between margins, and occasionally left abandoned on a forgotten shelf.

I step into the bookshop, one hand clutching my phone while the other smooths my shirt over my jeans. The warmth of the space wraps around me as I make my way to the back corner where the Dirty B's meet.

Our nook is fully decked out now—wingback chairs, throw pillows, and a rug that doesn't match the wallpaper but works anyway. Vivian insists it's the perfect vibe for "intellectual debauchery," and to be fair, I'm just impressed she has the word debauchery in her vocabulary.

I drop into the loveseat beside Lily, pulling out my phone. "Am I actually on time for once, or is Vivian late again?"

"Late," Tasia says, smirking over the rim of her wine

glass. She's already opened a bottle of red. Likely in case Vivian forgets to bring the booze.

"I figured," I reply, pulling my phone out. "It's practically tradition at this point."

"Tradition or personality flaw?" Lily asks with a soft smile as she flips through our latest read like she's trying to refresh her memory before a quiz.

"Can't it be both?" Carlie chimes in, grinning so wide that her dimples dig in deep.

Before I can respond, the door to the shop jingles, and Vivian breezes in, her heels clicking against the hardwood.

"Ladies and gentleman, the life of the party has arrived!" she announces, holding up two bottles of wine like they're trophies.

"There are no gentlemen here," I call out without looking up, "and you're late."

"Fashionably," she shoots back, making her way to her seat. "Before we get started, let's all take a moment to appreciate me for bringing the good stuff this week. French, full-bodied, and entirely too expensive for people like us."

Carlie raises her empty glass, her curls bouncing as she grins. "To Vivian. May her taste in wine always be better than her taste in men."

The group laughs again, but I just sink deeper into the loveseat, dropping my gaze to my phone and pretending to scroll.

"So, where's Quinn then? I thought he was supposed to be here," Vivian asks, settling into her chair with the effortless grace of someone who has never had a single awkward moment in their life.

"He'll be here soon. I have him training the new guy on inventory," Tasia says, uncorking one of the wine bottles Vivian brought.

"I hope he's here soon," Vivian says, fanning herself dramatically. "I *simply* must know what he thought of the tryst between Bradley and Ming. I didn't think I'd like his suggested read but it was so hawt!"

I snort under my breath, scrolling harder to avoid rolling my eyes. Who does Vivian think she's kidding? That scene wasn't hot because of the steamy descriptions. It was the emotional undertones—the way Bradley and Ming were finally on the same wavelength after all that tension. Matching intelligence, shared vulnerability, and genuine chemistry.

You know, actual *depth*.

But maybe that's giving her too much credit. For someone who claims she's all about passion and fireworks, Vivian is about as deep as a kiddie pool. Still, part of me wonders if her fascination with that scene has less to do with the romance and more to do with the fact that it's two men.

"Chang," Tasia says, turning to me with a wicked glint in her eye. "What's your excuse tonight? You've got that storm-cloud energy going on again."

"Storm-cloud energy?" I echo, not looking up. "Pretty sure that's just my face."

"Uh-huh," Vivian says, leaning back and crossing her

legs. "So, who pissed you off this time? Tech bros? Dumb clients? *Joel?*"

My fingers freeze over my phone screen.

"What?" I say, keeping my voice as neutral as possible.

"You know—Joel Price," Vivian continues, smirking like she's enjoying every second of this. "Your favorite subject to rant about. Haven't heard you complain about him in a while. What, did he finally drop off the face of the Earth?"

God, I could only wish.

"Maybe he got abducted by aliens," Lily suggests, her tone entirely too hopeful. "They could be testing the limits of his obnoxiousness in space."

"I think they'd send him back," I mutter, wishing *I* could send him back. The image of him sitting on my guest bed playing *my* song makes me clutch my phone a little too tightly. "Too much ego, not enough brainpower."

Vivian laughs, but it's the kind of laugh that says she knows she's hit a nerve. *Shit.*

"I don't know, Anna. You seem awfully opinionated about him for someone who supposedly doesn't care," she taunts.

I finally glance up from my phone, arching an eyebrow as I try to exude nonchalance. "I have opinions about a lot of things, Vivian. Doesn't mean I care."

"To be fair, Chang might be right," Tasia says, leaning forward and playing her forearms on her knees with a smirk "Her usual vibe is about one step away from 'resting bitch face.'"

"Exactly how I like it," I deadpan, earning another round of laughter.

Carlie waves a hand in the air. "Okay, let's cut Anna some slack. If she wanted to complain about Joel, or anything else for that matter, she would've already. Let's talk about the book. *Smoke and Sapphire* by Astrid Vaughn. I'm dying over here."

Vivian sits up straighter, her excitement palpable. "Yes—*finally*. That scene with Bradley and Ming in the library? I was fanning myself, literally. Astrid can write a smexy scene between two men like nobody's business."

I suppress a groan, leaning back against the loveseat as I drop my phone. "It wasn't about the tryst, though. You know that right?"

"What do you mean?" Vivian says, blinking her innocent eyes like a cartoon doe.

My face flatlines, but like an idiot, I bite. "It was the buildup—the way Bradley finally let his guard down, and Ming stopped trying to prove himself. The intimacy came from the emotional connection, not just the... *logistics*."

Vivian waves a dismissive hand. "You're overthinking it, Anna. It was hot, plain and simple."

"Maybe for you," I mutter under my breath, picking my phone back up. However, I rest a hand over my paperback, wondering if I'm the only one in here who can see the depth of the story.

Lily chimes in, her voice soft but thoughtful. "Anna's

right. That scene worked because the tension between them finally broke in a meaningful way. It wasn't just physical."

"Thank you," I say, tipping my head toward her without dropping my emotional security device.

Validation feels sweet.

"Ugh, you two and your deep thinking," Vivian says, rolling her eyes. "Sometimes it's okay for things to just be steamy."

"It's called layers," Carlie says, smirking as she pours herself her first glass of wine.

"Yeah, look into it sometime," I fire at Vivian.

Before Viv can respond, the bell above the shop door jingles, and all heads turn toward the entrance.

Quinn waltzes in like he owns the place, his white curls are tipped with red and bounce with every step. He's wearing a red and white sequined jacket that catches the dim light and shimmers like a disco ball, paired with combat boots that somehow don't clash. I don't know how he does it. He has a small bag slung over his shoulder that sways with his hips as he comes to a halt.

"Sorry I'm late, darlings," he says, his voice lilting as he sweeps into the nook. "The new guy was slower than molasses, and I had to teach him how to alphabetize like a functioning human being. Exhausting, really."

"You locked the door, right?" Tasia interjects, handing him a glass of wine.

"Of course," he says in mock indignation.

Vivian gasps dramatically, clutching her chest as she

stands and claps. "Oh my god, Quinn. Your hair. It's *everything*."

"Thank you," Quinn says, striking a pose. "I call it *'holiday inferno.'*"

"It's giving 'peppermint chaos' vibes," Tasia says, grinning. She shakes her head slightly and takes a sip of her wine.

Quinn places a hand over his heart, feigning offense. "Rude. But I'll allow it."

"You all realize Christmas is still three months away, right?" I ask, my brain doing a full-on record scratch at the timing.

Quinn grins, unfazed. "Darling, holiday spirit waits for no one. Besides, it's not about Christmas—it's about the aesthetic."

"The aesthetic of what? Looking like Santa's flamboyant backup dancer?" Tasia quips, taking another sip of wine.

Oh, she's salty tonight.

Quinn gasps, clutching his sequined lapel. "How dare you? Santa wishes he had this much flair."

Vivian laughs so hard she nearly spills her wine. "Quinn, I missed you. Never change."

"I never do, darling. Well, unless you include my hair, my wardrobe, and vibe," he replies, sinking into his wingback chair with a dramatic sigh. "Now, what did I miss? You better not have been gossiping without me."

"We were just about to analyze the *Smoke and Sapphire* library scene," Carlie says, holding up her copy of the book. "And by *analyze*, I mean arguing about whether it was hot because of the tryst or the emotional connection."

Quinn's eyes light up as he pulls his copy from his bag. "Oh, *finally*! That scene was everything. I need to know where everyone stands."

Vivian takes her seat, already looking vindicated. "Thank you! It was pure fire. No need to overthink it."

"It wasn't just fire," Lily says, her voice calm but firm. "It worked because of the buildup. The tension was finally resolved, and it felt earned."

"Ugh, here we go again," Vivian groans, rolling her eyes.

"Sexy without substance gets boring fast," I say, finally looking up from my phone. "The scene worked because it had layers. If it were just steamy without the emotional connection, no one would care."

"Preach," Quinn says, pointing his copy of the book at me like a microphone. "Bradley and Ming are perfection because of their vulnerabilities. The way they finally opened up to each other? Swoon-worthy. The tryst was just the cherry on top."

"You are all so exhausting," Vivian says, shaking her head. "Can't we just agree that it was hot and move on?"

"Nope," Tasia says, grinning as she leans back. "I'm with the group on this one. The angst and mutual respect made it work."

"Thank you," I say, raising my palm in approval.

"I tell it like it is," Tasia replies with a lopsided grin.

"Okay, but can we talk about the part where Bradley almost burned the library down with that candle?" Carlie says, laughing. "That felt a little excessive."

"Agreed," Lily says, nodding. "It's always a candle with these romance heroes. They need to learn about LED lighting."

I snicker under my breath.

Quinn shakes his hand dramatically. "Oh, but the candle was symbolic, darling. The burning passion, the reckless abandon—it's practically poetry."

"It's practically *arson*," Tasia counters, her grin widening. "Symbolism doesn't matter if you burn down the setting."

The group dissolves into laughter again, and I let out a small chuckle despite myself. It's these moments—when the Dirty B's are in full chaotic harmony—that almost make me forget about everything else.

Almost.

I shudder, thinking about who will be waiting for me at my house when I get there. With that, I reach out, pouring myself a generous glass of Vivian's expensive French wine. I take a big old sip, savoring the flavor and hoping it gives me the buzz I need to not care that my house has been invaded by the enemy.

Vivian claps her hands, reclaiming the spotlight. "Alright, enough about the book. Let's talk about something more exciting—like karaoke night."

Tasia groans. "You're still on about that?"

"Yes," Vivian says, her excitement undeterred. "Lily told me Nocté's doing a big karaoke night tomorrow and I want us to win it. It's going to be fabulous. Lights, drinks, and the chance to absolutely destroy a Britney Spears classic. What's not to love?"

"I can think of several things," I mutter, leaning back into the loveseat.

"Come on, Anna," Vivian says, pouting. "When was the last time you did something fun?"

"Fun is subjective," I reply.

"Viv's got a point," Lily adds. "You haven't been out in forever. Unless you count trips to the grocery store as wild nights."

"I'm busy," I say, shrugging. "Some of us have jobs."

"And some of us know how to multitask," Vivian retorts. "Besides, you don't have to work on Friday night. You work for yourself, woman. No excuses."

"I'll pass," I say, already scrolling again to signal the conversation is over.

But Lily, the only one in the world who knows my history with music chimes in, "Anna, it could be good for you. A chance to blow off some steam. You've seemed... tense lately."

"I'm fine," I reply quickly. *Too* quickly.

Lily tilts her head, her serene gaze locking onto me with that unnerving way she has of reading too much into everything. "You've been working non-stop, Anna. One night won't kill you. And honestly? It would mean a lot to me if you came."

"I'm literally out right now." I glance up from my phone, narrowing my eyes. "Wait, why would it mean a lot to *you*?"

"Because I've been planning this event for weeks,"

she says, a small smile tugging at her lips. "Do you know how hard it was to get London to approve a karaoke night? I practically had to write a thesis on how it would bring in a crowd. Now, it's my event, and I want my friends to be there. Is that so wrong?"

"Uh-oh, she's pulling the guilt card," Quinn says, hiding behind his wine glass.

"You bet I am," Lily replies cheerfully. "I worked my ass off to make this happen, and I'd really love it if we all went and made it awesome. Just for one night."

Vivian perks up immediately. "Well, you already know *I'm* in. I've been waiting for a good excuse to belt out some Britney."

"Same. Well, not the Britney part," Quinn says, rolling his hand slightly. "But I am calling dibs on 'Like a Prayer.' You can't stop me."

Tasia groans again, shaking her head. "You people are too much. But fine, I'll come. Someone needs to be the adult and keep you all from embarrassing yourselves."

Carlie raises her glass, her dimples showing as she grins. "I'm in too. Karaoke, booze, and friends? What's not to love?"

All eyes turn to me.

"Don't look at me," I say, sinking further into the loveseat in the hopes it swallows me whole. "I already said no."

Lily leans forward, her expression softening. "Anna, *please.* You don't have to sing. Just come, have a drink, and laugh at the rest of us. That's it."

My chest tightens. Part of me wants to tell her to let it

go, to leave me out of this and focus on her perfect, chaotic event.

But another part—the traitorous, buried part— wants to say yes. A night of witnessing these morons try to sing sounds mildly hilarious.

Plus, ever since Joel's been back, I can't ignore the part of me that remembers how it felt to stand on a stage, microphone in hand, and let the music take over. The part I've buried so deep that even acknowledging it feels like playing with fire.

Crap.

I swallow hard, pushing the thought aside. "Fine," I hear myself say. "But don't expect me to sing."

The group erupts in cheers, clinking glasses like we've just won a championship.

"You'll love it," Vivian says, beaming. "And if not, at least you'll have a bar close by."

"Or terrible performances to mock," Tasia adds.

"Probably both," Quinn says, winking at me.

Lily leans closer, her voice just loud enough for me to hear over the noise. "Thank you," she says softly.

I don't respond, just take a long sip of wine.

As the laughter swirls around me, I tell myself it's fine. It's just one night.

And yet, the thought of stepping into Nocté for a night of singing makes my chest ache with something I can't name.

CHAPTER 6

Joel

The morning sunlight spills across the kitchen, catching on the stainless steel appliances and bouncing off the ceramic mug in my hand. I've been up for a while, the house still and quiet in a way that's oddly calming. It's almost... *nice.*

Last night, though? Not so quiet.

Anna came home late, definitely not sober, and for a solid fifteen minutes, I thought I'd accidentally stepped into an alternate reality. She'd leaned against the counter, a crooked smile on her face, and made actual, borderline-friendly conversation. Something about "not all rockstars being terrible"—though I'm sure she threw in a dig about my ego. Then she stumbled off to bed, leaving me standing there like an idiot with no idea what had just happened.

Now, I'm leaning against the counter, sipping coffee, replaying her slurred words in my head, and wondering if maybe—just maybe—there's more to Anna Chang than a permanent scowl and cutting remarks. Not that I'd tell her that. I'd be likely to get my head bitten off.

The sound of shuffling feet pulls me out of my thoughts.

Here we go.

Anna trudges into the kitchen, her hair an uncharacteristic mess and her sweatshirt hanging off one shoulder. She squints at the light like it's personally offended her, then glares at me like I'm its accomplice.

"You're... awake," she mutters, her voice rough with sleep. Or maybe regret. Hard to tell.

"And good morning to you, too," I reply, raising my mug in mock cheer. "Rough night?"

She ignores me, heading straight for the coffee maker. "Don't talk to me until I've had caffeine."

I watch as she fumbles with the cupboard door, her movements slower and less precise than usual.

"Didn't know book club meetings got that wild," I tease, taking a sip from my own mug.

Her hand freezes on the coffee pot, and she turns her head slowly, her glare sharpening. "How do you know about book club?"

I shrug, smirking. "Uh, we talked last night. Something about romance novels and... "

Her cheeks flush, but not from the wine this time. "I don't know what you're talking about."

"Sure you don't," I say, leaning against the counter. "Must've been dreaming about me then."

Her scoff is immediate. "Clearly."

"Maybe I don't have to dream, Ace," I tease,

watching as she grabs a mug and fills it. "You were surprisingly nice last night. I didn't know you had it in you."

"Don't call me that." She stares into her coffee like it holds the answers to the universe, then mutters, "I was drunk. Doesn't count."

"Are you sure about that?" I ask, biting back a laugh. "I've still got some time here with you. Could it mean you'll be drinking more often? Because I've got to say, drunk Anna is way more fun than the sober version."

She raises the mug to her lips, takes a long sip, and then sets it down with a decisive clink. "Sober Anna is what you're stuck with, Price. And trust me, she's fun is not in her operating system."

I grin into my coffee, unable to resist. "Well, maybe it's time for a software update. I hear fun's all the rage these days."

Her eyes narrow over the rim of her mug, but the corner of her mouth twitches—just enough to make me wonder if she's fighting a smile. "Don't push it."

Oh, I'll push it.

It's strange, really. I'd expected this arrangement to be tense, awkward at best, but there's something about getting under Anna's skin that feels... familiar. Comfortable, almost. And yeah, I kind of like it.

"Don't worry, sober Anna," I say, leaning against the counter. "I'm a simple guy. I'll take scowls over silence. Keeps things interesting."

She rolls her eyes, but there's no real heat behind it.

"And here I thought you thrived on adoration and applause."

"True," I admit, shrugging. "But there's something refreshing about being hated on such a personal level. Makes a guy feel special."

Her cheeks flush again, and I can't decide if it's embarrassment or irritation.

Either way, it's fascinating.

I'm not used to seeing her caught off guard—she's usually too sharp, too quick. But here, in the soft light of her kitchen, with her hair still a mess and her sweatshirt sliding dangerously close to her elbow, she almost looks... *human*. Not the Korean equivalent of a *demon*.

God help me, I think it suits her.

"And here I thought you'd be too busy basking in your own reflection to notice," she shoots back, her voice dry but her eyes sharp.

"Touché," I say, holding up my hands in mock surrender. "Guess I'll leave the existential crises to you, Ace."

Her mug hovers midair, and for a moment, she looks like she might throw it at me. "*Stop* calling me that."

"Why? It suits you," I reply without missing a beat. "You're sharp, quick, and you've got that whole badass vibe going on. Plus, I bet you aced every test from kindergarten onward without even trying."

She blinks, clearly not expecting that. "You're ridiculous."

"Ridiculously right," I counter, watching as she shakes her head and takes another sip of coffee.

The silence stretches, but it's not uncomfortable. She leans against the counter, her gaze distant as she stares out the window. The sunlight catches on her profile, highlighting the delicate slope of her nose and the stubborn set of her jaw.

"You look like you didn't sleep," I say, surprising myself with the observation.

She shrugs, not meeting my eyes. "Maybe because I didn't. Wine and sleep don't exactly get along."

"Amateur," I tease lightly, earning another sharp look. But this time, there's something softer in her expression. Something... real.

"Some of us don't drink to relax," she says, her tone clipped. "Some of us actually have work to do."

I could let it go. I probably should. But instead, I find myself stepping closer, leaning against the counter beside her. "And what exactly do you think I do all day? Sit around and stare at the walls when not playing on stage?"

She glances at me, her brow furrowing. "Don't you?"

"Wow," I say, mock-offended. "For someone so smart, you really know how to oversimplify things."

"Enlighten me, then," she challenges, setting her cup on the counter and crossing her arms, her expression a mix of defiance and curiosity.

I take a breath, leaning back against the counter. "It wasn't always like this for me," I begin carefully, my tone steady. "At first, music was just... *fun*. A way to figure things out, make sense of things. You remember—those early days, you were right there with me."

Her expression doesn't change, but her hands clench into fists at her sides.

"But then I got caught up in the superficial stuff. It became about showing off, impressing people, chasing something I didn't really understand." I pause, the words coming slower now. "I lost track of what it was really about. What we used to talk about."

Anna doesn't say anything, but without a snarky comeback, I know she's listening.

"These days, though?" I continue, glancing at the ceiling as I gather my thoughts. "It's not just sitting around, strumming my guitar, or staring at the walls, like you think. It's *writing*. Tearing pieces out of myself and shaping them into something I hope someone else will feel. You'd know that if you listen to any of my new stuff. It's hours of trying to find the right words, the right sound, the right way to say something that matters. And yeah, it's *work*. Hard work."

Her gaze flickers, something soft and almost vulnerable crossing her face before she catches herself.

"It's more than just music," I add, my voice quieter. "It's the only thing that makes me feel like I'm exactly where I'm supposed to be. Like I'm giving people a piece of myself that actually matters."

She looks away, her jaw tightening as if she's chewing over what I've just said. For a moment, the kitchen feels too quiet, the tension thick and unspoken.

"You always did have a flair for the dramatic," she says finally, her voice quieter than before, but her sharpness isn't as convincing.

I let out a small laugh, shaking my head. "And you've always been good at pretending you don't understand things you understand perfectly."

Her lips twitch, like she's fighting a smile—or maybe another retort. She stares at me for a moment, her expression dropping back into her unreadable mask. Then she scoffs. "Maybe you do work. But we're still different. I don't need an audience to validate me."

Ouch. But, also, fair.

"Touché again," I say, smirking. "But you'd be surprised how much we have in common, Ace."

Her jaw tightens, and for a second, I think she's going to snap at me to tell me to stop calling her that. But instead, she just shakes her head and mutters, "You're impossible."

"And you're predictable," I fire back, watching as her lips press into a thin line.

But then, out of nowhere, she blushes again. It's faint, barely there, but it's enough to make me pause.

"Did—did you just blush?" I ask, my voice dropping to a teasing lilt. "Are you actually flustered?"

She huffs, grabbing her mug and retreating toward her office. "Don't flatter yourself, Price."

I grin, leaning against the counter as I watch her go. "Too late," I call out after her.

I watch the door to her office slam shut with a satisfying thud, and for a second, the house feels too quiet again.

But my grin? It stays.

Anna Chang—*flustered*.

If I hadn't seen it myself, I wouldn't have believed it. Hell, I'm still not sure it wasn't just some caffeine-deprived mirage. But no, it was there. The blush. The hesitation. The tiniest crack in her armor.

What the hell just happened?

What did I do? And how do I do it again?

I lean back against the counter, sipping my coffee as I replay the conversation in my head. She wasn't just firing off her usual quick comebacks. There was something else beneath it all. A flicker of connection, maybe? Or maybe I'm imagining things.

Still, I can't shake the feeling that this morning was different. The way her eyes softened, just for a moment, when I talked about music. Like she understood. Like she remembered.

And that blush. God, I'll be thinking about that for days.

I chuckle to myself, shaking my head. "Get a grip, Joel," I mutter, pushing off the counter and rinsing out my mug.

The last thing I need is to start reading too much into this. She probably hates my guts just as much as she always has.

Still, pushing her buttons? I'll admit, it's fun. A little too fun.

The thought lingers as I head back to the spare room. My guitar case leans against the wall, the scuffed leather reminding me of how far it's traveled. I glance at it, then at the notebook sitting on the desk—a mess of scribbles and half-formed lyrics.

That moment in the kitchen, the way Anna looked at me when I talked about music—it stirs something. A spark of an idea.

I sit down, grabbing the notebook and flipping to a clean page. The pen feels familiar in my hand, and for a second, the world outside this room fades away.

The words don't come easily, not at first. But as I start sketching out a melody in my head, the feelings take shape. Frustration, hope, the maddening pull of someone who drives you crazy in all the best and worst ways.

The song starts to form, the notes threading together like they've been waiting for this moment. And as I strum the opening chords, I can't help but think of Anna. I don't mean to, it just happens.

It's not just her quick wit or her impossible standards. It's the way she carries herself, like she's braced for the world to knock her down but refuses to give it the satisfaction. The way she can cut you to pieces with a single look but still make you wonder what's hiding underneath.

I pause, staring down at the strings. This song—it's not just about her. But she's in it, somehow. In the sharp edges and the soft notes. In the tension that won't go away.

The words start to flow, the melody weaving through my thoughts as the morning stretches on. And for the first time in a long time, it feels like I'm writing something that matters.

Something *real*.

Something that might even make her blush again.

CHAPTER 7

Anna

The soft glow of my monitor lights up my office, casting faint shadows across the cluttered desk. Lines of code stare back at me, a blinking cursor mocking my lack of progress. Normally, this is where I thrive— solving puzzles, creating order out of chaos.

But today?

My brain is a tangled mess, and it has nothing to do with the program I'm supposed to debug.

No. It's Joel *freaking* Price.

I lean back in my chair, letting out a frustrated groan.

Of all the houseguests in the world, why did it have to be him? Joel, with his infuriating smirks and annoyingly quick comebacks. Joel, who somehow managed to crack through my defenses this morning with just a few stupid, heartfelt words about music.

Music.

The very thing I've spent years trying to lock away in a mental vault and throw into the deepest part of the ocean. The thing I promised myself I would never think about or long to return to. And yet, here he is, dredging it back up with nothing more than a coffee mug in hand and that damn lopsided grin.

I twist the pen in my fingers, staring at the monitor but not really seeing it. His words keep replaying in my head, weaving through my thoughts like a melody I can't shake.

Why does he have to be so—*ugh*. No. Stop. I'm not doing this.

I roll my chair back, shoving to my feet and pacing the small space. The floor creaks under my socks as I mutter to myself. "Get a grip, Anna. He's just a guy. A frustrating, smug, overly emotional guy with zero empathy for others."

But a part of me—the part I'd rather pretend doesn't exist—whispers that maybe he's more than that. Maybe the Joel sitting in my kitchen this morning isn't the same Joel I shoved into the "irrelevant" folder years ago.

No. I refuse to go down that road. It's too dangerous. Too vulnerable. And if there's one thing I've learned, it's that vulnerability gets you nowhere but trampled on. Especially by him.

Shaking my head, I force myself to focus. "Code, Anna. Fix the damn code." I sit back down and try again, fingers hovering over the keyboard as I reread the lines.

But everything blurs together, and my thoughts slip back to Joel. How he leaned against the counter, looking so damn sure of himself yet... not. How his voice softened when he talked about music, like he wasn't just saying words but showing me something real.

Why does he have to be like that?

My fingers clench around the edge of my desk, and my eyes flick to the drawer on my left. That drawer. The one holding the envelope. It's ridiculous, sitting there like a Pandora's box of bad decisions, daring me to open it and ruin my day.

I almost reach for it, fingers twitching as if the pull of it is magnetic. What would it even change if I read it? It's just words—words from the same guy who turned everything into a joke when it mattered most.

I chew on my bottom lip, my hand hovering over the drawer handle. Curiosity burns in the back of my mind, but so does something else. A heavier, deeper weight that warns me not to look.

No. Not now. *Not ever.*

I yank my hand back and shove it into my lap like I've been burned.

Joel doesn't get to take up any more of my time—not then and certainly not now.

Enough.

I'm done letting him linger in my head like some unsolvable equation.

I scowl at my monitor, glaring at the blinking cursor. "Code, Anna. Fix the damn code," I mutter again, louder this time, as if saying it might make it true.

But it all still blurs together and it becomes painfully clear I'm not gonna get any work done.

I push back from the desk, standing so fast my chair wobbles.

"I need to get out of the house," I mutter to no one but myself.

Maybe some fresh air and distance will do the trick—anything to shut down the chaos in my mind.

❧

The lights of Nocté are warm and dim, the hum of chatter and clinking glasses filling the space. The Dirty B's have claimed a large semi-circular booth, and I slide in next to Tasia, feeling the bass of the music reverberate through the plush seat cushions.

"Look who decided to show up," Lily teases, pouring me a glass of what looks like Long Island Iced Tea. "I was starting to think you'd ghost us."

"Don't tempt me," I reply dryly, taking a sip. The flavor settles on my tongue, but I already know it won't be enough to make me forget Joel Price is somewhere out there being...*Joel*.

Quinn sits across from me, dressed to the nines in a sparkly silver blazer and matching tie. He's flipping through the karaoke book with a look of intense concentration. "Darling, I'm torn between Celine Dion and Elton John. Thoughts?"

"Neither," Tasia quips. "Spare us all and do Cher."

"Rude," Quinn replies with mock offense. "But not a terrible suggestion."

"Thought you were going to do 'Like a Prayer?'" Lily says, trying to eye the book over his shoulder.

"Oooh, that's right. Maybe two songs, then?" he responds, tapping his chin with his index finger as he flips the page.

Vivian suddenly drops into the booth, huffing dramatically as she plants her elbows on the table. "I swear to God, if Myles glares at me one more time tonight, I'm going to lose it."

Tasia snorts. "What did you do now?"

"Nothing—" Vivian protests, her eyes wide with innocence. "I was just trying to get a refill of my Old Fashioned, and she looked at me like I was personally ruining her night."

"Maybe you were," I mutter, earning a glare from Vivian.

"I'm a delight, thank you very much," she snaps, crossing her arms. "Myles just needs to get over herself."

"Wonder what the deal is? She's always been pretty cool with me," Lily says, glancing over to the bar.

"Jealousy," Vivian declares, flipping her blonde hair over her shoulder. "It's the only explanation."

The night rolls on, with the Dirty B's taking turns embarrassing themselves on stage. Vivian belts out a surprisingly decent rendition of *Oops!... I Did It Again*, complete with dramatic hip sways that have Quinn in stitches. Tasia tries *Smells Like Teen Spirit* but forgets half the lyrics, laughing her way through the rest.

Lily goes up with Carlie to do *Dancing Queen*, the

two of them harmonizing terribly but clearly having the time of their lives.

And me? I stay in the booth, sipping on my third Long Island and pretending to be entertained.

It's fine. Fun, even.

Until it's not.

Lily leans in, voice low as she nudges me with her shoulder. "You should go up next."

I snort. "Hard pass."

But she doesn't laugh like I expect her to. Instead, she gives me this look—one I don't like.

Like she sees something in me I don't want her to see.

Quinn perks up, flipping through the songbook. "Ohhh, yes. Do it. I bet you secretly have an incredible voice. You're giving me 'hidden talent' energy."

Tasia smirks. "She gives 'hidden everything' energy."

I roll my eyes, but my fingers tighten around my glass.

It's easy to dismiss their teasing. Easy to shake my head and act like it's ridiculous.

But Lily's still watching me. *Still waiting.*

I look away, take a long sip of my drink, but it doesn't do anything to steady me.

Why does she have to bring this up?

I used to love singing. I used to love the way music made me feel—like I was something more than just a girl with a sharp mouth and a brain full of code.

But that was *before*. Before it all went to hell.

I don't do music anymore.

And yet—

My fingers almost brush the edge of the songbook. Just to flip through it. Just to see.

"Come on, Anna," Quinn coaxes. "What's the worst that could happen? You suck and we laugh at you? That's, like, ninety percent of karaoke anyway."

Vivian smirks. "For what it's worth, I don't think she'll suck."

"Of course I wouldn't suck," I huff. "That's not the point."

"Then what is?" Lily asks, and the softness in her voice unsettles me more than all the teasing.

I don't answer. I can't.

Because I don't actually know.

My pulse picks up as I grab the book from Quinn and scan it. Just one song. Just to prove it means nothing to me anymore.

Something easy. Something light. Something so ridiculous that it won't mean a damn thing when I sing it.

Maybe *Call Me Maybe.* Or *Party in the USA.* Something fun. Stupid.

My fingers tighten on the corner of the page.

Maybe I could—

The mic crackles.

The emcee's voice cuts through the speakers. "While all you karaoke lovers out there pick your next victim— er, I mean your next song, we've got a special treat. Johnny Rivers is up next with an original track."

I glance toward the stage, expecting another butchered country ballad from someone in a cowboy hat. But then the spotlight hits him.

And of course, it's fucking not.

It's *Joel*.

He strides onto the stage like he belongs there, a microphone in one hand and his guitar slung over his shoulder. The room buzzes with scattered applause and murmurs of approval. My stomach plummets and I snap the book shut.

"What the hell is he doing here?" I hiss, leaning toward Lily, who has conveniently chosen this moment to sip her drink.

Her serene expression doesn't waver. "It's karaoke night. He's allowed to sing."

"He's not allowed to *exist*," I mutter, sinking back into the booth and gripping the edge of the table so hard my knuckles ache.

Quinn perks up beside me, his eyes lighting with recognition as he glances between me and the stage. "Wait, isn't that—"

"Don't," I cut him off, my glare sharp enough to silence even him.

Vivian, forever oblivious, leans in with a completely idiotic expression of confusion. "Who's Johnny Rivers? Is he, like, one of those indie guys?"

"Not exactly," I bite out, my voice tight.

Joel settles onto a stool at center stage, adjusting the mic stand with an ease that's both infuriating and magnetic. He doesn't look nervous. He doesn't even look like he's trying. He just... exists, completely at home in the spotlight. I remember when singing and being on stage was the single most terrifying thing he could think of doing.

The first chords of his guitar cut through the air, clean and deliberate, and the room seems to hold its breath.

And then he starts to sing.

Of course he can't just choose a damn karaoke song. It's gotta be something original and that thought makes me want to throw up.

The song is a raw, stripped-down melody—nothing like the flashy rockstar image I've spent years building up in my head from rage stalking his IG account. His voice is lower, softer, but it fills the space effortlessly. It's vulnerable in a way that feels too intimate, like he's peeling back a layer of himself and offering it to the room.

"Holy shit," Quinn whispers, his eyes wide. "He's good."

"Shut *up*," I mutter, my chest tightening with every note.

It's not flashy. It's not performative. It's just... real.

And I hate it.

I hate that I can't look away. I hate the way his voice tugs at something buried deep inside me, something I thought I'd locked up for good. I hate that he looks so at ease, like this is the most natural thing in the world for him.

My chest feels like it's caving in, the weight of it

pressing down harder with every word he sings. I grab my glass and down the rest of my drink in one long gulp, the sharp burn of the alcohol doing nothing to dull the ache in my chest.

"You okay?" Lily asks, her voice gentle as she leans closer.

"Nope," I reply, shoving out of the booth with more force than necessary. People around us glance over at me like I'm making a scene. Hell, I could show them a scene.

"Anna—" Lily starts, but I don't let her finish.

I storm toward the exit, feeling like the ghost of Valentine's Day past has come back to haunt me. With more force than necessary, I push open the door and step into the cool night air, the chill biting at my skin as I let out an exasperated cry.

My breath comes too fast, too sharp. I press my hands against my thighs, trying to steady myself.

What the hell was I thinking?

I almost did it—I almost went up there.

My hands are still shaking.

The thought makes me sick.

Because what if I *had?*

For a moment, I just stand there, trying to catch my breath, trying to block out the memory of his voice. The way his face looked and his body moved.

But it doesn't work. It lingers, haunting and infuriating, like an echo I can't escape.

I run my hands through my hair, frustration bubbling to the surface. "What the hell are you doing, Anna?" I mutter to myself. "Get it together."

But I can't shake it—not with him in there, baring his soul for everyone like the world is begging to hear it. Especially after our talk this morning. It feels like a sucker punch, a reminder that his words have already taken up too much space in my head.

The door swings open behind me, the muffled music spilling out for a brief moment before it closes again. I turn, half expecting it to be Joel.

It's not.

It's Lily.

"Hey," she says softly, her expression full of empathy. "You okay?"

I force a tight smile, crossing my arms over my chest. "Just needed some air."

She doesn't buy it. Lily never buys it. But she doesn't push. "Take your time," she says, her voice calm and steady. "But... don't let him get to you."

Too late.

I nod, watching as she heads back inside, leaving me alone with my thoughts.

The door clicks shut, and the night settles around me, too quiet, too heavy. Joel's voice lingers in my mind, raw and uninvited, like it's found a crack in the walls I've built and refuses to leave.

I glance toward the glowing sign for Nocté, the bass from inside thumping faintly under my feet. Maybe I should've stayed. Maybe I shouldn't have come at all.

My phone feels cool in my hand as I pull it out, the screen lighting up my face in the dark.

Screw this.

I tap the screen, ordering my Uber.

Joel Price might think he's rewritten himself, but no song is going to rewrite me. Not again.

CHAPTER 8

Joel

There's a moment when you're playing a song— when the world narrows, when it's just you and the music, nothing else. The chords settle into muscle memory, the words roll off your tongue like they were always meant to be there, and for a little while, nothing else matters.

This was supposed to be one of those moments.

At least, that's what I'd hoped for when I stepped onto the stage.

I'm testing something out tonight. A song I finished this afternoon, still a little rough around the edges, the kind that needs to be played out loud, felt out loud, before I can tell if it actually holds. It's got that half-finished ache to it—one of those songs that feels like it means something, but I won't know for sure until I hear it outside my own damn head.

That's why I'm here.

Not for the crowd. Not for the rush of performing.

Just to see if the words hold, if the melody lands the way I want it to.

And for the first half, it's going... *fine*.

I'm a little tense, but that's normal with a new song. My voice is steady. The guitar stays in sync. A few heads turn, some people nod along. At the bar, a girl sways a little to the rhythm, fingers tapping against the side of her drink, and I take it as a good sign.

It's not perfect, but it's getting there.

Then, halfway through—it happens.

A flicker of movement in my peripheral.

At first, it barely registers—just another shifting body, another face in a blur of dim lighting and half-drunk conversations. People are always coming and going, weaving in and out of focus.

But something about it pulls at me anyway.

Like a sharp tug on a loose thread.

I glance up.

And there she is.

Anna.

Leaving.

Fast.

And okay, that shouldn't bother me.

I should just keep my head down, finish my damn song, move on with my life like a normal, functioning human.

But instead, my fingers almost falter over the strings, my throat tightening around the next lyric.

Because this isn't just Anna stepping outside for fresh air.

That much is clear in the way she moves—stiff shoulders, clipped strides, the kind of exit that isn't just about leaving a place but getting the hell away from something.

From me.

And somehow, I know—deep in that annoying, traitorous part of me that still gives a damn—that I'm the reason.

Which is just fantastic.

Because I wasn't trying to piss her off. *Again.*

Hell, I didn't even know she was here.

And yet, apparently, I've developed some kind of personalized Anna Chang Radar, because now that I do know she was here—*now that I know she's not*—it's like I can still feel her absence.

Like she took all the oxygen with her when she left.

Like she left the whole damn room off-balance.

I exhale slowly, forcing my fingers to stay steady on the strings, but something shifts.

The song was already raw, already unfinished, but now it feels hollow in places. Like I'm missing something.

Like the melody doesn't quite sit the way it should.

Like it's waiting for something *more.*

And before I even know what I'm doing, before I can talk myself out of it—

I find it.

The words slip out, unplanned, tumbling past my lips in a way that wasn't in the original draft. A line I didn't write, a feeling I hadn't meant to put here, but now that it's out in the open, I know it belongs.

I know it's hers.

Shit.

I don't stop.

I can't.

Because suddenly, this song—this thing I thought I understood, thought I had control over—is shifting under my hands, finding new meaning in real time.

And I don't know what that means.

But I know it's because of her.

I push through the last chords, fingers tightening slightly on the strings, trying to make sense of the feeling curling low in my chest.

Trying not to think about the fact that even after she's gone, she's still here.

I'll give her space.

For now.

But the words she left behind?

I don't think they're going anywhere.

The house is dark when I get back, but she's here.

I don't know how I know, but I do. Some weird, messed-up instinct that's been on hyper-alert since I watched her leave.

I toe off my boots and step inside, expecting—well, I don't know what I'm expecting. But definitely not this.

She's in the kitchen, arms crossed, hip against the counter, eyes locked on me like she's been waiting.

It's almost... *unsettling.*

Like walking into a room where you know you're about to get wrecked. I do my best to brace for the onslaught.

"Anna," I start, but I don't even get her name out before she's cutting me off.

"Don't."

I pause, tipping my head. "Okay, but just so we're clear—what are we *not* doing?"

Her eyes narrow. "This."

She gestures vaguely between us, and something about it makes me want to smirk. Which is not the right reaction, but hey, when have I ever made good choices?

"I feel like I need a little more context." I lean against the opposite counter, mirroring her stance. "Because from where I'm standing, we're just two adults having a totally normal, not at all hostile post-club conversation."

Her glare sharpens. "You know what I mean."

"Ehhh, do I?"

She exhales sharply, like she's barely holding on. "I don't need you pulling this crap with me."

"What crap?"

"The thing you do." She gestures again, this time toward me. "With your stupid guitar and your soulful, heartfelt... whatever the hell that was. You knew I was there. You knew I'd hear it."

I blink. "What?"

"Don't play dumb."

"I'm not playing." I push off the counter, frowning. "I *didn't know you were there.*"

That stops her.

Just for a second, her brows pull together, like she's processing, recalibrating. But Anna Chang does not hesitate long. She recovers fast.

Too fast.

"Oh, that makes it better?" she fires back, voice sharper than before.

"I don't know. Does it?"

Her jaw clenches. "Jesus, you are infuriating."

"So I've been told."

She lets out a sharp, humorless laugh, shaking her head. "You don't get it."

"Then make me get it."

"I don't want to."

And that? That one stings.

Because *I* do.

I want to understand. I want to get it, to know why every damn thing I do seems to hit a nerve with her.

Hell, I wanna know why she can't just open the goddamn envelope and forgive me already?

And I want to know why—why even now, even when we're standing here, practically snarling at each other in her stupidly pristine kitchen, I still can't seem to let it go.

We're close now.

Somewhere between our back-and-forth, we got too close.

And maybe she notices it at the same time I do, because suddenly, she shifts. Her breath is shallow, her posture tense. Her fingers twitch at her sides, like she doesn't know whether to push me away or pull me closer.

And me?

I should step back.

I should give her room.

But I don't.

Instead, my fingers graze hers—just barely.

Not enough to call it an accident.

Not enough to ignore.

She freezes.

We both stare down at the point of contact.

And for a second—*a split second*—the air between us shifts.

Then she jerks her hand back like I just electrocuted her.

"What the—" She takes a full step away, bumping into the counter. "I—God, just move."

She won't look at me. Which is interesting.

Because Anna Chang is a lot of things, but she's not the type to back down. Not from a fight. Not from an argument. And definitely not from me.

So what the hell is this?

I lean back against the counter, watching her with what appears to be way too much amusement for her liking because she full on growls at me.

"Did you just flinch?"

She snorts under her breath. "No."

"You did."

"Joel," she says my name with far too much exasperation and it makes me grin.

"Anna."

Her name feels way too good in my mouth.

She exhales sharply, nostrils flaring. "You are so goddamn infuriating."

"Yeah, so I've heard."

Something in her eyes flickers, but she's already moving, already retreating to the fridge. Because of course she is. Classic Anna move—make it seem like she's in control when we both know she's two seconds away from combusting.

She yanks open the fridge with a little too much force, stares into it like she's hunting for a solution to her problems next to the oat milk.

"You didn't have to run out, you know," I say, my voice low.

She goes still.

"I don't know what you're talking about."

"Sure you do." I keep my voice even, watching her shoulders tighten. "You left before I finished."

"So?"

"So... you don't run, Anna." I tilt my head, watching her process. Watching her brain work. "At least, you didn't used to."

She lets out a sharp, humorless laugh, shaking her head. "You think you know me?"

I don't answer right away.

And that hesitation is dangerous.

Because yeah, I do.

At least, if the past is any indication.

I know that she sleeps curled up on her side because she thinks it's the most efficient way to conserve heat.

I know she hates surprises but loves puzzles, which is kind of the same thing, if you think about it.

I know she overthinks and overanalyzes everything.

And I know she's lying through her damn teeth right now.

"You don't," she says before I can get a word in.

She moves to step past me, but at the last second, she hesitates. Just for a fraction of a second—like she's reconsidering. Then she squares her shoulders, brushing my arm as she walks by.

I should let her go.

I should let this drop.

But my mouth? It has other plans.

"What did you think of the song?"

She stops.

Back still turned.

Not facing me, not running either.

For a second, I wonder if she'll ignore it. If she'll pretend she didn't hear me, pretend like it didn't mean anything.

Then she speaks.

"I don't know what you're talking about."

A slow grin spreads across my face.

Because that?

That right there?

That's not a no.

I take a slow step forward, testing the waters.

"You don't know what I'm talking about?" I repeat,

drawing out the words. "That's interesting. Because I was under the impression you left Nocté halfway through my song."

Anna stiffens. Just the slightest twitch in her shoulders, like I caught her.

"Coincidence," she mutters, still not turning around. "Not everything is about you, Joel."

"True." I nod, even though she can't see me. "But this *was* about me. Specifically, a song I wrote. One you *definitely* heard."

"I hear a lot of things."

I can't help it—I smirk.

"And yet, you ran."

That does it.

She whirls around, arms crossed tight over her chest, chin tilted up in that *classic* Anna way.

"I did *not* run."

I raise an eyebrow. "Mmhmm."

"I *left*."

"Uh-huh."

"There's a difference."

"Right," I say, dragging the word out. "One is controlled. The other is running away because you felt something you didn't want to feel."

Did my song really make her *feel* something?

Her glare sharpens to *murderous levels*.

"You are *so* full of yourself," she hisses.

"I mean, I'm not the one who stormed out mid-song."

"Oh my god." She presses her fingers to her temples

like she's literally trying to keep her head from exploding. "I left because I was bored, Price. That's it. Not everything is some *deep*, emotional moment just because you played a few sad chords."

"A few sad chords?" I place a hand on my chest, mock-offended. "Wow. That almost hurt, Ace."

"Stop calling me that."

"Not a chance," I fire back, taking another step into her space.

She groans, muttering something under her breath that sounds a lot like *I hate you* but with significantly more aggression.

Then she pivots sharply, ready to stalk off, but I mirror her step, shifting just enough that she stops short.

"Move," she demands.

"Admit it," I counter, grinning. "You liked the song."

"I *hate* the song."

"You don't even remember it."

"I remember *enough*."

"Oh yeah?" I tip my head. "Then tell me. What was it about?"

She opens her mouth. Then shuts it. Her jaw tightens.

I watch as she fights with herself, scrambling for something to say, something *vague* enough to avoid proving me right.

It's fascinating.

"It was... moody."

"Uh-huh."

"A little whiny."

"Rude."

"And," she adds, eyes flashing as she finds her footing again, "an *obvious* attempt to get people to feel sorry for you."

I let out a low laugh, shaking my head. "God, you're the worst liar."

"And you're insufferable," she snaps, brushing past me with more force than necessary.

This time, I let her go.

Because as much as she *pretends* to be unaffected, her entire reaction just proved my point.

She *felt something*.

And whether she likes it or not?

I'm not letting that go.

Not yet.

CHAPTER 9

Anna

My brain is malfunctioning.

Like, actual system failure. Like, blue screen of death. Like, Anna's not here anymore,

Why? Because she's dead.

I stand frozen in my bedroom, heart racing, chest tight, every nerve ending on high alert. My body is stuck in DEFCON-1 Mode for no good reason.

No. That's a lie. I know exactly why.

Because for one stupid second—one fleeting moment of insanity—Joel touched me. And he *meant* to do it.

And worse?

I noticed.

Okay, another lie. I not only noticed—I became *hyper-aware.*

Like some psychotic live broadcast where all I could focus on was the heat of his fingers barely grazing mine. And then I became aware that I was aware. And then I was aware that I was aware that I was aware. God, how is that even a thing? So stupid.

And then I ran—because what the hell else was I supposed to do?

Now, I'm here. Still spiraling. Still grossly aware of my own pulse, beating a little too fast, a little too erratic, like my body is rebelling against me.

I press my hands to my face, groaning into my palms.

"Get a grip, Anna," I mutter, voice muffled. "It was barely a touch. A millisecond of contact. Less than a tap on a damn keyboard."

But it doesn't matter.

Because Joel doesn't get to take up space in my head. He doesn't get to sit there, all smug and unreadable, and worm his way under my skin like he belongs there.

I rip off my sweatshirt and fling it across the room, where it lands in a heap on my floor. It's childish, but I don't care. My skin feels too hot, too constricted, like his presence is still lingering, clinging to me, and I need it off.

Next, I yank out my hair tie, shaking my head like that'll somehow dislodge him from my thoughts. A few strands get caught in the elastic, yanking at my scalp as I pull it free.

Great. Now I'm losing hair over Joel Price.

I glare at my reflection in the mirror above my dresser, my face still flushed, my expression tight.

You're losing it, Anna. I mutter the words under my breath, pressing my palms against the cool wood surface, willing myself to calm the hell down.

Routine. That's what I need. Something mindless. Something to pull me out of my own damn head.

I drop onto the small stool at my desk—the one my grandma gave me when I moved out, the same one my mom wouldn't let me say no to. It's an antique, or at least that's what she told me when she forced it into my new apartment.

"A lady should have a proper vanity, Anna."

Like I was suddenly going to start sitting here in silk robes, brushing my hair a hundred times like some 1950s housewife.

But tonight, I'm grateful for it. The routine. The ritual. The mirror is small, slightly warped from age, but it reflects the tired mess of my face just fine.

I grab my makeup wipes and scrub at my skin, a little harder than necessary, like I can physically erase the memory of his voice, his stupid smirk, the way his fingers barely grazed mine but still managed to set my nerve endings on fire. I work my way through my skincare— cleanser, toner, moisturizer—focusing on the motions, forcing my brain into autopilot.

By the time I smooth the last bit of lotion over my skin, I feel marginally better. Not *great.* But like maybe, maybe, I'll be able to shut my brain off long enough to sleep.

But first—a shower.

The thought hits me, and I hesitate, glancing toward my door. I should go now, while I have the chance. The last thing I need is to risk running into him again in the hallway.

I exhale sharply, pressing my fingers to my temples. This is ridiculous. I live here. I shouldn't have to feel like I'm sneaking around my own damn house.

Decision made, I push off the stool, reaching for my pajamas so I can head to the bathroom—

Then I hear it.

The telltale creak of the hallway floor. Slow. Unhurried.

The bathroom door clicking shut.

And then—

The unmistakable hiss of the shower turning on.

Oh. *Oh.*

My brain short-circuits so hard I physically sit back down.

Because Joel Price is in my house.

In my bathroom.

About to be completely, 100% naked... if he isn't already.

The thought hits differently as I hear the shower curtain being pulled back. The water running, the faint reverberation of the pipes—it's all undeniable proof that there is a wet, very bare Joel standing approximately fifteen feet away.

I feel my soul leave my body.

How have I not thought about this before? I'm the logical one. My contingency plans have contingency plans.

And why, *why*, is it the only thing I can think about now?

About him.

In there.

Water running down his broad, stupidly defined shoulders. Steam curling around his too-tall, too-annoying frame. Soap trailing down—

NOPE. NO. STOP IT.

ABORT.

I shoot up like I've been electrocuted, then sit right back down because my legs are no longer trustworthy.

No. No, no, *no.*

This is not happening.

I refuse to let this happen.

I grab my face towel and scrub at my cheeks, like I can physically exorcise the thought from my brain. It doesn't work.

I lunge for my headphones, pure survival instinct, scrolling through my phone with hands that are shaking slightly.

I land on Lily's playlist for me. She made it last year and I could use it now.

I slam my thumb against play on *"Zen as Fuck."*

Soft piano drifts into my ears, followed by some deep, meditative voice telling me to inhale peace and exhale stress.

Breathe in. Breathe out.

Don't think about Joel Price being naked in your house.

Breathe in. Breathe out.

Don't think about his arms. His back. His hands—

I yank the blanket over my head and crank up the volume.

This. This is my life now.

&

I don't remember falling asleep. One second, I'm buried under my blankets, trying to drown out the fact that Joel is naked somewhere in my house, and the next, I'm fourteen again—sitting cross-legged on the floor of my childhood bedroom, my notebook balanced on my knee.

Joel is next to me, his seventeen-year-old self sprawled out lazily with my old acoustic guitar, plucking out chords like it's the easiest thing in the world.

It always was, for him.

"Okay, what if we tried this?" He strums a few notes, then hums under his breath, testing out different melodies. His brows furrow in concentration, lips pressing together like he's actually taking this seriously.

Which, honestly, is shocking.

Because when I showed him my lyrics—when I nervously, stupidly, let him peek into my world—I half expected him to laugh. To make some dumb joke.

Instead, he'd read them. Really *read* them.

And then, he wanted to help.

Even now, my stomach tightens at the memory of him staring at my notebook, scanning every word, and asking, *So, who's it about?*

And me?

I panicked. Obviously.

Because how the hell was I supposed to tell him the truth?

That every single line was about *him*?

That my stupid, ridiculous, massive crush on my brother's best friend had bled onto the page?

So I lied.

"Just a guy in my class," I'd mumbled, shrugging way too hard. "No one special."

I'd felt the lie burning the whole way out.

But he'd bought it. Maybe because he didn't care to dig too deep. That suited me fine.

And now, here we were, working on the melody together—co-creating a song about him that he didn't even know was about him.

I watch as he plays through the first verse again, nodding slightly as the melody takes shape.

"Yeah," he murmurs, more to himself than to me. "I think this works. It's got that..." He gestures vaguely with his hand. "You know, that feeling."

I do know.

Because it's *my* feeling.

Because this song is the closest I'll ever come to telling him.

I bite my lip, forcing my voice to stay steady. "You think it's good?"

He grins at me, so effortlessly Joel, like he doesn't even realize what that smile does to me. "Yeah, Ace. It's good."

Oh my god, that stupid nickname. It didn't bother me so much back then.

I tuck my chin, trying to fight back the warmth in my chest.

For a second—just one stupid second—I let myself believe that maybe this moment matters.

That maybe this song means something to him, too.

And then—

It all shatters.

The dream shifts. Warps.

Suddenly, I'm not in my bedroom anymore.

I'm standing in the school auditorium.

The lights are low, the air buzzing with anticipation.

And he's onstage.

Joel Price, seventeen and stupidly charming, sitting on a stool with my guitar in his lap.

He shifts on the stool, his fingers moving over the strings like he was born with a guitar in his hands. The soft glow of the stage lights casts him in warm gold, turning the world around us dim, unimportant.

And then—he looks at me.

Straight at me.

Like I'm the only person in the room.

The first chord hums through the auditorium, soft and familiar, wrapping around my ribs like a memory I never wanted to share. I know this song. I *wrote* this song.

My breath catches as his voice drifts through the speakers.

Do you see me, even when I'm quiet?
Do you hear me, when I don't know what to say?
I don't have the words, I don't have the courage—
But maybe I don't have to, if you feel the
same way.

The lyrics slam into me, knocking the breath from my lungs.

Because they're mine. My heart laid bare, my secret stitched into every word, every aching note.

Because they carry every silent wish, every stolen glance, every impossible hope—that maybe, just maybe, *he'd see me.*

And now...

Now he's singing it.

To me.

His gaze doesn't waver, his voice steady, like this moment—this song—means something.

And suddenly, I believe it.

My heart pounds so hard I think it might crack my ribs. This is it. This is the moment.

He's finally seeing me. *Finally.*

A lump forms in my throat, emotions crashing over me all at once. I barely notice the other students murmuring around me, their whispers blending into the background. My whole body feels electric, like the universe is rewriting itself in real time.

This is happening.

He feels it, too.

I swallow hard, barely breathing as the last chord rings out.

Then Joel lowers the guitar, shifting on the stool.

He takes a breath, running a hand through his messy, too-long hair.

And then—

Then he smiles.

"Hey, Jessica," he says, voice warm, smooth.

My stomach drops.

I can't move.

I can't breathe.

He's still smiling, turning just slightly in his seat—just enough for me to realize...

He wasn't looking at me at all.

He was looking past me.

Straight at Jessica Carson.

And then—

"Would you wanna go to prom with me?"

The world tilts.

There's a moment—a brief, brutal moment—where my brain refuses to process what just happened.

Because it doesn't make sense.

Because this song—*my song*—was supposed to be ours. It was supposed to be private.

And now?

Now Jessica is laughing, giggling, her hands flying to her mouth like she's in a goddamn romance movie.

Now the entire auditorium is watching, waiting for her to answer.

Now my heart is breaking, splintering right there in my chest, because he never meant it for me at all.

I want to move. Want to turn around and walk away before I have to witness any more of this train wreck.

But I can't.

I just stand there, frozen in place, as Jessica throws herself into his arms.

And Joel—Joel grins like he just won the lottery.

Like this was always about her.

Like I was never even part of the story.

Like I never existed.

The realization is slow and excruciating.

I gave him this.

And he gave it away.

My breath catches. The auditorium fades. The crowd vanishes.

And then—

I wake up.

My chest is tight, my pulse hammering against my ribs. For a few seconds, I can't move.

My skin feels too hot. My sheets? Suffocating. I kick them off, swing my legs over the side of the bed, and press my bare feet into the floor, trying to ground myself.

Just a dream. Just a stupid dream.

But it's not, is it? It's a memory.

I squeeze my eyes shut, but it's too late—the past is unspooling whether I want it to or not.

After that day, I stopped answering his texts.

Joel had no idea why.

He thought it was just about the song—thought I was just mad that he played it without asking. And sure, that was part of it. But it wasn't the real reason.

The real reason was that I couldn't breathe.

I couldn't sit next to him, couldn't watch him pluck at the guitar strings like nothing had changed—like the whole world hadn't just caved in on me.

Because he didn't know. He didn't *know* what he took from me.

I remember the way his brows furrowed in confusion when I told him I was busy and to go away.

How he tried again the next day. And the next. And the next.

Because Joel was always at our house. Always around.

When Ethan was busy, he hung out with me. Not because he had to, but because it was better than being at his own house, dealing with his parents' divorce, pretending it wasn't breaking him in half.

I was his backup person. His in-between. His safe place.

And I—*stupid, stupid me*—let myself believe I was something more.

But after that night? I snapped my shell shut. I was colder. Sharper. Shorter. I had to be.

I cut him off with sarcastic jabs and thinly veiled irritation. I stopped writing. I stopped singing.

I stopped being the girl he knew.

And when he looked at me—really looked at me—he saw the difference.

I'll never forget the way his face fell the last time he asked if I wanted to work on a new song. The way he stared at me like I was a stranger. Like he couldn't figure out what he'd done to make me hate him.

And I never told him.

Never told him that he was the song.

Never told him that he was the heartbreak.

Never told him that every time he smiled at me like nothing was wrong, it felt like a knife to the ribs.

So he stopped asking.

And I stopped caring.

Or at least, I tried.

I drag my hands through my hair, exhaling slowly. Years. It's been years.

I should be over this. I *am* over this.

And yet—

The stupid envelope comes to mind through the tiny crack in my already vulnerable shield.

No.

I will not go digging up the past.

Instead, I close my eyes as tight as I can.

Deep breath in. Deep breath out.

I can sleep. I can move on. I can—

I don't realize I've gotten out of bed until I'm already standing in the doorway.

My office is dark, except for the faint glow of my monitor in sleep mode, pulsing like a quiet heartbeat. My chair is tucked in, my desk neat—except for the drawer.

The drawer.

The one I shoved shut the last time I let myself get too close to this mess.

But suddenly, my fingers itch. My breath is still uneven. My body is still running too hot, the ghosts of old memories simmering under my skin.

And I know exactly what's inside.

Waiting.

I stare at it, at the handle, at the stupid pull that would take all of two seconds to slide open. My hand hovers, hesitation tightening in my chest.

I could read it. I could finally see whatever bullshit excuse he tried to give me.

But what if... what if it changes nothing?

Or worse—what if it changes everything?

My throat tightens. My fingers curl into a fist, shaking slightly at my side.

No.

Not now. *Not ever.*

I'm not that girl anymore.

My breath catches in my throat, but I rip my gaze away, spin on my heel, and march straight back to my bedroom.

And if I slam my door shut behind me?

That's no one's business but mine.

CHAPTER 10

Joel

I wake up feeling like I got hit by a freight train.

Not from alcohol. I wasn't drinking last night—not enough to explain the heavy ache in my skull or the knots in my stomach, anyway.

No, this has to do with one thing an one thing only.

Anna.

Anna and the storm that's been brewing between us since the moment I set foot back in Duluth. Since the moment I saw her again.

Since the moment she looked at me with something other than loathing—something that might've been fear.

Not fear of me, necessarily. At least, I hope to hell that's not it.

I push up onto my elbows, staring at the ceiling. It's too early for this shit.

And yet, my brain is already spinning out of control, playing and replaying last night. The way she bolted from Nocté like she couldn't get away fast enough, the way I found her waiting when I got home —calm on the surface, but with that barely restrained tension humming beneath. The way we argued in the doorway, her voice sharp, then wavering, then something else entirely. Something I don't know how to name.

I squeeze my eyes shut and exhale through my nose.

Get a grip, Joel.

This isn't a second chance or a rekindled spark.

Anna Chang *hates* me. And she has every right to.

But that *look*. I can't shake it.

Something sharp. Something unguarded. Something that cracked through all the walls she's built between us and let me see what's still underneath.

I run a hand through my hair, frustration bubbling up beneath my skin. I'm not supposed to think about her like this. Not supposed to remember the way she used to be—before I screwed it all up.

But my mind won't let it go.

And I know exactly when it started...

Ethan ditched me that night.

Classic Ethan move—meet up at his house, then disappear the second some girl from the soccer team texted him. Which left me stuck, trying to decide whether to hang out in his basement alone or deal with the fact that my dad was on another one of his self-destructive benders at home.

I picked option C. The back porch.

And that's where I found her.

She didn't see me at first. She was sitting on the steps,

guitar in her lap, strumming out something soft, something unpolished, something *real*.

Something that made my chest go tight, like I was hearing a secret I wasn't meant to know.

Then I stepped on a loose board, and she jumped.

"Jesus, Joel," she scowled, fingers fumbling over the strings. "Ever heard of knocking?"

"It's a porch." I smirked, leaning against the railing. "Not a private recording studio."

She rolled her eyes, but she didn't tell me to leave.

And that should've been my first warning. I mean, alarm bells were going off, but what harm was there in sitting down?

So, I sat next to her, stretching my legs out. "What are you working on?"

She hesitated. Just for a second.

Then she did something that caught me off guard— she slammed the notebook shut.

"Nothing," she muttered, shifting so her elbow covered it, like she was shielding it from view.

That was new.

Anna never cared when I saw her notes before. She used to shove them in my face—riddles, puzzles, random facts she found interesting. And whenever Ethan bailed on me—which was often in our teenage years—she'd show up like it was a given, dropping onto the porch beside me with her notebook in hand. She'd toss out lyric ideas, let me mess with chord progressions while she scribbled down adjustments.

It was easy. *Effortless.*

A game we played without overthinking it.

But this?

This was different.

"Didn't sound like nothing," I teased, nudging her shoulder in the hopes of softening her edges.

"Well, it is," she shot back, still not looking at me. Instead, she stared straight ahead, fingers gripping the edges of her notebook like it might fly away if she didn't hold tight enough.

I studied her, brow furrowing. "Okay, now I really want to see it."

She scoffed, shaking her head. "Of course you do. That's exactly why you won't."

"That's not fair."

"Life's not fair, Joel," she said, but the insult had no bite. If anything, she sounded—flustered. Like she was thinking too hard about something.

Which meant I was right. This wasn't just another song. This wasn't just a random melody she was messing with.

This *meant* something.

I leaned in, lowering my voice. "Come on, Ace. I taught you your first chord. I think that earns me some rights."

She finally turned to me, expression unreadable. "Oh, you think you have *rights* to my inner thoughts? Get stuffed, Joel."

"Okay, poor choice of words," I admitted, holding up my hands. "But seriously, you're good. You know that, right? I'd just like to hear it—help if I can."

She exhaled through her nose, staring down at her notebook, fingers tapping a restless rhythm against the cover.

"I was just messing around," she muttered.

"Sounded better than messing around," I pointed out.

Another pause.

A war was waging inside her, and I could see it in the way she bit her lip, in the way her grip tightened around the spiral binding like she was physically holding herself back.

And for the first time, I really *looked* at her.

Anna had always been this tiny force of nature—sharp, relentless, always keeping up, even when she wasn't invited. But sometime in the past year, she'd started to change. The roundness of childhood had faded from her face, leaving behind something more defined, more striking. Her eyes—dark, intense—held something deeper now, something that made my chest tighten if I thought about it too much.

And right now, with the porch light casting a soft glow around her, I could almost see the woman she'd become one day.

The realization came like a slap—hot, sudden, and so fucking wrong that my whole body tensed against it. I felt it everywhere—too much, too fast, like stepping off a curb I hadn't seen coming. I swallowed hard, forcing my gaze away before my thoughts could go anywhere worse.

Shit.

Bury it. Pretend it never happened.

I shoved the thought away, clearing my throat, refocusing on the moment.

Then, slowly, she shifted.

"Fine," she huffed, flipping the notebook open—but not to the song.

No, she skipped a few pages forward and landed on something else. Some random collection of lyrics, unfinished lines that she probably didn't care about.

She handed it over. "Here. Enjoy my garbage."

I smirked. "Generous."

I skimmed the page, picking up on the structure immediately. The lines had potential, but they weren't what she'd just been playing.

"You know this isn't what you were singing, right?"

Her jaw tensed. "Just take it or leave it, Joel."

That should have been my cue to drop it.

To take what she was willing to give and move on.

But I was seventeen, and an idiot.

And, more than that, I was curious.

So instead of backing off, I tapped the corner of the notebook, waiting until she finally met my eyes.

"Why don't you want me to hear it?"

Her lips parted slightly, like she had an answer locked and loaded, but then she snapped her mouth shut. Her shoulders hunched, and her fingers curled around the edge of the page like she wanted to rip it out and set it on fire.

And that's when it hit me.

This wasn't just a song.

This was personal.

And personal meant—

Shit.

I straightened, scanning her face, piecing together what should have been obvious.

"It's about someone you like, isn't it?"

Her whole body jerked, eyes going wide before she could stop herself.

That was it. That was my answer.

It *was* about someone.

But before I could process what that meant—before I could even think to ask who—she ripped the notebook out of my hands and slammed it shut.

"You're so annoying," she muttered, standing abruptly.

"Hey—"

But she was already moving, grabbing her guitar, tucking the notebook under her arm like she was making a run for it.

"Where are you going?" I asked, standing too.

"Bed."

"Bed? It's barely ten on a Friday night."

She shot me a glare over her shoulder. "Well, some of us don't have endless energy reserves fueled by bad decisions."

I rolled my eyes. "Drama much?"

She didn't answer, just shoved open the back door, stepping inside before glancing at me one last time.

Something flickered across her face—hesitation, conflict, something I didn't understand at the time.

Then she sighed. "Goodnight, Joel."

The door clicked shut, leaving me standing there, staring at the spot she'd just been.

And for the first time in my life, I wondered—

Who the hell had Anna Chang been writing about?

I never got my answer.

Not then.

Not until it was too late.

And by then, I'd already ruined everything.

I scrub a hand down my face, dragging myself out of the memory, but it lingers—like smoke, like something burned deep into my brain that I'll never fully scrub out.

Because I know this is where I messed up.

I just don't know *why* I still can't let it go.

I tell myself it's guilt. That's the easy answer. That's the one I can live with.

I stole her song.

That beautiful song full of longing and embedded with a part of her soul.

That's why she hates me.

That's why she stormed out of Nocté like she couldn't escape fast enough. Why, when I found her waiting for me at her place, she had that look in her eyes —braced, like she knew exactly how much this would hurt. And maybe that should have been enough.

Maybe I should have just left things well enough alone.

But I can't. Around Anna, it seems like I never could.

Because back then? That's exactly what I was trying to do.

I was trying to get her to hate me.

I just never expected to hate myself for it.

I don't know what made her change her mind that day—why she finally let me see the song she'd been working on.

Maybe she got tired of me pushing. Maybe she figured I'd just keep annoying her until she caved.

Or maybe—*maybe she finally trusted me.*

That thought twists something in my chest, even now.

Because I didn't deserve it.

Not then. Definitely not now.

But she gave it to me anyway.

She sat cross-legged on the floor of her room, her back against the bedframe, fingers twitching against her notebook like she was still second-guessing whether this was a mistake. Her face was unreadable—her tell, I knew that much.

Anna wore her emotions like armor, but not this time.

This time, she was handing me something fragile.

So when she slid the notebook toward me, my stomach clenched.

I took it carefully, flipping to the page she had marked, letting my eyes move over the lyrics.

And shit.

I was right.

It *wasn't* just another song.

It was her.

Every single line felt like she had pulled pieces of herself from somewhere deep, raw, real—like she had unraveled something private and laid it bare on the page.

It wasn't perfect. The melody wasn't locked in yet, the words weren't as polished as they could be, but it was *real*. It had weight.

It made me want to hold onto it. And worse—it made me want to hold onto *her*.

Not as Ethan's little sister. Not as the stubborn, sharp-witted girl always trying to keep up.

As something more.

And that scared the hell out of me.

Because she was fourteen.

And I was seventeen.

I might have been a stupid teen, but I wasn't dumb.

I knew damn well I *wasn't* supposed to be feeling like that about her.

I wasn't supposed to feel like that. Wasn't supposed to notice the way she bit her lip when she was thinking, or how she tucked her hair behind her ear when she was nervous. Wasn't supposed to feel that low, sinking pull when she leaned into me, laughing under her breath as she fixed a note.

But I did.

Even though it was wrong, she became the only thing I could think about. I stopped going to Ethan's house for him. I went, hoping he'd bail so I could spend more time with her.

I knew it couldn't last, but I did it anyway. At least, until it became obvious I was going to get us both in deep shit.

So I did the only thing I could think of.

I buried it.

I shoved it down, locked it away, forced myself to forget it was even there.

And then I made the worst mistake of my life.

I made her *believe* that song—her song—meant nothing to me.

I told myself it wasn't a big deal.

That if I played it in front of the whole school, it would mean nothing. It would turn into just another performance.

It would break whatever was happening between us before it could become something more—something worse.

And I needed that.

I *needed* her to hate me.

Because maybe if she hated me, I could stop hating myself for the way I had started seeing her.

So I did it.

I walked onto that stage, sat on that stool, and I played *her* song.

And at first, it was fine.

The auditorium was packed, students buzzing, the usual pep rally chaos filling the air. I let my fingers move over the strings, let my voice find the melody we had pieced together.

When I found her, I couldn't help it—I poured every last feeling into it for her, knowing full well I was about to shred it all to pieces. Part of me hoped she'd feel me, though. Feel the real reason I was doing all of this.

And for one impossible second, I thought... maybe she did. Maybe she felt it too. Maybe she knew, even if I never said it out loud.

Her expression in that moment—it was open in a way I'd never seen before. Like she was waiting for something, bracing for it. Like this song meant just as much to her as it did to me.

And if I had let myself hold onto that look—if I had let myself believe that maybe, just maybe, we were standing at the edge of the same feeling—I never would have done what I did next.

Because this performance couldn't be personal. The song wasn't supposed to be hers anymore.

So, I turned it into something else.

And when the last note rang out, I made sure to make it loud and clear—I made sure *everyone* knew who it was for.

Not her.

Not the person who had poured her heart into it.

Not the person I wanted to be focusing on.

I turned my head, locked eyes with the first girl from my class I could see, Jessica Carson, and said the words like they had always been meant for her.

"Hey, Jessica. Would you wanna go to prom with me?"

The crowd erupted.

Jessica gasped, her hands flying to her mouth in that over-the-top way she did whenever she wanted attention.

And Anna—

I didn't look at her.

I *couldn't* look at her.

But I *felt* her.

I felt the second she realized.

The second she understood what I had done.

And then—

She was gone. Just like she had done on Valentine's Day. Just like she had done last night.

She didn't wait for the applause, didn't stay to watch Jessica squeal her answer. She just turned and ran out.

And for the first time in my life, I felt like a part of myself had died.

I just sat there, let Jessica launch herself at me, let the school cheer like this was some perfect teen movie moment.

I let it happen.

Because I told myself it was for the best.

That I had done the right thing.

That nothing was ruined. It was *saved*.

I saved *her*.

That's the lie I told myself.

But the truth? I was only saving myself.

I knew it the second I saw her the next day—the way she *didn't* look at me, the way she *didn't* say anything, the way something in her had gone cold.

And I knew it last night, when she walked out of Nocté—when she looked at me like I was something that had happened to her, not someone she used to trust.

And now?

Now I can't live with it.

And I don't know why.

I *got what I wanted* back then.

I wanted her hate. I just never thought she'd stop writing.

But that's exactly what she did.

And the worst part?

I think I knew she would.

Did I destroy her to keep from wanting her?

Did I steal that part of her—so I wouldn't have to watch her give it to someone else?

If I did, I'm an asshole.

And now? There's nothing left but ashes. And I have to live in the wreckage.

CHAPTER 11

Anna

The smell of coffee is supposed to be something nice to wake up to.

But not when you live alone.

My brain takes a second to boot up, caught in the sluggish limbo between sleep and reality, but as soon as I hear the low hum of someone singing—*ugh, Joel*—I'm officially done with this morning and I haven't even gotten out of bed.

I crack one eye open, willing myself to be wrong.

But no.

Somewhere on the other side of my bedroom door, I catch the sound of a cabinet closing, then the distinct clink of pans being placed on my stovetop.

What. The. Hell.

I groan, shoving the blankets off and rolling out of bed. I don't even bother checking the mirror—I already know I look like I've lost a fight with my pillow, and honestly? That's the energy I'm bringing into today.

Fuck it.

Joel should not be in my kitchen. He should not be existing in my space like some kind of domestic rock god, humming to himself like he has some sort of right to my kitchen.

Did he even buy his own food? Because if that man so much as touched my last pack of kimchi noodles, I'm committing a crime.

I need coffee. And I need him to not be here.

Flinging open my dresser, I grab the first hoodie I can find and pull it over my sleep shirt, already deciding I'm heading straight to *Bean There, Done That*. If I have to be awake and conscious enough to deal with Price, I need massive amounts of caffeine for my suffering. Maybe I'll even catch Carlie there because I need to *vent*.

I yank my bedroom door open and step into the kitchen, prepared to fight for my sanity, my caffeine, and my last shred of peace.

Joel is standing at the stove, flipping something in a pan with way too much ease, like this is *his* apartment and *his* morning routine, and I'm just some visitor in his domestic fantasy land.

His hair is a tangled mess, his sweatpants are hanging loose on his hips—something I totally did *not* notice—and he's barefoot, which for some reason annoys me more than anything else.

"What," I say, voice still rough from sleep, "the actual hell are you doing?"

Joel barely glances at me before returning his attention to whatever he's cooking. "What does it look like, Ace? I'm making breakfast."

I squint at him. "For who?"

He grins. "Us."

I snort, heading straight for the coffee pot because it's full and I might need a weapon. "Absolutely not."

Joel flips the spatula dramatically, sending something golden brown into the air before catching it. "Wow. So much hostility so early in the morning. It's almost like you don't appreciate my efforts."

I glare at him, yanking the coffee pot off it's warmer with more force than necessary, then slam it back into place.

I hate how good it smells.

I cross my arms. "Did you poison this?"

Joel turns off the burner, feigning deep thought. "Depends. Do you consider a dash of cinnamon poison?"

I blink at him. "Cinnamon?"

He sighs dramatically. "Yes, cinnamon. It brings out the flavor of the beans. Now, I know what you're thinking. We're eternal enemies, doomed to cohabitate under one roof for the next couple of weeks. *Why* on earth is he making me a delicious breakfast and coffee that tastes like it was blessed by the gods?" He picks up a plate and gestures toward me. "So, want some pancakes, or should I throw these in the trash in a fit of heartbreak?"

I narrow my eyes at the stack of perfectly golden pancakes sitting on a plate. I have to admit, I'm slightly impressed—more than I should be. My stomach, the traitor, tightens with interest, but I ignore it. "Go to hell, Price."

He gestures at himself. "Me? What did I do?"

"You exist. That's enough."

"I forgot you are *not* a morning person." He throws his head back and laughs, and I hate that my stomach does something weird over it.

I cross my arms. "Did you even buy this food? Or did you just *forage* from my kitchen like some kind of musical raccoon?"

Joel places a hand over his heart, like I've just mortally wounded him.

"I'll have you know, I bought it. I do have money, you know," he says, pointing toward a reusable grocery bag sitting on the counter. "See? Eggs, coffee, butter, all mine. You should be thanking me for upgrading your kitchen staples. You didn't even have real milk, Anna. Not everything has to be a Korean staple."

"I don't drink almond milk because it's Korean, dumbass," I say, grabbing a mug from the cupboard. "Some of us don't trust cow juice."

His eyebrows lift. "Cow juice?"

"Don't act like that's weird. You were literally just singing to your pancakes."

Joel grins again and leans against the counter, watching as I hover next to the coffee pot, waging an internal war.

I could pour a cup of coffee.

The pot is right there and I'm clutching my cup like a lifeline—which, to be fair, isn't far from the truth.

The wake-up juice is already made…

I bite the side of my lip, deliberating.

For some reason, it smells like sin and temptation.

Joel watches me with a lopsided grin that I wish I could wipe off his stupid, smug face.

"You gonna drink it, or are you afraid it'll make you start liking me?"

I drop the mug. Not on the floor—just on the counter a little too aggressively.

"I have places to be," I announce. "I'll get my coffee at *Bean There, Done That*. You know, from an actual barista who knows what they're doing."

Joel snorts. "You mean you're gonna pay five bucks for the same caffeine that's right here?"

"It's about *principle*," I say, heading for the door.

If I have to cut my nose off to spite my face, I can at least push home the point.

Joel leans against the counter, fully amused, sipping his own coffee as he watches me actively avoid the free caffeine in my own goddamn kitchen.

"Suit yourself," he says, voice far too smug.

I'm still mentally cursing him as I fling the door open—

And nearly face-plant into Ethan's chest.

His entire form blocks my getaway and the hand that's poised to knock, drops to my shoulder.

"Jesus, Anna," he grunts, steadying me like I'm some fragile thing. "Are you running from something?"

I smooth down my hoodie, straightening like I haven't just been caught mid-escape. "*Yes.* You."

But then I see who's standing behind him.

My mother.

Oh for the love.

Every ounce of irritation, exhaustion, and general desire to commit crimes against Joel is immediately buried under years of ingrained filial obedience.

I smile. A little too tight. A little too forced.

"Hi, Mom," I say sweetly, like I wasn't just moments away from throwing a coffee mug at Joel's head.

Her eyebrows lift, gaze flicking from me, to Ethan, to inside the house—where, unfortunately, Joel is very much visible and very much looking amused. I wanna throat punch that smug grin off his face.

I can feel the exact moment my mother spots him.

Because her entire expression shifts.

The smile sharpens, just a little. Like she knows something I don't.

I don't like it. Not one little bit.

Joel, the human disaster that he is, chooses that exact moment to walk up behind me, boxing me in.

"Morning, Mrs. Chang," he says, all polite charm. Fake. Calculated.

I'm going to kill him.

Mom smiles back. "Joel, darling, It's so great to see you. I heard you might be here."

Oh my god, gag me.

Mom's expression shifts—just the slightest knowing tilt of her head as she glances at me. I narrow my gaze when she turns her back to me so she can face Joel.

"You're looking well," she adds, stepping past Ethan

to glide into my kitchen like she owns the place. She pats Joel's arm as she passes.

Pats.

His.

Arm.

I watch in horror as she gives him the kind of warm, affectionate look that is usually reserved for the good Korean sons who become doctors or lawyers, not the should-be exiled best friend of my brother who ruined *my* goddamn life.

Joel grins like he knows exactly what's happening and is enjoying every second of it. I envision that throat punch again.

I grab Ethan's sleeve, dragging him slightly onto my back porch so I can hiss, "You *told* her. Why would you tell her about Joel?"

He pulls back with mock horror. "She's our mother, Anna. She gets things out of people."

I glare harder. "Good god, grow a spine, man."

He shrugs like the traitor he is. "She might've mentioned you've been MIA the past few days, and I *might've* let it slip that Joel's been staying in your spare room, so you're probably occupied with all of that."

Fantastic. *Just fantastic.*

I head inside to find Mom now perched in my dining chair, completely at home, like she's settling in for a long chat.

"Well," she says, giving me her most innocent smile. "Since we're here to finalize plans for Mina's doljanchi, Joel suggested we might as well have breakfast together."

I whip around so fast I nearly give myself whiplash. "I'm sorry, Joel suggested what now? It's not even *his* house."

Joel sips his coffee, looking as pleased as a cat who just knocked a vase off the counter. "I just thought, since everyone is here, why not make it a family affair?"

A family affair.

I stare at him, then at my mother—who is beaming for som god awful reason—then at Ethan, who is already helping himself to the pancakes like a traitorous bastard.

This cannot be happening.

But it is.

Because my mother is nodding like this is the best idea she's ever heard, and Joel is setting out plates like he's a charming and respectable member of society instead of the actual bane of my existence.

I pinch the bridge of my nose. "Mom, I was heading out. We don't need to—"

"Nonsense," she says, waving a dismissive hand. "We have so much to discuss. And you know food always makes planning easier. We were going to see if you'd like to go to Perkins, but this is better."

Joel grins like he knows exactly how much I want to throw something at him. "See, Ace? Even your mom agrees with me."

I whip back around. "I swear to god, if you don't stop calling me that—"

"Sit," Mom orders, voice sharp with motherly authority.

My entire body moves against my will. Damn it.

I drop into the chair next to Ethan, who is already on his second pancake. He nudges my plate toward me. "Might as well eat. You're gonna need the energy."

I grab a pancake and stab it with my fork, ignoring the way Joel sits across from me, looking far too smug for someone I am actively considering murdering.

Mom, oblivious to my suffering, takes a delicate sip of her tea—and when the hell did she have time to make that? Come to think of it, why is there a bag of her favorite tea bags on my counter?

"Ethan, you and Tessa need to help set up the venue. Anna, we need final RSVPs from our side of the family. And of course, the big thing is the dol table. Everything has to be set up perfectly for Mina's doljabi. And don't forget—everyone needs to have their hanbok ready."

I nearly choke on my coffee. "Wait. What?"

I mean, it's not like I didn't see this coming, but still.

Mom gives me the look. The one that says she is prepared to fight me if I open my mouth again. "You heard me, Anna. You're wearing your hanbok. End of story."

Joel, the worst person alive, perks up. "Oh, hell yes. Do I get to see this?"

I glare at him. "I will burn this entire house down first."

"Of course you'll see it. You'll be there, won't you Joel?" Mom says, ignoring my outburst entirely.

"I wouldn't miss it for the world," Joel grins, patting my mother's hand. "Mina's practically my niece."

I glare in his general direction and witness my mother sigh contently.

I hope all of them choke on their breakfast.

Joel tilts his head, looking genuinely interested. "Wait, what's a dol table? I don't think I've heard of that before."

Mom lights up.

Oh, god. No.

Joel has just made a critical mistake.

My mother might not be born Korean, but when she married in, she immersed herself so deep into the culture, you'd think she was a direct descendant of Shilla royalty.

"The doljabi is a tradition where we set up a table of symbolic objects," she explains, eyes glowing with excitement. "Mina will pick one, and it's supposed to predict her future. Like, if she picks a stethoscope, she might become a doctor. If she picks money, she'll be wealthy. Things like that."

Joel blinks. "So, like, baby fortune telling?"

Ethan snorts. "Pretty much."

Mom swats his arm. "Ethan, it's a serious tradition."

Joel, being the worst person alive, grins. "What if she picks, like, a drumstick? Or a microphone?"

I groan, already seeing where this is going. "That just means she's doomed to a life of financial instability."

Mom gives me a look of incredulousness..

Joel fake gasps. "Anna, that's a terrible thing to say about your niece. Are you telling me you wouldn't support little Mina if she wanted to become a world-famous musician like her uncle Joel?"

I glare at him. "I'm saying I wouldn't actively encourage her to starve."

Mom sighs. "Just because your appa thinks the same way, doesn't mean you need to follow in his footsteps, Anna. You used to love music. Just like any profession, you can be successful if you're truly skilled."

There it is.

I stab my pancake a little harder than necessary.

Ethan, sensing danger, shovels more food into his mouth like he did when we were kids.

Joel leans back in his chair, sipping his coffee like he's enjoying a particularly juicy drama. "Speaking of your appa, where is he? Doesn't he want to help out with all of this."

Mom waves a dismissive hand. "Oh, you know Min-woo. He loves tradition, but he says planning parties is 'too much of a spectacle.'"

Ethan snorts. "That's his way of saying he'd rather read research papers and judge his students."

I nod. "And critique my life choices."

Mom shoots me another look.

Joel chuckles. "Still the same Min-woo, huh?"

Mom's expression softens. "Always. He's looking forward to the ceremony, though. And don't let him fool you—he's the one who insisted we use the university's cafeteria for it."

I roll my eyes. Of course. My father might not be into "spectacles," but he'd make sure the event looked presti-gious enough to represent his name.

Joel hums, still too interested. "Well, can't wait to see him there. Hope he still remembers me."

Mom smiles, too pleased. "Oh, he remembers. *Trust* me."

I squint. "What's that supposed to mean?"

Joel hums into his coffee, far too entertained. "So, just to be clear—when he sees me, should I expect an immediate disowning glare or will there be a *buffer* period before he tells me I'm a disappointment for going into music?"

"Oh, Joel, Min-woo doesn't *say* things like that," Mom says with another exasperated sigh.

Ethan snorts. "No, he just stares at you until you feel like *you* should apologize for existing."

I groan, already anticipating the headache this is going to cause. "I can attest to that."

Mom gives me a pointed look over the rim of her teacup. "Anna, don't be dramatic. Your appa is proud of you."

I scoff. "Sure. In an *'if only she had gone into engineering instead of app development'* kind of way."

Ethan nods. "Or in a *'she has a good job, but imagine if she'd gone to med school'* way."

I point at Ethan and nod.

Mom purses her lips but doesn't deny it.

Joel, of course, is soaking all of this in. "Man, I really did miss you guys."

I glare at him. "Don't be weird."

"Oh, I'm sorry," he says, resting an elbow on the table like he's settling in for a show. "Am I *not* supposed to enjoy the family drama I was deprived of for years?"

Ethan gestures with his fork. "See? That's the real tragedy here."

Mom, as if sensing my rising frustration, smooths a hand over the table like she's tidying up the air around us. "Min-woo is looking forward to the doljanchi, end of story. And," she adds, looking at Joel, "he *does* know you're back in town."

Joel arches a brow. "That's good, I guess."

"And?" I say, drawing out the word, knowing full well there's probably more to it than that.

Mom shrugs. "And nothing. He just said *hmm.*"

I deadpan, but counter, catching Joel's curious gaze. "I'd be scared. That's worse than *ah.*"

Joel frowns, looking between us. "What's the ranking system here? I need context."

Ethan sets his fork down, suddenly invested. "Okay, so *hmm* means he's filing it away for later, possibly as evidence against you. Anna's right. You should be on high alert."

I nod. "And *ah* means he already knows and has *thoughts* he will reveal at the most inconvenient time."

Joel blinks. "What about *oh?*"

Ethan and I exchange a look.

I grimace. "That's when you *run.*"

"You are all so dramatic." Mom rolls her eyes. "I just think it'll be nice to have everyone together again. We're all family, after all."

Joel, to his credit, doesn't gloat at that.

But he does meet my eyes again.

And for a second, just one second, something in his expression shifts—like he wants to say something, but isn't sure he should.

I push my chair back, grabbing my now-cold coffee. "Great. Can't wait for the inevitable disaster this turns into."

Joel shifts in his seat, the corner of his mouth quirking up as I stand. "What's the matter, Ace? Afraid you'll have too much fun?"

I snort under my breath. "Oh yeah, Joel. *So* much fun. Being trapped in a room with you, my family, and my father's inevitable disapproval sounds like an *absolute blast.*"

Mom clears her throat, and I immediately regret my words.

"I'm sure your father will be delighted to see both of you," she says sweetly, but there's an unmistakable edge of *fix your attitude* to it. "And it'll be good for the family to be together again to celebrate Mina. Just like old times."

Joel leans back, still watching me with that stupid amused smirk. "Exactly. What's a little nostalgia between childhood friends?"

I glare. "We were never *friends.*"

"Oh, don't be ridiculous, Anna," Mom says, already rising from the table and smoothing out her cardigan. "You and Joel were *inseparable* when you were young."

I nearly choke on thin air. "That's revisionist history,

and you *know it*. He's always been *Ethan's* inseparable friend. Not mine."

Mom merely hums as she gathers her things, but before she can fully make her exit, she pauses and turns to Joel. "Oh, by the way, darling, I need your hanbok measurements, as well. Can you get them to me?"

Joel blinks. "Uh—"

"He's not wearing a hanbok," I blurt, horrified.

Mom looks offended. "Of course he is. He's *practically family.*"

Joel, to my utter horror, beams. *Beams* like she just told him he won the lottery. "Wow, Mrs. Chang. I'm touched."

I'm going to die.

Mom nods, satisfied. "I'll make sure it's ready for the ceremony. Just get me your measurements." She turns to me, and her smile sharpens. "And I expect *you* to wear yours properly this time."

I groan. "I wore it properly last time."

"You tied the norigae onto your wrist like a bracelet," she says flatly.

"...Fashion is subjective."

She sighs. "Just be ready, Anna."

With that, she gives Joel's arm one last pat—*traitor*—before gathering her purse. "Ethan, come on, I need you to drive me to the store so I can order the food."

Ethan groans but gets up, stretching before pointing his fork at me. "You're gonna have to wear the hanbok, you know. There's no getting out of it."

I narrow my eyes at him. "You're dead to me."

"Love you, too," Joel says, chuckling under his breath as he follows after our mother.

Joel snickers, clearly reveling in my suffering. "I can't wait to see this. You all dressed up, looking like the perfect little—"

I whip around, pointing a menacing finger at him. "Finish that sentence, Price, and I swear to god—"

His hand catches my wrist.

Not hard. Not yanking. Just—*firm*.

Intentional. Like a silent demand that I look at him.

A shiver ghosts up my arm, unwelcome, unwanted.

My brain stutters, short-circuiting for the briefest second. Because this touch—his touch—is different from the casual, infuriating Joel I know. There's no smirk, no teasing. Just the weight of something unspoken stretching between us and because he's not talking, my brain is sputtering.

His thumb barely brushes my pulse, like he's testing something. Like he's waiting for me to pull away—or waiting to see if I won't.

I should yank my hand back. I should roll my eyes and tell him to shove off. But for a fraction of a heartbeat, I don't.

Joel notices. I can tell by the way his grip tightens, just slightly.

And then—

"Oh, I forgot my tea bags."

My mother bustles in, completely unaware that she just shattered whatever this was into a thousand tiny, irretrievable pieces.

Joel's hand disappears. Like it never happened.

I exhale too sharply. Step back like I wasn't just standing there, waiting for—

I wasn't.

I wasn't.

Mom plucks her tea bags off the counter, then gives us both a knowing smile that makes my stomach twist.

"Well," she says, eyes far too observant, "see you both soon."

Joel smirks, like he's enjoying this way too much. "Can't wait."

I don't even have a clapback for that.

Because my wrist still tingles.

Because I have no idea what just happened.

Because I don't want to know what would have happened if my mother hadn't walked back in.

And that thought?

That's what really terrifies me

CHAPTER 12

Joel

The club is alive with energy, buzzing with the anticipation of a sold-out crowd. The sound techs are running cables, the lighting guys are testing strobes, and Mark, the stage manager, is barking orders like he's leading an army.

And I should be in it—feeling the electricity in my veins, the familiar rush of performing.

But all I can think about is this morning.

That moment.

That fucking moment.

Her wrist under my fingers, pulse fluttering just once before her mom interrupted. The way her lips parted, like she was about to say something—but didn't. The way something unspoken cracked between us, and for the first time, I had no idea what she was thinking.

Hell, I forgot what *I* was thinking.

For a split second, if I didn't know Anna was Anna, I

would have sworn there was something else in her eyes. Something I shouldn't even entertain.

But no.

That's not possible.

Anna would rather slide down a banister of razor blades into a pool of alcohol than admit to even tolerating my existence—let alone being attracted to me.

Still.

I keep replaying it. The feel of her skin. The way she didn't pull away. The way my brain short-circuited because suddenly, all I wanted to do was push that button again.

And now, standing in the middle of soundcheck for my fucking opening show at Nocté, I can't get my head straight. She's all I could think about all damn day and it's bleeding into my night.

Mark snaps his fingers in front of my face. "Hey, rockstar. You planning to check in with the rest of us anytime soon?"

I blink. The mic is in my hand, the band is waiting for me to run through the set, and I have no idea how long I've been standing here like an idiot.

I scrub a hand down my face. "Yeah, yeah. Just—late night."

Mark narrows his eyes and huffs. "That's not what this is."

I let out a staccato laugh. "What? You got mind-reading powers?"

Mark folds his arms, unimpressed. "Please. I've seen performers run on nothing but Red Bull and bad decisions. I've seen them drunk, hungover, jet-lagged, and fresh off a breakup. But you?" He gives me a slow once-over. "You're in la-la land, Price. Where the hell did you go?"

I roll my shoulders back, grip the mic tighter. "I'm right here."

Mark snorts. "Sure you are. You've just been staring into the void like it owes you money."

I glance toward Myles over at the bar, half expecting her to jump in, but she just arches a brow, looking equally entertained and unimpressed. Great. Now I have a damn audience.

"I'm fine." It's a lie, and we all know it.

Mark sighs through his nose, muttering something about *musicians and their melodramatic bullshit* before waving to the band. "Alright, let's run it again. Try not to sound like you're thinking about your grocery list this time."

I flip him off before adjusting my stance, nodding at the guys to start from the top.

The first notes hum through the club, deep and familiar. I roll into the song, the chords flowing through my hands like muscle memory. The mic is hot, the sound balanced.

And yet...

It feels off.

I go through the motions, hitting every note, every beat, every moment I've practiced a thousand times before. But there's no fire behind it. It's flat, and I hate that I know exactly why.

She's not gonna be here.

There's no way in hell she'll be here tonight.

She'd rather chew glass than deliberately walk into my opening night, especially if she thought I expected her to. Had I asked, she'd probably have made some smart-ass remark about how there aren't enough earplugs in the world to endure my set.

And yet, something in my chest sinks at the fact that she's not here.

Because it means she doesn't care.

Or worse, she *does* care—and that's exactly why she stayed away.

By the time we finish the run-through, Mark gives me a slow clap. "Well, that was soulless. Congrats. You've officially become a pop machine."

I sigh. "Jesus, Mark. You're a pleasure, you know that?"

He shrugs. "Don't Jesus me. You're the one phoning it in. Fix whatever's broken before you get up there for real."

I roll my eyes, but he's right. I gotta get my shit together.

❧

The house lights drop. The roar of the crowd rips through the club like a thunderclap.

This is it.

This is what I *live* for.

The band starts up, the first heavy pulse of the bass

rattling the floor beneath my boots. I step onto the stage, and for a second, I forget everything.

Because when the lights hit, when the music kicks in, when the crowd starts moving, screaming, reaching—I usually become someone else.

Someone *untouchable*.

Someone who doesn't care that Anna isn't in the room.

But tonight?

That someone doesn't show up no matter how much I try to summon him.

The set goes fine. Technically, I kill it. The energy is high, the sound is tight, and the crowd gives me everything I want from them.

But it still feels empty.

Every lyric, every riff, every moment that should hit like a rush just feels like an echo of what it should be. Like I'm watching myself perform instead of living in it.

No matter what I do, my brain keeps looping back to this morning.

To *her*.

To that fucking second where I felt something I shouldn't have—something I thought I stamped out when I was seventeen.

Backstage, after the set, I peel off my jacket and toss it onto the couch in the green room.

I expect a moment to myself to collect my thoughts, but Myles strides in, arms crossed, looking half-amused, half-unimpressed.

"Tessa said you'd be good," she says, tilting her head. "And you were. *Technically.*"

I let out a slow breath, already on edge. "But?"

Myles shrugs. "But it felt a little... I don't know. Off? I thought you'd have more, like, rockstar energy."

I roll my shoulders, avoiding her gaze. The last thing I want to do is to have tonight's performance get back to Tessa. Thank god she and Ethan weren't able to make it tonight. "Sorry, I just wasn't feeling it. A little distracted, I guess. Tomorrow night will be better."

She studies me for a beat, then shakes her head. "Well, London's thrilled. Packed house. Drinks flowing. The club made a killing. So, don't sweat it too much."

I don't respond. Because none of that means anything when I feel like I just played a set on autopilot.

Myles watches me a second longer, then exhales through her nose. "Anyway, I came back here to let you know we've got a space for you and the crew for the after-party in the Upper Tier."

I glance up at that. "Upper Tier?"

She nods but shifts slightly, like she's choosing her words carefully. "Yeah. The VIP area upstairs."

But there's something in her expression—just a flicker of hesitation before she shrugs it off.

I catch it, though. Evidently, all this time around Anna has my subtle expression antennae up. Super.

"You got something against this Upper Tier?" I ask before I can stop myself.

She quickly shakes her head. "Nah. Just... it's not usually used for this. But tonight, it's all yours, rockstar."

That gets my attention. "Not usually used for what?"

Myles waves a dismissive hand. "Don't worry about it."

Okay. That's weird.

But before I can press, she jerks her chin toward the door. "You coming?"

I hesitate, because something about this whole thing feels off. I just don't know why.

But I need a drink before heading back into the lion's den that is Anna's place.

I need something to take my mind off her—*that touch*—before I lose it completely.

"Yeah," I say, grabbing my jacket. "Let's go."

The moment I step inside, I know something is a little different.

The club's main floor was electric—wild and loud, full of people riding the high of the show. Drinks were flowing, people were dancing.

But this?

This is something else.

The lighting is lower, casting a golden glow over plush seating. The air is thicker, the music softer—a deep, slow bass vibrating under conversation.

And the people?

Sure, they're drinking and chatting to each other. But they're also doing something else that makes the hairs on my neck stand on end.

They're *watching*.

And not in the '*Oh, there's the rockstar*' way, either. But I can't seem to put my finger on it.

There's something about the way bodies lean too close, linger too long. The way laughter rolls under hushed voices, like there's an inside joke I'm not part of.

Don't get me wrong, I'm used to post-show flirting. The occasional groupie trying to stick around. But this? This isn't that.

I settle at the bar, ordering a whiskey, but I can't shake the feeling that I've walked into something I wasn't supposed to see.

I lean toward the bartender. "Upper Tier always this... quiet?"

The guy smirks as he slides me my drink. "Quiet? No. Can't say it's ever *quiet*."

I lift a brow, but he's already walking away.

Great.

I take a sip, scanning the room.

Some of my crew is already here, sprawled out on couches, laughing, drinking. A few industry people mingle, doing the usual handshake networking bullshit.

But beyond them—there's a vibe that says I've stepped into another world, and I'm not entirely welcome. Odd.

Then, I hear it in passing.

Whispers.

Little things, caught in flickers of conversation.

"London must really like this guy if he roped off the rooms for the night."

"Yeah, well, can't exactly have rockstars walking in the middle of..."

"But it would be so fun to have an actual rockstar to..."

The voices fade, but I get the idea.

And now that I get it, I can't *un*-get it.

I shift my weight, frowning slightly, finally noticing the velvet rope sectioning off the hallway at the side of the lounge. A guy stands at the entrance—not a bouncer, exactly, but definitely there to keep people out by the looks of it.

I don't have to guess what's behind those doors.

And I definitely don't mean VIP bottle service.

As I watch, a couple approaches the rope. A woman —elegant, poised, confident in a way that suggests she knows exactly how this works—leans in close to the guy at the entrance.

He nods, lifts the rope, and lets them through.

They disappear down the hall.

I should look away.

But, like an idiot, I don't.

Because the guy's hand slides down her back, fingertips grazing just under the hem of her dress as they approach one of the closed doors.

He presses her against it. Murmurs something against her lips.

She laughs—soft and knowing—right before the door clicks open and they disappear inside.

The hallway door shuts.

And just like that, it's cemented.

This Upper Tier isn't just a VIP lounge.

It's a playground.

And now, my brain that was already spinning out is a fucking traitor.

Because instead of shaking it off and moving on, all I can think about is Anna.

No.

Nope.

I grip the glass tighter.

Because it shouldn't be like this.

I shouldn't be standing here, surrounded by the unmistakable vibe of sexual debauchery, and thinking about *her.*

About how her pulse kicked under my fingers this morning. About how, for a fraction of a second, she didn't pull away.

But my brain? It makes the connection anyway.

Anna.

Sex.

Fuck.

I toss back the rest of my drink.

I need to get out of my own head. *Now.*

I scan the room for a distraction, but all I can think about is why the hell I'm tying Anna to any of this. She'd think I was cracked.

I exhale slowly, fingers tightening into a fist as the thought creeps in.

What would that pulse feel like under my tongue instead of my fingertips?

For the briefest of moments, I envision running my tongue up the tender side of her neck.

The idea shouldn't hit the way it does.

It shouldn't sink into my skin, heat low in my stomach, making my body react before my brain can shut it down.

But I let it linger for just a second—long enough to feel it. To picture it.

Too long.

I grit my teeth, spinning around to face the bar, so no one can witness what the thought is doing to my lower half.

I exhale sharply, setting the glass down as a decision settles over me. It's a *bad* fucking decision, but a decision nonetheless.

Somehow, I *need* to push that button again to see if the attraction was really there. I need to know if I imagined it.

Because if it's not there?

Then I'm completely fucked.

CHAPTER 13

Anna

The best thing about Joel Price being such a *hotshot* rockstar?

He has to leave sometime.

And tonight? Tonight is blissfully Joel-free.

No humming. No guitar. No frustratingly loud presence lingering in my space, waiting to get under my skin.

Which means tonight is just me, my couch, and an uninterrupted night of my favorite K-drama.

I stretch out, arms wide, luxuriating in the freedom of it all.

Finally.

Finally, I get one damn night without his voice in my ears, without the constant reminder that he exists too close, too often. It might only be a few days since he invaded, but it feels like years at this point.

I exhale, letting my body sink deeper into the cushions. This is exactly what I need. A night of soft blankets, takeout, and brain-melting romance with an emotionally unavailable male lead who *isn't* Joel Price.

I hit play on the next episode and grab my takeout box to settle in.

The music swells, dramatic and sweeping, pulling me in even though I know *exactly* how this scene will go.

The hero is standing on the edge of a city sidewalk, his knuckles white around a crumpled letter, his jaw tight like he's trying to swallow a thousand things he should have said. He watches her walk away, shoulders stiff, not looking back, even though we know she wants to.

I dig into my takeout container, swirling noodles around my chopsticks without looking away from the screen.

God, I love this shit.

The camera cuts to his expression—the heartbreak in his eyes, the devastation, the quiet plea he won't say aloud. He shifts forward, like he might run after her, like he wants to so badly he's physically stopping himself.

I let out a small huff through my nose. "Just go after her, dumbass."

Of course, he doesn't. That's not how these scenes work.

Instead, it starts to rain.

Classic.

Fat droplets hitting the pavement, soaking through his jacket, his hair. He doesn't move. He just stands there, watching her disappear into the night, drowning in his own silence.

I scoop up another bite of noodles, chewing slowly as I watch him suffer.

Ugh. So angsty. So dramatic. I love it.

The heroine stops.

Not fully—just a pause in her step, like something tugged her back for half a second. She doesn't turn, doesn't give him the satisfaction of seeing her face.

But it's enough.

Enough to let him know she feels it too.

I shift slightly, twirling my chopsticks against the rim of the container.

It's stupid. Just a TV show.

Except—

Except the way he looks at her—like he's waiting for her to turn around, like he needs her to but can't ask her to—

My breath catches.

Because for a split second, I remember the way Joel looked at me before he left tonight.

Like he wasn't going to ask.

Like he wasn't going to say a single thing about the show, but he wanted *me* to.

Like he was waiting for something—anything.

My fingers tighten around the blanket in my lap.

Nope, I do *not* like this train of thought.

I don't care about his stupid show. I don't care about whatever expression he had on *his* face.

I'm only here for the K-drama and to witness these two finally get over their stupid differences.

And yet—

My stomach twists again.

I force my attention back to the screen, but the drama doesn't feel as fun anymore.

Because now my thoughts are spiraling.

He's probably on stage right now.

Probably standing in the spotlight, playing *my fucking song,* and I'm sitting here letting him take up space in my head like a complete idiot.

My jaw tightens.

It's not like *he* invited *me.*

Not that I would have gone. But still, he could have mentioned it. Could have asked, even knowing I'd say no.

But he didn't.

I grab another bite of noodles, but they taste flat now, like cardboard in my mouth. I push the takeout container onto the coffee table, suddenly restless. My skin feels too tight and my blood feels itchy in my veins.

This is stupid.

I should be enjoying this—a night of *peace.* But instead, my brain is doing exactly what I swore I wouldn't let it do.

Thinking about *he-who-shall-not-be-named.*

Or thinking about the way he looked at me before he left, like he desperately wanted me to say I'd come with.

I shake my head, pulling my blanket tighter around me.

No.

Maybe a night alone was a bad idea.

I need a distraction.

I could put on another episode.

I could call Lily. No, she's probably at the stupid club watching the stupid performance since she practically lives there now.

I could—

My gaze flicks toward the hallway.

Toward my office.

My stomach flips over and my noodles try to make a comeback.

Nope.

No, no, no.

If I could disappear into the couch, I would. Instead, I tuck my legs under me. I am not doing this.

I am not thinking about that god forsaken envelope.

It's been sitting in my desk drawer for over a *year* now, untouched.

For good reason.

It doesn't *matter*. It's just another attempt to make me feel bad for poor old Joel. Misunderstood musician.

Whatever bullshit is inside, it won't change anything.

I cross my arms, planting myself firmly on the couch.

I'm not opening it.

I don't care what it says.

I don't.

My eyes drifted to the television. The drama is still playing, but I'm not watching it anymore.

My fingers tap against the blanket, restless.

My knees bounce.

I exhale slowly, trying to force my body to settle. Of course, it doesn't.

My eyes flick to the hallway again.

Damn it.

Just forget about it, Anna. Nothing has changed.

I reach for my drink, take a slow sip, then set it down.

A beat passes, then I reach for the remote, pressing pause.

I mean, I could just read it.

Not because I care—but because it's unfinished business.

I hate unfinished business.

And if I read it—if I finally open the stupid thing—then maybe I can stop thinking about it. Besides, knowledge is power right?

Maybe I can shove it back in his face later.

Maybe I can use it against him.

Or maybe you're just looking for an excuse.

The thought slithers through my mind before I can stop it.

My jaw tightens.

No.

That's not what this is.

This is practical. This is self-preservation.

This is me taking control.

Before I can talk myself out of it, I throw off the blanket, stand up, and march down the hall.

My feet hesitate for half a second at the office door. Then I shove it open before I can second-guess myself.

The room is dim, the desk lamp casting a soft glow over the papers stacked neatly beside my laptop.

The drawer is closed. But I'm all too aware of what's inside.

It's been in there since the day he gave it to me.

I reach out, fingers hovering over the handle.

My pulse kicks up.

I tell myself it's just irritation.

I tell myself I don't feel *anything* else.

And then I pull the drawer open.

The envelope sits exactly where I left it, tucked beneath a few random bills and old receipts.

For a moment, I just stare at it.

This is a mistake.

I know it.

I can *feel* it.

But my hand moves anyway, fingers curling around the edge of the envelope, pulling it free.

It feels heavier than it should.

I don't breathe as I tear it open.

The torn edges of the envelope feel sharp against my fingertips, the weight of it settling like a stone in my palm. My heart kicks against my ribs, loud in the quiet room.

I tell myself I don't care what's inside.

I tell myself I won't let it mean anything.

But my hands shake just a little as I reach inside.

The first thing I pull out is a thick stack of papers, folded neatly. I smooth them open, my brows furrowing.

Legal documents.

The words Copyright Transfer Agreement stare back at me, official and cold, stamped with dates and signatures—Joel's and someone else's, probably his lawyer's.

My pulse jumps.

I scan the details, my brain sluggishly piecing them together.

He signed over everything.

Every right. Every royalty. Every single cent the song has ever made.

My fingers tighten around the pages.

What the hell?

Something slips free from between the documents, landing on my lap.

I blink.

A check.

The number printed across it makes my stomach drop.

My breath catches, my mind struggling to wrap around the figure staring back at me.

This isn't some small payout. This isn't a token sum to clear his conscience.

This is hundreds of thousands of dollars.

My fingers tremble as I grip the edges, like the weight of it might be too much to hold.

There's a sticky note attached.

> Anna,
> This is what I owe you. It should have always been yours.
> —Joel

I press my lips together, pulse pounding.

This isn't just an apology.

This is a debt paid in full.

I grip the check so tightly the paper creases under my fingers.

This is too much.

Too real.

Too final.

My heart lurches, and I hate that I feel anything at all.

I press my lips together, forcing my breath steady.

This is just guilt. This is him trying to erase what he did. It doesn't change the past. It doesn't undo the fact that he stole my words and made them his.

My stomach twists as I set the contract aside.

I don't want it.

I don't want anything from him.

And yet, my hand moves back to the envelope, pulling out the next thing.

It's a single sheet of lined paper, edges curled slightly, like it's been handled too many times.

My breath catches.

I know this paper.

I know the way the ink bleeds at the edges, the way my own handwriting slants unevenly, the lyrics crammed into the margins because I never learned to write neatly in a notebook.

My original lyrics.

The ones I wrote before he ever touched them.

But they're not just mine anymore.

Joel's handwriting is all over them.

Messy scrawls in the empty spaces, words circled, lines rewritten.

His notes.

My throat closes up.

I scan them, my eyes catching on his edits, his thoughts—

This line is perfect.

Feels raw, don't change it.

What if this is the second verse instead?

I swallow hard.

I shouldn't care.

I shouldn't care that he cared. That he didn't just steal it outright.

That he saw something in my words.

That he understood what they meant, even back then.

The ache in my chest sharpens, spreading like a bruise beneath my ribs.

I shove the lyrics aside before I can think too hard about them.

The last thing in the envelope is a letter.

The paper is smooth beneath my fingertips, heavier than the notebook paper, the kind of stationary that looks expensive but understated.

The date catches my eye before anything else.

February 14th—last year.

Valentine's Day.

I frown.

That was the day he gave me this stupid envelope.

My pulse pounds as I unfold the letter.

Anna,

I know this doesn't fix anything. I know it doesn't change what I did. I stole from you and I don't expect forgiveness.

But I want you to have what was always yours. The song, the rights—every cent it's ever made. It belongs to you. It always has.

I never should have taken it from you, and if I could go back and change it, I would. But I can't. So instead, I'll do the only thing I can.

After tonight, I won't play it again.

Not on stage. Not in interviews. Not for an encore. It's yours. I had no right to it.

I'm sorry, Ace.

—Joel

The words blur as I read them again.

And again.

After tonight, I won't play it again.

My throat tightens.

He thought I'd open this letter that night.

That I'd read it immediately.

He thought I'd know.

And all this time—a year and a half later—I had no clue. Hell, he's been in my house for four days and he hasn't even said anything.

The song is his biggest hit. He could have played it forever and no one would have questioned it.

I grab my phone with numb fingers, pulling up YouTube.

I type his name, my breath coming faster as I scroll through the search results.

Tour dates. Interviews. Live performances.

But the song?

I can't find it.

I switch to Google.

I dig through fan sites and forums.

Why did Joel Price suddenly stop playing his biggest hit?

Did something happen? Did he lose the rights?

Is he planning an acoustic rerelease? He HAS to bring it back!!

My heart slams against my ribs.

He really stopped.

He really meant it.

I stare at the letter in my hands, fingers trembling.

The sound of the front door opening shatters the silence.

My body jolts so hard I nearly knock my laptop off my desk.

Shit.

Shit, shit, shit.

Joel's home.

My pulse kicks up, panic slamming through me as I scramble to shove everything back into the envelope.

The check, the contract, the lyrics, the letter—*all of it.*

I shove the envelope back into the drawer, slamming it shut just as his footsteps hit the hallway.

My hands are too hot.

The paper lingers on my fingertips, phantom-weighted, like it's burned itself into my skin. I flex my fingers, pressing my palms flat against my desk, trying to force the feeling to go away.

I barely have a second to school my features, to erase every single emotion clawing up my throat before he appears in the doorway.

I am *calm*. I am *normal*. I am totally *fine*.

I force my shoulders to relax, casually reaching for my laptop like I wasn't just on the verge of a full-blown existential crisis.

Joel leans against the doorframe, arms crossed, his gaze too sharp, too knowing as it sweeps over me.

Something is different.

I can feel it before he even speaks.

I don't like it.

I *really* don't like it.

But I pretend not to notice.

Instead, I lift my chin, blinking at him with forced disinterest. "You're back early. Not enough groupies tonight?"

Joel doesn't answer right away.

His gaze flicks to the desk—to the drawer.

My stomach clenches.

Oh god, does he know?

He doesn't say anything, but I can feel it in the shift of his stance, the slight tilt of his head, the way he watches me like he's putting something together.

I tighten my grip on my laptop, tilting the screen slightly as if I was deep in work—as if I wasn't just reading a letter that's completely fucked with my entire night.

"Busy?" he asks, voice low, amused.

I lift a brow, forcing a casual shrug. "I'm *always* busy, Price."

Joel huffs a laugh, stepping further into the office. "Yeah? What are you working on?"

My stomach twists.

He's too close.

I cannot do this right now.

So I go with distraction and deflection, the only tools I have left.

I tap my keyboard like I'm totally focused. "Oh, you know. World domination. The usual."

Joel hums, taking another step closer.

And then—

He reaches out.

Before I can react, before I can shift away, his fingers brush just behind my ear, tucking a loose strand of hair back into place.

Every single muscle in my body locks up.

Heat flares under my skin, sharp and startling, as his

fingertips graze the edge of my jaw for a fraction of a second too long.

It's nothing.

A tiny movement. A brief touch.

But my pulse fucking jumps.

My breath catches in my throat.

I can't move.

Can't breathe.

Joel is standing too close, touching me too softly, looking at me too intently.

And why the hell does he smell so good after a performance?

His lips twitch, like he knows exactly what he just did.

Like he can hear the way my heartbeat just spiked.

I snap out of it.

I jerk back, reaching up and pointedly tucking my hair behind my own damn ear.

Joel's smirk deepens, his gaze flicking to my hands before dragging back up to my face.

"Relax, Ace," he murmurs. "Just a little hair out of place."

I hate him.

I hate that my face is warm.

I hate that my pulse is still hammering.

I hate that he looks so fucking pleased with himself.

I cross my arms, leaning back in my chair, forcing every ounce of disinterest into my expression.

"Well, thanks for that life-changing gesture," I

deadpan. "Truly. I don't know how I would have survived without it."

Joel chuckles.

It's a low sound, smooth and slow, like he knows something I don't.

He doesn't leave right away. He lingers.

Just a second too long.

Like he's weighing something. Like he's putting together a puzzle and just found the missing piece.

Then, so softly I almost miss it—

He nods once to himself.

Like he's confirming something.

The realization settles behind his smirk.

Not cocky.

Not teasing.

Just certain.

And then, finally, he steps back.

"Don't work too hard," he says, turning toward the hallway.

I don't respond.

Because I can't. I'm still reeling.

I wait until I hear his bedroom door click shut, the sound far too loud in the quiet apartment.

Then, slowly, my gaze flits to the drawer.

I don't know what's worse.

The fact that I finally caved in and opened that stupid envelope—

Or the fact that now, for the first time in a decade, I don't know what to think of Joel.

What alternate universe is this?

CHAPTER 14

Joel

I should be feeling smug.

Anna was flustered. *Really* flustered.

And that's becoming something I enjoy more than anything. I love seeing her unravel.

She always has control. *Always*.

She's built from fire and sharp edges—a master at throwing up walls the second anyone gets too close. She cuts with words before anyone else can. She's made an art of keeping herself untouchable.

But tonight?

She slipped.

And I saw it happen.

I *felt* it.

The small, barely-there hitch in her breath. The way her chest rose sharply before she forced it down, like her body had betrayed her first and her brain was scrambling to cover it up. I can relate to that.

The way color bloomed along her cheekbones, so

faint it might've gone unnoticed if I hadn't been watching for it.

And I *was* watching.

I was waiting.

Waiting for the inhale, the hesitation, the second it took her to shut it all down.

I meant to catch every single tell.

However, what I didn't mean was for it to hit me just as hard.

I can still feel it—*her.*

I let out a slow breath, rolling onto my side, my body still buzzing like I just stepped offstage.

But this isn't stage adrenaline. This is something else.

Something tangled and restless, coiling under my skin.

I scrub a hand down my face, but it doesn't erase the memory of the way her hair slipped through my fingers, the way she froze under my touch. The way she swallowed hard, forcing down whatever emotions were coming up.

And that's what's messing me up the most. All this time I thought she hated me—plain and simple.

Never in a million years did I think she might still feel something else. Something I tried to kill when we were teens.

That's not my ego talking. It's not wishful thinking or some bullshit fantasy.

It happened.

And now I don't know what the hell to do with that or why it was so important to test it.

I shouldn't be thinking about any of this—but I am.

And it's not stopping.

I close my eyes, willing the feeling away, but it's already under my skin. It's still running through me, a live wire, sizzling along my nerves, making it impossible to sit still.

I roll onto my back, rubbing my hands over my face.

Fuck.

This is not how this was supposed to go.

I was just pushing her. Testing her, because something about that moment at Nocté told me I should. Hell, it was probably the whisky.

But I wasn't supposed to be here, alone in my room, replaying it over and over like some lovesick idiot.

I mean, I'm Joel fucking Price. Rock god. *Legend.*

At least, that's what I've been telling myself as I build by career.

But Anna tears that all away, stripping me back to that stupid kid who just loved the music.

I let out a slow breath, willing my pulse to settle. But the second I do, my mind slides into dangerous territory.

Because a flicker of recognition tickles at the back of my mind.

None of this is new.

This feeling—the way my body reacts to her, the way my chest tightens when I remember the look on her face —it's not the first time.

I just never let myself sink into it before.

And now, I'm back there.

I had just turned seventeen.

It was a random Saturday. Nothing important. No big moment.

I had crashed at Ethan's the night before, as I had a thousand times before that.

I'd just gotten out of the shower, towel-drying and barely paying attention to anything except trying to shake the water out of my ears.

Anna was sprawled out on the Ethan's bed—Ethan, of course, nowhere in sight—watching something on Ethan's laptop.

She was almost fourteen—still had her hair in those half-braids she always used to wear back then.

I was half-distracted thinking about who the fuck knows what. I was hardly aware of her as I walked by to grab my phone. But when I leaned down, my arm brushing against hers, and something shifted.

The shift was so small, so barely there, that if I hadn't been standing right next to her, I might've missed it.

But I *did* notice.

The air between us changed.

She didn't move away. Didn't roll her eyes or huff dramatically like she normally did whenever Ethan or I got too close.

She just... stopped.

Completely still.

Like she was waiting for something.

And that's when I became acutely aware of myself. Of the way water still clung to my skin, trailing slowly from my hair down my chest. Of the way the towel hung low on my hips, the only thing between me and a whole lot of awkward if my grip slipped.

For the first time, standing there, half-naked in Ethan's room, I suddenly felt hyperconscious of Anna's presence.

It wasn't like before, when she was just Ethan's annoying little sister, tagging along because she had no one else to hang out with.

We'd spent the last six months working on music together. Just the two of us.

And sometime in between her scribbling lyrics in her notebook and me teaching her chords, something had changed. Something I hadn't noticed—until this moment.

Until she sat frozen on that bed, gaze locked on the screen, pretending I wasn't standing next to her in a towel.

I should have walked away then. I *knew* I should have. I should have grabbed my phone and left the room to get dressed, just like I'd done a hundred times before.

But instead, I hesitated. Instead, I lingered. For just a second too long.

My fingers curled around my phone, but my eyes flicked back to her.

And there it was.

The way her breath shuddered in her chest before she covered it up. The way her hands tightened around the laptop. The way her jaw flexed, like she was forcing herself to look unaffected. Like she knew I saw it and she was mad at herself for slipping.

It was so quick, so fleeting, that for weeks afterward, I convinced myself it was nothing. That I had imagined it. Because just as fast as it happened, she shut it down.

She scoffed. Rolled her eyes in true Anna fashion.

And before I could process the moment we just had, she chucked a pillow straight at my face.

"Jesus, put some clothes on, Price," she huffed. "Nobody wants to see that."

I laughed.

Not because it was funny—but because it was safe. Because that's what we did. We covered things up with deflection and sarcasm.

And just like that, the moment was gone. But it wasn't forgotten.

I remember walking out of that room feeling... off kilter.

Like I had seen something I wasn't supposed to see— just like I had tonight at Nocté.

Like I had *felt* something I wasn't supposed to feel.

And just like she did, I began to bury it.

I told myself it meant nothing. Because it *had* to mean nothing. She was Ethan's little sister. No way was I stepping into that's hornet's nest.

So I told myself, whatever that was, whatever I *thought* I saw—it didn't matter.

Except, what if it did?

Because tonight?

She looked at me the exact same way. She *reacted* the exact same way.

And this time, she can't blame it on being thirteen, or some dumb childhood crush she outgrew.

This time, it's real.

And I don't know what the hell to do with that.

I press the heels of my hands against my eyes, but it doesn't help.

Because now, I can't stop thinking about her.

Not just the way she reacted tonight.

What if she stopped fighting it? Would she still come undone—breath hitching, cheeks flushing—before she shoved it all back down?

Does she bring that kind of fire to the bedroom?

A flare of anger ignites, hot and irrational, and I push it aside. I don't want to think about Anna with anyone else. I *won't*.

I sit up, blinking hard at that thought.

Anyone else?

Holy shit. Do I wish it were me?

I play out that thought for a moment and find myself circling the drain.

Would she fight it at first? Would she let me—

Fuck.

I sit up fast, running my hands through my hair, forcing the thought right the fuck out.

What the hell is wrong with me?

This isn't supposed to happen. I wasn't supposed to want this.

Not like this. Not with *her*.

I was here to get her forgiveness so I could move on

and focus on my music career without the dark cloud over my head. *That's all.*

I swing my legs over the bed, breathing hard, trying to push past the heat creeping into my skin.

I need a distraction. *Now.*

A cold shower.

Something.

Anything.

Marching to the bathroom, I stare at my reflection in the bathroom mirror, my chest rising and falling like I just ran a marathon.

This is so fucked.

I'm standing here, trying to will my body into submission like some horny teenager.

What the hell? Where did that even come from?

I undress quickly and step into the shower, twisting the knob all the way to cold.

The first blast of water makes me suck in a sharp breath, my body jolting at the icy sting.

Good. I need it.

I brace my hands against the tile, letting the water pummel me, trying to drown out the fire in my blood.

But it doesn't work.

Because my brain is still spinning, caught on a loop of what ifs.

What if I touched her again?

What if she didn't stop me next time?

What would her lips taste like if I kissed her?

What if—

Fuck.

I close my eyes, groaning as I grip myself, trying—*failing*—to think about anything else. But all I see is Anna. The flush on her skin. The way her lips parted. The sharp inhale of breath before she forced it down.

My hand moves like it has a mind of its own.

I should stop. I don't.

My free hand fists against the wall. My breath shudders as I bite back her name.

Fuck. *Fuck.*

A minute later, I stand there, head tipped back against the tile, feeling nothing but regret.

So much for a cold shower.

I blow out another captive breath, releasing myself as I let the water cascade over my head and torso.

I stay there as long as I can, allowing the water to wash away any evidence of my indiscretion.

I can't tell her—can't admit to any of this. Hell, I can't even talk about this to my best friend because he'd literally *kill me.* But I also can't just sit here waiting for her to crack again.

She won't.

Anna's too damn stubborn.

She'll patch up the cracks, reinforce the walls, and pretend nothing happened.

And I can't let her.

Not after this.

I scrub a hand through my wet hair, thinking.

She won't give me an inch.

She won't open the damn envelope.

She won't let herself be vulnerable.

But there's one thing she can't resist. I *know* she can't.

So maybe—

Maybe I don't push her.

Maybe I let her pull herself in.

If I pretend to struggle with a song—something off, just enough to get under her skin—she won't be able to help herself.

She'll correct me.

She'll engage.

She'll forget, just for a second, that she's supposed to hate me.

And once she lets herself lean in once—she'll do it again.

This is it.

I shut off the shower and step out, gripping the sink, my pulse still too fast.

I don't know if this will work. But I need to try.

If I can get the old Anna back, even for one night—

Maybe she'll let me in.

And maybe—*just maybe*—she won't want to shut me out again.

I smirk to myself, grabbing a towel and heading for my guitar.

Let's see if she takes the bait.

CHAPTER 15

Anna

I'm fine.

I am totally, completely, *100% fine.*

Sure, I spent the last twenty minutes laying on my bed, thinking about the envelope that completely ruined my night—and the man who gave it to me. No biggie. Right?

Somehow, Joel Price has wormed his way back into my head, and now I can't shake him loose. My brain keeps replaying the past few moments. The way his fingers slid through my hair. The way my body reacted before my brain could catch up. The way I *let it happen* for a fraction of a second too long.

What the hell is *wrong* with me?

I knew letting him stay here was a bad idea.

My stomach twists. I throw an arm over my face and groan, willing the feeling away, but my chest is still tight and my heart rate is at a highly concerning level for someone who has been lying still.

But it's fine. *I'm* fine. This is *fine*.

I exhale sharply, smoothing my palm over the top of my head before forcing myself upright.

Bathroom.

That's what I need. A reset. I'll splash some cold water on my face, brush my teeth, and erase this entire day from my brain.

I push off the bed, my limbs feeling heavier than they should as I step into the hall. My mind is still buzzing, stuck in an endless loop of *why did I react like that?* and *what the hell does it mean?* Mixed with a bit of *why am I even thinking about any of this?*

I reach for the bathroom doorknob, desperate for the distraction.

But my hand hesitates midair.

Water's running.

Good god, how many showers does one guy need to take?

My jaw tightens. Okay. Not ideal, but whatever. I can wait. *I'm an adult. I can do hard things.*

He was on stage tonight. He probably worked up a sweat. Maybe he really *does* need another shower.

I take a breath, doing my best not to think about him all sweaty or soapy. I'm about to turn back toward my room, when—

I hear it.

A low, muffled sound. Barely audible over the running water.

I freeze.

At first, I think maybe I imagined it. This is an old house. It was probably a pipe whining or something.

Then it happens again.

Only, this time—

Oh my god.

My entire body locks up, my blood draining straight to my feet.

It's not my imagination.

Because I know *exactly* what that sound is.

It's Joel.

It's Joel in the shower.

And he's not just *showering.*

Oh god. *Oh my fucking god.*

My stomach twists into a violent knot. Heat crashes over me in a tidal wave of secondhand embarrassment and *something else* I refuse to name because somewhere low in my abdomen, a warm tingling sensation floods my senses.

No. Nope. No way. That's not what I heard. I'm being ridiculous.

He could be... stretching.

Or groaning about how sore he is from his stupid performance.

Or yawning. *Yeah. A yawn. A totally normal, in-the-shower yawn.*

There are squishing noises and another low, barely contained sound, and my soul is about to leave my body.

I swear to god—

Wait, what?

Did he just say my name?

My pulse flatlines and my lungs forget how to function.

No—*no way*. That's not what I heard. My brain is just short-circuiting from the sheer *horror* of this situation. There is no universe where Joel Price is in that shower—doing *that*—and thinking about *me*.

Except...

Except I *did* hear it.

And now I can't *unhear* it. In fact, the sound of him groaning my name as he—well, it's burned forever into my brain now.

Holy fuck.

My whole body locks up as if staying perfectly still will somehow make this situation not real. If I don't move, maybe the fabric of reality will shift, and I will be back in my room, blissfully unaware of whatever the *hell* this is.

Anna, don't just stand there like an idiot. You need to leave.

You need to walk away, right now. Immediately. Stop hesitating, for fucksake.

But I don't.

Because my traitorous brain is still making connections, and every single one of them is worse than the last.

The stupid letter and contract.

The check.

The way he was acting earlier.

The way he looked at me.

The way *I* reacted.

The *shower.*

A pulse of something hot and electric shoots down

my spine, and I slam the lid on it so fast, I nearly give myself whiplash.

Absolutely not.

I am *not* having this reaction.

Not to him.

He is the villain in this story. He is the reckless, arrogant bastard who stole my song and shattered my trust—the one person I swore I would never, under any circumstances, let get under my skin again. So why is my body acting like it didn't get the memo? The fucking bitch.

The heat in my face burns like a warning light, flashing DANGER, DANGER, DO NOT PROCEED.

Move, Anna!

I need to burn this house to the ground.

I need to—

The water shuts off.

Oh, *shit.*

But instead of walking away—

Instead of saving myself—

Instead of doing *literally anything* that makes sense—

I freeze.

Why?

How the hell am I supposed to know?

What kind of moronic self-preservation instinct is this?!

Move Anna. Now—

The door swings open.

And my entire body malfunctions. My limbs forget

how to move. My brain forgets how to form a single coherent thought. My breath stalls halfway up my throat, and *oh god,* I am so, *so* screwed.

Joel steps out, still dripping wet despite a towel hanging obscenely low on his hips. His chiseled torso is on full display—like some reckless god of destruction sent solely to dismantle my last shred of sanity.

I think I actually black out for a second.

His shoulder length hair is damp, messy, curling slightly at the ends and it reminds me of how he used to look when we were kids. A single droplet slides from his shoulder down his chest—

Nope.

Absolutely not.

Do not pass go. Do not collect $200.

Do not, *under any circumstances,* let your eyes go any lower, Anna.

My gaze jerks up to his face so fast, it's a miracle I don't snap my own neck.

Of course Joel notices.

His lips twitch, amusement flickering behind his way too curious eyes. Something else flashes across his features and his face flushes.

And just like that, I know.

He *knows.*

He knows that *I* know.

Heat bursts up my neck and into my own goddamn cheeks.

I need to fix this. Right now.

I clear my throat, crossing my arms so tightly, I might cut off my own circulation. "Took you long enough."

Joel tilts his head, a hint of entertainment spreading across his lips as he gives me a lopsided grin. "Something wrong, Ace?"

Yes. Everything is wrong. Wrong, wrong, *wrong*.

But then he shifts his weight slightly, and—

Oh my *god*, the towel *dips*.

Panic explodes in my chest.

My brain flatlines.

I snap my gaze back to his face with the force of a thousand nuclear reactors.

Joel's smirk deepens.

Fuck my life.

"Did you, ah…" He pauses, dragging my torture out as he runs his hand through his wet hair, making his bicep flex in the motion. "Were you standing outside the bathroom door long?"

I scoff—too fast, too sharp. "What? Psh. No. Jesus, Price, I was—"

Too defensive. Absolutely zero chill.

Joel's breath catches slightly, a little flush tinting his cheeks, but then—oh no.

Oh no.

His grin turns lethal.

He adjusts his towel, purposefully slow.

My eyes drop *before I can stop them*.

He catches it.

I *hate* him.

"Happen to hear anything of interest, Ace?" His voice dips just slightly, teasing—*knowing*.

Okay, maybe he didn't know before. But he most certainly does now.

I swallow hard, raising my chin high as I force my face into an expression of total indifference. "Oh, yes. The sound of water is an utter fascination of mine. I listen for it whenever I can."

Joel hums, amusement flickering behind those green eyes of his like he knows exactly what game I'm playing and is more than happy to let me lose.

Joel steps in closer, his body radiating heat, his towel slung low enough that my brain issues an immediate evacuation order.

He's too close, too smug, too... unfairly gorgeous for a man who just did what he did while thinking about me.

My pulse hammers against my ribs. This isn't happening. This *cannot* be happening.

"Good to know." His voice is silky smooth, smug as hell. "Wouldn't want you to be bored."

My pulse spikes dangerously, and I have to clench my fists to keep from doing something insane—like smacking that stupid smirk off his face. Or worse, wondering what it would feel like pressed against my skin.

Nope. No. *Absolutely* not.

Joel shifts again, his towel dipping another fraction of an inch, and my fight-or-flight instinct short-circuits enough to make me whimper under my breath.

I need to go.

I need to go *now*.

But my feet are still rooted to the spot, and Joel—because he is the actual worst—takes a slow, deliberate step toward me.

Finally, my stupid feet move as I back up.

He follows.

The hallway wall stops me cold.

His grin grows when all I can do is blink back at him, my words held captive in an alternate universe.

I swear to god, this is how I die.

Joel braces one arm against the wall next to my head, caging me in. His scent—clean soap, a hint of spice, something inherently *him*—fills the space between us, and I can't breathe.

I can't do *anything* except exist in the molten chaos of this moment.

He leans in, his voice dropping low. *Dangerously* low. "You sure you weren't listening for something else?"

My stomach flips and another whimper escapes my lips before I finally bite out, "Go to hell, Price. I wasn't spying on you, if that's what you're getting at."

His eyes flick to my mouth. My breath catches.

Oh no. *Oh no.*

His free hand lifts—slow, deliberate.

And then—

His fingertips slide along my jaw and the pad of his thumb grazes my lower lip, featherlight and completely devastating.

But my entire body *shatters*.

This isn't a brush of a hand or a wrist grab. It's

definitely not tucking a strand of hair behind my ear. This is...

What the fuck *is* this?

My stomach swoops, my nerves spark like live wires, and a full-body shudder runs through me before I can stop it.

My lips part—just a fraction, just enough to take in a single sharp inhale of breath, but the moment it happens his lips curl slightly, his pupils wide as he takes in my reaction.

Like he knows he *won*.

And then—just as fast as he cornered me—he steps back.

He turns, flashing me one last devastating smirk over his shoulder.

"Night, Ace."

Then he disappears into his room, leaving me standing in the hallway, wrecked.

My entire body is still locked in place, like a system crash I can't reboot. My skin is flushed, my breath too sharp, my pulse a runaway train I can't slow down.

And the worst part? I can still feel it.

The burn of his touch. The heavy weight of his gaze. The way my breath stuttered when his thumb grazed my lip—like he knew exactly what he was doing—like he wanted to see me come undone.

Like he *liked* it.

Like he wanted *me* to like it, too.

My insides flip violently, and for a horrifying second, I feel something dangerously close to anticipation. A pulse of heat, sharp and unmistakable, twisting low in my stomach before I slam the brakes so hard, I nearly give myself a migraine.

Oh, no. Nope. Nope. I am NOT doing this.

And yet, my entire body is trembling—not in fear, not in anger, but in something far, far worse.

Desire.

Not possible. That is not what this is.

And yet... my fingers lift to my lips, tracing the spot where his thumb had just been.

It tingles.

I groan, letting my head fall back against the wall, praying for divine intervention, or maybe an EMP for my brain so it will erase the last ten minutes from existence.

Because this isn't just about the fact that Joel got under my skin. It's the fact that I LET him.

And worse? For one terrifying second—a part of me actually wanted him to.

No. NO. Nope. That is NOT reality. That is a brain malfunction. A temporary lapse in judgment due to prolonged exposure to his bullshit.

This is fixable.

This is salvageable.

I just need to never, ever, in the history of time, be alone with Joel Price again.

I hate him. I really, *really* hate him.

Only for one single, excruciating moment—

I didn't.

CHAPTER 16

Joel

Well, that sure as shit didn't go as planned.

But in some weird way, it actually works.

I exhale sharply, dragging a hand through my damp hair as I lean back against the door. My pulse is still too fast—*way* too fast—and not just because of the shower.

Not just because of what I *did* in the shower, either.

Did she hear me?

I squeeze my eyes shut, already knowing the answer.

Of course she did.

She was practically standing outside the damn door.

And instead of walking away—she stayed.

She *listened*.

A groan builds in my chest, half frustration, half disbelief. My heart is *still* hammering, which is objectively fucking stupid. I should be mortified. I should be figuring out how to avoid eye contact for the next week after the shit she just overheard.

But all I can think about is the way her breath hitched.

The way her face flushed when she realized I *knew*.

Jesus.

This is not how I wanted to confirm Anna might actually be into me. There were—*are*—a thousand better ways to push her buttons.

But this? This is...

Oddly hot.

It *shouldn't* be, and yet, all I can think about is the way she *looked* at me.

Wide eyes. Parted lips. Cheeks flushed like *she'd* been the one caught.

And the second she realized I *knew*?

She *shut down.*

Too late, though. Because I saw it.

I push off the door, shaking my head.

Anna Chang is *attracted* to me. There's no doubt in my mind.

She might wanna pretend she hates my guts and thinks I'm the worst human on the planet, but I know the truth. It's all one big cover-up to protect how she really feels.

And now? Now I'm going to push until she stops fighting it because, damn, *I miss her.*

I brace my hands against the dresser, taking a slow breath, trying to piece together the mess in my head.

I mean, at least we're no longer on the questionable side of an age gap. We're adults now, not seventeen and fourteen.

She's still *Ethan's sister*, though.

That's the only problem here.

Or at least, it *should* be.

Right?

Would he kill me if he knew I was thinking about making a move on his sister?

I snort. Ethan isn't the person I should be worried about.

No, the *real* threat is the woman currently sitting in her room—probably plotting my murder.

And if Anna decides I need to be eliminated, it won't be quick. It'll be *methodical*. I'll probably wake up with my guitar strings cut, my coffee mysteriously replaced with salt water, and my phone rigged to play nothing but K-pop girl groups at full volume whenever I try to open Spotify.

I grin.

I could *totally* see her doing all of that.

But the thing is, if Anna is *that* mad, it means she felt something.

And if she felt something once? I can make sure she feels it again.

I exhale, my pulse *finally* starting to level out as I drop my towel to the floor and sit on the edge of the bed.

Tomorrow, I push a little further.

Tomorrow, I *make* her engage.

I lay back on the bed and stretch my arms behind my head, my mind already flipping through the possibilities.

She sure as shit won't let herself admit she feels

something, so I have to make her *forget* she's supposed to be fighting it.

And I *can't wait* to do it.

Over the years, I've learned that the trick to getting under Anna's skin isn't pushing her.

It's giving her something to fix.

That's why I'm not in my room right now.

I could easily work on this song behind closed doors, where she wouldn't be forced to acknowledge me. But that would defeat the purpose.

Instead, I'm sprawled across the couch in the living room, guitar resting on my thigh, fingers lazily strumming out the chords to the song I sang at Nocté.

It's good—but it's not *right* yet.

There's something missing.

And while I could probably mess with it until things click, I need *Anna* to help me find it.

Finally, I hear her bedroom door creak open, and I school my expression into one of deep, brooding concentration, my fingers idly plucking at the strings as I hum the melody under my breath.

I don't look up. I don't need to.

I can *feel* her glare.

And then—the hesitation.

That fraction of a second where she almost asks what I'm doing before catching herself.

I bite back a smirk.

Hook.

Line.

Sinker.

I drag out a sigh, shifting slightly on the couch as I deliberately botch the next chord.

Wince. Groan. Shake my head like I'm frustrated.

Damn, I'm good. I should have gone into acting.

Anna still doesn't move.

She's trying *so damn hard* not to take the bait.

It's so fucking hard not to grin like an idiot.

I strum again—worse this time.

Oh, it's a deliberate mess. A sound so wrong, so painfully off-key, it could haunt a *nun's* nightmares.

Anna *huffs.*

I fight back the grin.

Almost there.

I strum again, singing under my breath a set of lyrics that obviously don't work.

She growls.

Hooked.

"You're kidding me, right?"

Bingo.

I glance over to her, keeping my expression neutral. "Hmm?"

Anna is standing in the kitchen now, one hand wrapped around a coffee mug. I guess she's over needing to run out for her morning java. Her other hand is planted on her hip and her glare is scalding enough to burn through concrete.

"Why the hell are you in the living room?" She spits out, her brows tugged in tightly.

I barely keep my lips from twitching as I spin around to face her. "Closed-in rooms mess with my process."

Anna blinks. Then she glares harder. "Your *process?*"

I nod, looking solemn. "Yeah. Creativity needs *space* to breathe, Ace. The energy in my room felt... stifling."

She tilts her head, studying me like she's debating whether to murder me or just kick me out entirely.

I strum another *dissonant* chord.

Anna inhales sharply through her nose, like she's practicing restraint—which, honestly, is impressive considering I just *massacred* a chord progression right in front of her.

I strum again, letting the wrong notes linger, watching as her grip on her coffee mug tightens.

Then, with a slow, calculated exhale, she sets her mug down a little too hard.

I bite the inside of my cheek to keep from smirking.

"I need one morning," she mutters, rubbing her temples. "One single, solitary, Joel-free morning where I can drink my coffee in peace without whatever the hell this is." She gestures vaguely in my direction.

I give her my most innocent look. "Music?"

She scowls, jabbing her index finger at me. "That's *not* music. That's a war crime."

I fight back a chuckle, tapping my fingers idly against the body of the guitar. "So, you agree it's bad?"

Anna narrows her eyes.

Damn, she's salty today.

Which... makes sense. After last night, she's probably still reeling. Not just from hearing me in the shower. But from the fact that she *listened* and then got caught.

A flicker of heat slides down my spine, completely uninvited. I shut it down before it can go anywhere dangerous, but then—

Another thought blindsides me—one I wasn't expecting.

One I should not be fucking having.

Was she...?

My fingers falter on the strings. My stomach free-falls. My pulse rockets.

Oh. Fuck.

I was so caught up in what *she* heard—*what she knew*—that I didn't even consider what she might have done about it.

What if she was just as turned on? What if she touched herself last night—because of me?

Why didn't I listen for—

Fuck.

The thought punches me in the gut so hard, I physically shake my head, like I can dislodge it before it goes any further.

Nope. Nope. Shut it down. Now.

Because if I don't?

I will not be able to function today.

I shift on the couch, clearing my throat, forcing my fingers back into motion on the fretboard.

Focus, Price. *Mission first.*

"I still don't understand why you're out *here*." Anna

folds her arms, glaring like she wants to incinerate me on the spot. I'm actually starting to love it.

I sigh like she's exhausting me. "I told you. *Creativity needs space.* You should know that."

Anna's eye twitches.

"Go to Nocté." She waves a dismissive hand. "Play in the green room. Hell, play in the walk-in fridge for all I care. Just get out of my space."

I pluck a few more strings, cocking my head like I'm analyzing the sound. "Mm. Yeah, no. That won't work."

"Why *not?*"

I shrug. "Nocté doesn't have the right energy."

She stares at me, deadpan. "The *right energy.* What, are you some sort of New Age nutter now?"

I nod.

Anna closes her eyes, her lips parting slightly like she's praying for strength.

It's adorable.

She inhales through her nose. Exhales through her teeth like some sort of banshee.

Then she grabs her coffee, turning on her heel.

My heart sinks and my stomach flips.

Mission *failed.*

Or so I think.

Because just as she steps into the hallway—I play the wrong chord again.

I make sure it's *bad.*

Like *nails-on-a-chalkboard, send-a-music-teacher-into-cardiac-arrest* bad.

Anna stops.

Her entire body locks up—very similar to last night.

She stays frozen there, gripping her coffee mug like it's the only thing tethering her to sanity.

I pluck another atrocious note, dragging it out long enough to make even an AI-generated music bot short-circuit.

Anna stiffens like I just personally insulted three generations of her ancestors.

She's fighting it.

Come on, Ace. You know you want to.

I strum again—slow, wrong, and offensive to the very concept of sound.

Her shoulders inch up some more and I can practically hear the gears in that big, beautiful brain of hers turning.

Almost there.

She shakes her head, muttering something under her breath, like she's cursing the gods for putting her through this. A small lopsided grin slips through.

One more.

I strum—a truly heinous combination of notes that would make a ghost pack up and leave a haunted house.

Damn, I'm getting good at these analogies.

Her entire body jerks like I just set off a nuclear detonation.

And then—she cracks.

Anna spins so fast, I barely have time to school my expression before she's stomping toward me, murder evident in her dark eyes.

She drops her mug to the coffee table with a loud thud. *"Move."*

I do as I'm told.

But I make sure there's not much space.

She drops onto the couch beside me, her knee barely brushing mine as she yanks the guitar from my hands, her scowl deep enough to level a city.

But she's here. She's *engaging.*

And as her fingers settle over the frets, something in my chest tightens.

Because for the first time in years...

She's not just arguing with me.

She's creating with me.

And fuck, if that doesn't feel a little like hope.

CHAPTER 17

Anna

I have no idea how this happened.

One minute, I was drinking my coffee, minding my own damn business.

The next, I'm sitting on the couch with Joel's guitar in my hands.

Why?

Why am I like this?

You know, scratch that. I know exactly what happened.

I know *exactly* what he was doing.

He played like absolute garbage until I cracked.

And like a complete idiot, I fell for it. It's like I was possessed and a demon took over my body. At least, that's what I'm telling myself.

I stare down at the guitar like it personally betrayed me, my fingers already positioned over the right progression. My hands move like they remember this.

Because they do.

Damn it.

Damn *him.*

Joel doesn't say anything.

He just sits there, all relaxed and smug, like he didn't just manipulate me into fixing his stupid song.

Like he wasn't sitting here, ruining music until I had no choice but to intervene.

I grit my teeth, determined to fix this disaster as quickly as possible.

Because that's the only reason I'm doing this.

For the *music.*

Not for him.

I shift on the couch, fingers plucking out the melody, smoothing it into something natural. Something right.

Joel hums along, nodding slightly. "Better."

I shoot him a glare. "Obviously."

His lips twitch.

Damn it.

I walked right into that.

I curse under my breath and strum again, deliberately focusing only on the frets, the strings—*not* on the way he's watching me. Or the fact that his knee just barely brushes against mine.

Nope.

Not noticing that *at all.*

I shift slightly, just to see if he moves away.

He doesn't.

Great.

Now I have to commit to sitting exactly like this, or he'll know he's getting to me.

Joel taps his fingers against his knees, following my rhythm like it's second nature.

Like we've done this a thousand times before. I mean, I guess we have.

Before.

A memory tries to slip in—

I slam the door shut.

Nope.

No nostalgia.

No warm fuzzies.

Just fixing this damn song.

And yet, as I shift my grip and adjust the chord, something familiar slides into place.

Like a missing piece.

Like it belongs.

Joel exhales, almost softly.

The sound settles into the space between us.

I hate it.

I hate how easy this is.

How *natural.*

How good it feels.

I grit my teeth and ignore the flicker of warmth in my chest.

I clear my throat, shifting my grip on the guitar, my fingers pressing into the strings, adjusting the chord progression again.

"Try it like this," I mutter, playing through the new

transition, smoothing it out where it had been a little clunky before.

Joel watches my hands carefully, his expression serious for once. Focused.

"Yeah," he murmurs. "That works much better." He reaches out, tapping a spot on the fretboard. "But if you move this finger here, I wonder if it'll give it a little more tension before the resolve."

My pulse does something stupid, but I ignore it, shifting my fingers the way he suggests.

I play the sequence again, and—

Damn it.

It's better.

It's so much better.

I shoot him a begrudging look, but he just smirks, his fingers twitching like he wants the guitar back.

I roll my eyes and shove it toward him.

"Fine. Your turn."

Joel takes the guitar, and without hesitation, he picks up where I left off, his fingers finding the notes like he already knew them. Like we were always going to end up here.

He plays through the whole section, adjusting where necessary, and I hate—*hate*—how easy this feels.

How natural.

How we fall into the same rhythm we used to have, like no time has passed at all.

I cross my arms over my chest, biting the inside of my cheek to keep myself steady.

Joel glances at me. "Well?"

I exhale sharply, refusing to look at him.

"I guess it doesn't suck," I grumble. "But you need to work on the lyrics at some point."

"Yeah, I know." He chuckles, fiddling with the strings like he's perfectly at ease. No sign of the terrible player from earlier. Go figure.

Instead, he's acting like he isn't pushing all my buttons just by existing.

I glare at the guitar, trying to focus only on the song.

But why does it feel like something more?

Joel shifts beside me, his fingers still resting on the body of the guitar, but his focus is somewhere else.

On me.

I feel it before I see it. The quiet weight of his attention.

And then—his voice, lower than before. Softer.

"Can I use it?"

I blink at him, not sure I heard him right. "What?"

He nods toward the guitar. "The changes. The way we fixed it."

Eh-hem, he must mean the way *I* fixed it.

However, something flickers in my chest, sharp and fast.

I shove it down. Bury it.

It's a simple question.

A *normal* one.

Not a big deal.

And yet—

Joel doesn't ask permission for anything.

Not for the song he stole.

Not for the years he let pass without a word while he played it all over the eastern seaboard.

Not for the way he walked back into my life, acting like it didn't matter.

But now—*now*—he's asking.

Something about that doesn't compute.

Something about it makes my throat tight.

I lift my chin, grasping for the safest response. "Do whatever you want."

The words are sharp. Distant. An automatic response to keep me safe because nothing about this feels safe.

Joel's gaze flickers, his lips parting like he wants to say something.

Then, he hesitates. Just for a second. Just long enough that I see something shift behind his eyes, something quieter, more reserved. It's not the usual cocky self-assurance, not the easy confidence that usually drives me up the wall. This is different. Measured.

He sets the guitar aside, his fingers still resting lightly on the wood, and then—before I can prepare for it—his hand covers mine.

Not cocky. Not teasing.

Steady.

"Anna."

Just my name. No sarcasm. No challenge. Just him trying to get me to listen.

I should pull away.

I should snatch my hand back, roll my eyes, remind him that he lost the right to say my name like that a long time ago.

But I don't.

Because my body doesn't seem to be listening to my brain lately. Instead, it replays the way he said it last night in the shower, the traitorous bitch.

I swallow hard, forcing my gaze to stay locked on our hands instead of his face.

Joel's thumb moves, the lightest brush against my knuckles. My stomach clenches, my skin burning beneath his touch.

"I need to explain," he says, voice lower now. "The envelope—"

Panic lurches up my throat.

No.

I'm not doing this. Not now.

I wrench my hand away and shove to my feet so fast, I bump the coffee table and my coffee nearly spills.

Joel follows, reaching for me again, but I step back.

"Forget it," I say quickly, my pulse thundering against my ribs. "Seriously. Go have fun doing... whatever it is you do with the song tonight. I have work to do."

His brows pull together, like he's debating whether or not to let me go.

I don't give him the choice. I turn on my heel and walk away.

Unfortunately, I don't make it two steps before Joel is following.

"Anna, *wait.*"

Not a chance.

I pick up the pace, but he's faster. He catches up just

as I reach my office, his hand grazing my arm—just barely, just enough to send a jolt down my spine.

"Hey." His voice is quieter now, lower, more careful. "Can we just—can you let me—"

I yank away before he can finish. "I have work to do."

Joel exhales sharply. "Come on, you're really gonna lock yourself in there under the bullshit pretense of *work?*"

"Yup."

He shoots me a look. "That's mature."

"Says the guy who butchered his own song just to get my attention."

At least he has the good sense to look chagrined.

I turn the doorknob, but he moves closer, not touching me this time, just... *there*. Too close. Too much.

"Anna," he murmurs.

It's careful. Like he's afraid I'll bolt.

I hate that it *almost* makes me stop. That for a fraction of a second, I feel it—something small, something sharp, catching against my ribs.

His voice is softer when he speaks again. "Please, just let me—"

I don't let him finish.

I push into the office and shut the door behind me so fast, the frame rattles.

A beat of silence.

Then, on the other side—

Joel sighs.

Not dramatic. Not exaggerated. Just... tired.

A pause.

And then, his voice, quiet through the wood. "I guess I'll see you later, Ace."

I close my eyes, back pressed against the door.

I wait. Listening.

His footsteps don't retreat right away.

For a second I think maybe he's going to knock again.

But then, finally, his steps fade down the hall and back toward the great room. I hear him shuffling around and then the front door clicks shut.

I let out a breath I didn't realize I was holding, my heartbeat throbbing in my ears.

And then I sit at my desk and stare at my screen, doing everything in my power *not* to think about the way his voice sounded when he said my name. Any of the damn times.

I shake my head, hard, and roll my shoulders back, forcing myself to focus.

This is better.

Him leaving is better.

I don't have to deal with his presence, his stupid smirks, or the way his voice keeps doing that low, careful thing like he's trying to *reach* me.

Nope. None of that. He's off to play rockstar.

And now, I can *work*.

I adjust my desk chair and pull my laptop closer, fingers hovering over the keyboard as I scan the lines of code I was working on last. My inbox is manageable, my task list is light. I could get a solid head start on the week if I really buckle down.

I crack my knuckles, then start typing, sinking into the logic, the numbers, the structure.

This is good.

This makes sense.

Unlike Joel *freaking* Price.

Unlike his stupid song.

Unlike the way his fingers brushed against mine, slow and unhurried, like he was *testing* me.

My typing falters.

I grit my teeth, delete the last string of nonsense I just wrote, and refocus.

This is no big deal.

Everything is under control.

I pull in a deep breath and keep coding, my eyes scanning for errors, my brain shifting back into work mode.

One line at a time. One function at a time.

I settle into the rhythm of it, into the comfort of something logical, structured, *safe*.

And then—

I realize I'm humming.

I freeze.

My fingers hover motionless over the keyboard as my own voice hums the very melody I *swore* I wasn't going to think about.

My stomach plummets.

No.

No, no, no, *no*.

I clamp my mouth shut so fast, my teeth nearly click together.

I did *not* just do that.

I did *not* just hum *his* song.

The same song he's playing live right now.

Heat prickles at the back of my neck, frustration twisting through my ribs.

I lean back in my chair, glaring at the ceiling.

It doesn't mean anything.

It's just a song. A song I improved, by the way. A song I fixed because I *had* to.

That's all this is.

I drop my hands into my lap, exhaling hard.

I refuse to let this get to me.

I refuse to let *him* get to me.

I click back into my code, eyes narrowed, fingers poised—

And then, like some cruel joke from the universe, I hear it again.

The melody.

Playing in my head.

Clear as day.

My jaw clenches so tight, my temples throb.

This is *not* happening. It's been years since I heard the music like this.

I squeeze my eyes shut and press my palms into my forehead, trying to erase it, trying to push it out, trying to get my damn brain back from this hostile takeover.

But the melody lingers.

Soft. Persistent. *Unshakable.*

Like him.

I dig my nails into my palms, exhaling sharply.

No.

I refuse to give in. Joel is an asshole and that's the hill I'm willing to die on.

And yet...

Somewhere, beneath all my frustration, all my denial—

I'm not sure I believe it.

Tonight feels different.

From the moment I step onto the stage, something in me locks into place. Not all the way—there's still that hollow space in my ribs, still that restless ache—but it's quieter. More manageable somehow.

The weight of my guitar is steady in my hands, the hum of anticipation in my veins more fire than nerves. The set already feels stronger than last night.

Because tonight, I have *this* song.

The one she helped me fix.

The one shaped by her hands—sharpened by her mind.

The one I haven't let myself fully admit is *ours* now.

I tighten my grip on the neck of my guitar, strumming the first chord. It echoes through the room, clear and sure, settling into the pulse of the crowd. The band holds back, letting me take the lead. My fingers move like they've always known where to go, like this song existed in me long before I found the right shape for it.

Not until today.

Not until *her*.

She ran the second it was finished—like the fire we struck between us was too much to touch.

Maybe she was overwhelmed.

Or maybe she's scared of what it means.

The thought digs in deep as I play, because I *get it*.

I spent years running from things I didn't want to face, too. But I stopped. I turned around.

And maybe, just maybe, I can get her to stop, too.

The next chord lands cleaner than it ever has. The melody is richer. *Fuller*. Almost like she's here, just outside my reach, muttering about my phrasing and adjusting my damn fingering.

The song is alive now.

And the words—they finally come.

I'd been chasing them for days, losing them every time I reached out. But under the stage lights, with her carved into my memory, they spill from my lips effortlessly.

Like they were always meant for her.

The crowd fades. The energy of the room hums at the edges of my awareness, but my focus is locked. The pulse in my ears. The sound in the mic. The words on my tongue.

When the last note rings out, I barely hear the cheers.

Because this—this *feels* right.

I sling my guitar over my back, still grinning as I make my way toward the bar. People reach out as I pass—clapping me on the back, calling my name and raising their drinks in toast.

It's electric.

London steps in my path before I make it to the bar. "Good set," he says, nodding once. "Final shows next weekend should be solid. Gotta say, I'm looking forward to them."

There's weight in the words—something that tells me I've passed whatever silent judgment he was making.

"Appreciate it, man."

He claps me on the shoulder once before slipping back into the crowd, disappearing just as Myles catches my attention behind the bar.

She's already pulling down a glass. "Look who finally decided to show up for his own damn performance," she drawls.

I smirk, leaning against the counter. "Told you it'd be better tonight."

She snorts. "And thank fuck for that."

Setting a whiskey in front of me, she tips her head. "Good job tonight. You really did slay."

Something about that settles inside me.

I nod, rolling the glass between my fingers. "Yeah. It felt better."

More than better.

It felt right. At least, the music did. One thing could make it even better.

But for now, the song is almost there.

The lyrics—they finally came to me.

And I know exactly why.

I glance toward the exit, half-expecting to see her standing there, arms crossed, unimpressed, pretending she isn't completely mesmerized by the way I played *our* song.

But she's not here. Of course she's not.

She's probably at home, buried in her laptop, convincing herself she doesn't still love music.

I swallow back the disappointment, pressing the edge of my glass to my lips.

"Joel, you *rocked* tonight, man."

I turn to find Ethan and Tessa pushing their way through the post-show crowd.

Looks like they actually made it this time. Something about that makes my chest warm.

I tip my drink toward him. "I know."

Tessa rolls her eyes. "Jesus, I swear your ego is *worse* than it was when you were twenty."

Ethan shakes his head. "Nah, he's *always* been like this."

I let their teasing roll off me, still caught up in the lingering high of the performance.

"Anna would've *loved* it," Ethan says so flippantly that I'm sure he has no idea how he just slammed be back to reality,

My stomach knots.

The words hit too fast, sharp and unexpected.

I take a slow sip of whiskey, steadying my voice. "Yeah? What makes you think that?"

Ethan nods like it's obvious. "I mean, I get why she's being... well, *her*. But if she actually let herself watch you play, she'd fucking love it the way she used to. Then she'd *see* what I see."

The glass in my hand suddenly feels too heavy.

"See what?" I try to come off as nonchalant, but I swear there's a glint in Tessa's eyes that tells me I've failed. At least to her.

Ethan, thank fuck, is clueless as he shrugs. "That you're different now. Whatever grudge match she's got going with you might actually come to an end if she saw it. You know? God, I miss when we all got along. Well, mostly."

The weight of his words drops in my chest.

Because whatever this is I've been tiptoeing around with Anna isn't just about her—or me.

She's *his* sister.

Not just *Anna*. Not just the girl who has been in my head since the second I got back.

Ethan's *sister*.

The realization knocks the breath out of me, slamming me with something I haven't let myself *fully* consider.

I mean, I thought about it, but only in terms of Anna being the bigger worry. But is she? What would he think? Would he hate me? Would I I ruin our friendship with all of this? God, if he knew I—

I shake away the thought of Anna catching me after

my shower last night.

This isn't just complicated.

This is *Ethan*.

The person who has *always* had my back. My best friend since childhood. The guy who has been more of a brother to me than anyone else in my life.

And I'm standing here, gut-deep in *whatever the fuck this is* with his *little sister*.

I see flashes of her as a kid—hovering at the edges of our games, tagging along when she wasn't supposed to, scowling when we teased her for it.

Shit, maybe he wouldn't want me anywhere near her. Not in *that* way.

Hell, if he knew how I've been thinking about Anna, the things I've done—he'd *kill* me.

And maybe he should.

Because I already hurt her once. Before this was anything, before I even understood what she meant to me. I screwed it all up.

And now I want *more*?

Guilt coils tight in my stomach, warring with the part of me that doesn't care. The part that still wants to run straight to her and make her admit she feels this, too.

"I agree. She'd really love your performance, Joel. There's so much heart to it." Tessa nudges Ethan, but locks her bright blue eyes on me. "She still loves music. I know she pretends she doesn't, but it's *still there*."

My fingers tighten around my glass.

I know. I *saw* it. I *felt* it.

"You know, I can't say Anna's brain has ever made

sense to me, but for what it's worth, I don't even think she's mad at you. She's just afraid to admit she isn't," Ethan says, shaking his head like he didn't just say something that totally snaps my insides.

I exhale hard, setting my glass down too fast.

He has no idea what I did to her. No idea why she was so pissed.

"I gotta go."

Ethan looks startled. "What?"

"I just—" I shake my head. "Thanks for coming. I'll see you guys later."

I don't wait for their response. I need air. I need to *think*.

I need to get to her.

And maybe that should scare me more than it does.

The ride home is a blur of streetlights and static. The uber took way too long to arrive and I'm fucking spinning out.

Ethan's words keep looping in my head, burrowing under my skin.

I miss when we all got along.

She's just afraid to admit she isn't mad at you.

I tap out the rhythm to our song on my knees, counting down the seconds until we pull into her driveway.

His words shouldn't mess with me as much as they are. But fuck if they aren't setting something loose in my chest— something restless, something desperate to get through to her. Even if that means dealing with Ethan in the aftermath. I've gotta know—

I need to put this to rest so I can get her out of my head.

Finally, the driver pulls into the driveway. He cuts the engine and turns around. I barely hear him chirp out a price, which I pay on autopilot.

When I get out, I take a deep breath and exhale slowly as I stare at her house. For the most part, it's dark, but a golden glow from her living room tells me she must still be awake somewhere. No way would she leave a light on for me.

The late September breeze smells like leaves and the whisper of winter wind.

Deep breaths, Price.

She's probably holed up in her office still pretending to work. Already avoiding me like it's her full-time job.

But when I step inside… she's on the couch.

Reading.

My brows furrow as I step further in, toeing out of my boots. She doesn't acknowledge me, which isn't surprising, but the fact that she's out in the open instead of hiding in her office is.

She's curled into the corner of the couch, legs tucked up beneath her, holding a paperback and looking completely enthralled. Beside her, on the end table, is a glass of wine and a half-empty bottle.

As I move toward her, I stop short, blinking hard.

There is a *naked man* on the cover of her book.

Well, okay, to be fair, it's just his chest, but still. Close enough.

"What the hell are you reading?" I blurt out before I can think better of it.

Anna flinches—*actually flinches*—like she forgot I existed for a second.

Her eyes snap up, dark and defensive, but I don't miss the way she clutches the book to her chest like I'm about to snatch it out of her hands.

Which, to be fair, I absolutely was.

She glares. "None of your damn business."

I step closer, peering over the edge of the book before she can react.

Oh.

Oh, this is gold.

I barely suppress a grin as I read the title aloud. "*Taken by the Barbarian King?*"

Anna's face goes nuclear.

She snaps the book shut and launches off the couch so fast, I almost stumble back.

"Do you have a fucking problem with what I'm reading?" she snaps, tucking the book behind her like that'll somehow erase what just happened.

I grin, slow and easy. "I mean... I have questions."

She scowls, but a rosy color tints her cheeks. "Well, I don't have any answers."

I chuckle, leaning against the back of the couch, arms crossed, fully enjoying the way she's absolutely flustered.

"Didn't take you for the type, Ace," I muse, eyes twinkling. "I thought you were all about intellectual thrillers and feminist dystopias. But here you are, indulging in some good ol' fashioned *smut*."

Her eyes narrow dangerously. "Oh, I'm sorry—would you rather I read about emotionally constipated rockstars with bad impulse control?"

I laugh, but Anna looks ready to murder me in cold blood.

"Seriously," I say, still grinning. "A Barbarian King, huh? Didn't peg you for the type. I mean, you're *terrifyingly* smart. And if emotionally constipated men are such a turnoff, why the hell are you drooling over one whose mode of communication is with a battle axe?"

She lifts her chin and quirks an eyebrow. "Maybe I like a man who isn't afraid to *cross swords.*"

I choke. Pretty sure there was a double entendre buried in there.

Anna's demeanor shifts slightly—victorious, almost —as she turns on her heel to head toward the hallway. "Have fun sussing out that one, Price."

Like hell I'm letting her escape. And you bet I'll be Googling whatever that meant later.

I follow her, too riled up to let this go. Maybe it's the post-show adrenaline wearing off. Maybe it's the fact that I need to find a way to get Anna out from under my skin before I blow up my friendship with Ethan.

"You know, I had a pretty great show tonight," I say casually, like I'm just making conversation.

Anna keeps walking. "Good for you."

"I mean, you wouldn't know. Since you weren't there."

She freezes. The tension thickens, coiling between us like a live wire.

Anna turns slowly, arms crossed, her expression unreadable. "Oh, *poor Joel*. Was the crowd of drunk, barely clothed girlies not enough for you? You needed a few hecklers, too?"

I exhale sharply, running a hand through my hair. "I just don't get it, Anna. You could've come to the show. Just to see how the new song sounded."

She scoffs. "What would be the point of that?"

"Because you love music. And maybe you'd see—"

"See *what* exactly?" She cuts in.

"That I'm—I'm *different*." I blurt out, Ethan's words racing through me.

She actually laughs. A cold, sharp sound. "Oh, you're different?"

"Yes."

"Bullshit."

My patience snaps.

"What the fuck do you want from me, Ace?" I take a step closer, heat rising under my skin. "Do you want me to beg for your forgiveness? Do you want me to say I don't regret anything I did when we were kids? Because I *do*, Anna. I fucking do. If you'd just open the damn envelope, you'd—"

Her arms tighten around herself, but she holds her ground. "It wouldn't change anything if I did."

"It *could* if you'd let it."

She flinches, just slightly, but I see it.

She realizes it too, because she turns away like she can physically shut me out.

But I'm done letting her. We've been living in this space for a week and I can feel her defenses cracking. Hell, mine have already gone to shit. May as well see if she'll join me.

She doesn't want to be angry with me. I can kinda see that now. She just doesn't know how to let it go. To let me back in.

I step in, crowding her space, voice lower now— rougher.

"Admit it. You don't hate me," I murmur.

Anna exhales sharply, dropping her hands to her sides. "Oh my god."

"You're just afraid to admit that you don't."

She turns back, eyes blazing. "You think you know me that well?"

I nod, not backing down. "I know you better than you think, Ace. Hell, I'd wager that I know you better than just about anyone else."

She huffs a dry laugh, but I catch the small shiver. The flicker of something akin to fear in her deep brown eyes.

The space between us is razor-thin now, heat crackling between us like an exposed wire.

Her breath hitches, just slightly.

I see the way her gaze flickers, her body locked tight like she's fighting herself. Fighting *me*.

She won't admit it, but she's thinking about it.

She's *feeling* it.

That pull. The same one I've been trying to ignore—and failing miserably—since I got back.

Her eyes drop, just for a second, to my mouth, and I stop breathing.

Holy shit.

I could close the space between us.

It would take nothing.

A tilt of my head, a shift forward, and I'd have her. I'd feel her lips on mine, the heat of her skin.

She'd hate herself for it. Hell, maybe she wants a reason to hate me again.

But I can feel the battle in her. The warring between *get out of my life* and *come closer.*

Her fingers twitch at her sides, knuckles tight like she's bracing for impact.

I don't move.

I let her decide because I refuse to force her.

Then, just when I think she's about to—

The front door swings open.

"Yo, Anna, you home?"

We snap apart like we've been burned.

I take a step back, jaw clenched, while Anna exhales sharply and *shakes herself out of it.*

Fuck.

I run my hands through my hair and breathe out.

Ethan's voice is casual, easy—completely oblivious to the fact that I was a breath away from making *a very bad decision.*

Tessa follows behind him, her gaze flicking between

us like she knows *something* just happened but can't quite put her finger on it.

Anna recovers faster than I do.

She crosses her arms, her entire stance shifting like she wasn't just about to kiss me. Like she wasn't just considering something dangerous.

"Yeah, I'm here," she says, voice impressively steady. "What's up?"

Ethan lifts a brow, glancing between us again, his gaze lingering just long enough to make my pulse spike before he shrugs it off. "Just a heads up—Mom's gonna call you about Mina's party bright and early tomorrow. She's in full *Korean grandmother event planning mode*, so brace yourself. Sounds like the party will be Saturday, so we need to get serious."

Tessa laughs it off at the same time Anna groans, dragging a hand down her face. "Great. Can't wait."

Tessa shifts, leaning against the doorway, still looking at me like she *knows*.

Like she *feels* the shift in the air.

"So, how was the show?" Anna asks, voice overly nonchalant.

Too nonchalant.

She didn't even call me a name or make a snide remark about it.

Tessa smirks.

Ethan, bless him, launches into the recap, and I use it as an excuse to take a step back. To shake off whatever the hell that moment was because I knew I wanted to get her to admit she doesn't hate me.

But I sure as shit wasn't expecting to nearly *kiss* her.

While Ethan talks about my performance like it's the most important thing in the world, I walk back to my room and close the door.

Somehow, my show feels like a lifetime ago. Because all I can think about is the way Anna looked at me.

Like she wanted it—wanted *me*. And I would have given her everything if she had.

And fuck me, I don't know what to do with that.

CHAPTER 19

Anna

I am never drinking wine again.

Okay, that's a lie. I love wine. Wine and I have been through *a lot* together. And the Dirty B's would kill me. But after last night? I need a solid twenty-four hours of sobriety before I even look at my Merlot bottle again.

I groan into my pillow, but the betrayal of my own brain continues. It *replays* the scene like I'm watching my own downfall in slow motion.

The way he stepped closer. The heat in his eyes. The *gravity* between us, pulling me in like I was caught in some stupid, reckless orbit.

And the worst part? The absolute *worst* fucking part? *I almost kissed him.*

Not the other way around. *Me.* I was the one who lost my goddamn mind.

I shove my face deeper into the pillow, willing myself to suffocate on sheer embarrassment alone.

It was the *wine*. It *had* to be.

Well, the wine and the fact that he walked in *right* when I was reading the filthiest sword-crossing scene imaginable. It was the hottest thing I've read in a long time and I was seriously considering heading to my bedroom for some "alone time" before Joel got home. But no… It was *strategic timing sabotage* by the universe.

What are the odds?

Actually, *high*, considering my current luck.

Joel's shower situation crops up in my mind unbidden, making my insides heat.

God, I hope he doesn't say anything.

What if he thinks I actually *wanted* the kiss?

Worse—what if he doesn't mention it at all?

Actually, I don't know which is worse, him pretending it never happened or me knowing that he knows and him smirking about it every time he looks at me.

Which, let's be honest, he's definitely going to do.

He's probably already storing it as ammo. The next time I roll my eyes at him, he'll just grin and say, "What? You weren't rolling your eyes last night when you almost kissed me, Ace."

Of course he is. I bet he's been smiling to himself, perfectly smug in his stupid, rockstar arrogance. Someone send help.

I groan and throw my pillow across the room.

I exhale sharply, shifting onto my back to stare at the ceiling.

Why did I even mention sword crossing? Good god, Anna.

What if he looked it up? I wouldn't put it past him.

The thought makes my stomach *plummet*.

Joel Price, Googling "sword crossing romance novel meaning" like some oblivious idiot, only to be *slapped in the face* with the dirtiest excerpts from the internet?

I physically cringe and I can literally feel the blood rushing to my cheeks.

What if he finds a Reddit thread?

What if he clicks on some fanfic?

What if he learns things I can never un-know?!

Oh my god. What have I done?

I shut my eyes, fingers pressing into my temples.

No. He wouldn't.

...Would he?

No, Anna. You don't care.

I *do* care.

I don't *want* to care.

I groan again and pull the blanket over my head.

This is fine. Everything is fine.

I'm fan-fucking-tastic.

Besides, if I ignore it long enough, my mortification will fade. That's how it works, right?

I reach for my phone on my nightstand, desperate for distraction, only to find a missed call from Mom.

And a text.

Shit.

> Mom: Call me back ASAP. Important.
> Love you! 😘

I stare at the screen like it's rigged to explode.

I don't want to talk about Mina's doljanchi at seven thirty in the morning.

I debate my options. I could pretend I didn't see it. I could fake sleep. But if I *don't* respond soon, she'll assume I'm dead and start calling *Ethan*.

And if Ethan gets dragged into this first, he will *absolutely* call me to demand why I didn't intervene sooner. And if I don't answer *him*, he'll be straight down here, bursting through my door and stealing my leftovers.

With a sigh, I dial her number and press the phone to my ear.

She picks up on the first ring.

"Anna, sweetie. Finally. I was starting to think you'd fallen off the face of the earth."

Oh my god, you'd think I'd been ignoring her for days.

I sigh, already regretting this. "Hi, Mom. What's up?"

"I wanted to check in about Mina's doljanchi. I know we talked about you helping with RSVPs and the dol table, but you don't have to worry about that anymore."

I frown, wishing I had gotten coffee before making this call. "Wait—what?"

"Tessa and I have it all handled," she says breezily, like this isn't a huge revelation. "Invitations were sent weeks ago, and the dol table is already planned. I found the perfect hanbok for Mina, the baekseolgi cake is ordered, and the doljabi setup is going to be *so* cute. Tessa has been wonderful—she made sure we got the traditional bokjori for luck and even found a silk table runner to match Mina's outfit."

I blink, trying to process. "Wait… that means when you came over a few days ago, you already had this stuff organized. And you're only telling me now?"

"Of course, sweetie," she says, like this is totally normal. "I'm telling you *and* Ethan now so neither of you can back out by dragging your feet the way you both tend to do. Besides, did you honestly think I'd put either of you on something as important as the invites and dol table?"

I let out a slow breath, oddly impressed. "Wow. That's… *calculated*."

Mom *tsks* like she didn't just admit to a Taylor Swift level mastermind. "I *knew* you'd say something like that. But it's *Mina's* day, Anna. We just want it to be special."

I pinch the bridge of my nose. "Okay, so if you and Tessa did everything, what exactly do you need me for? I mean, other than to show up in full Korean garb."

"Oh—" Her voice brightens, and I instantly regret asking. "I need you on the music."

I sit up so fast my phone almost slips from my hand. "I'm sorry, *what*?"

"The music," she repeats, like this isn't a big deal. "You'll be in charge of it."

I scoff. "Mom. Mina's *one*. She doesn't care what's playing. Hell, I could put on an endless stream of Ni Hao, Kai-Lan in the background and she'd be happier."

"You're right," she agrees easily, and for a second, I think I've won.

Then she lands the *real* punch. Because, she's my mother.

"So I guess you and Joel can just play some music together."

I choke. "I'm sorry, *say huh*?"

"You used to love playing together all the tine," she says, like this is a fond nostalgia moment and not an absolute nightmare. "I still remember when you and Joel would practice in Ethan's room for hours. Oh, you were *so* cute. You'd get all serious when he'd try to improvise, and he'd just laugh and say you were too structured— remember that?"

Oh, I remember. I remember *all too well*.

"Mom—" I warn, shaking my head.

"I used to love hearing you two," she sighs wistfully, completely ignoring the abject panic rolling through me. "You were always in sync, even when you pretended you weren't. I bet if you tried, you'd still sound just as good together."

Yeah. Because *that's* the problem.

Mom sighs again. The *drama* in this sigh. The full-weight *K-drama protagonist has been betrayed* sigh.

"You know," she says, voice soft, *dangerously* soft, "when you were ten, you and Joel wrote a whole song for Appa's birthday. Do you remember that?"

I freeze.

I forgot about that. Well, actually, pretty sure I suppressed it, but whatever.

But now that she's said it, the memory crashes over me in full detail—Joel, sitting cross-legged on my bedroom floor, plucking clumsily at the guitar while I insisted that he had to learn the right chord progression.

"Dude, this is a masterpiece," he'd said dramatically, flipping his hair. "We're gonna be famous one day."

And then the actual lyrics come back, and—

Oh.

Oh God.

"Appa, you're the best, better than the rest, even when you make us clean, you're still the dream—"

It was dumb. but we spent days perfecting it, sneaking around the house trying to practice without him hearing.

And the way my father smiled when we played it?

I slap a hand over my face.

We were so stupid.

And Appa loved it anyway.

My throat tightens.

Mom, clearly sensing weakness, presses forward.

"He kept that little recording on his phone for *years,* you know. He'd play it every once in a while and tell me, *'They're going to do something big someday.'*" She laughs softly. "He loved hearing you two together."

"Appa? My Appa?" I gape. "Are you sure we're talking about the same man?"

"Of course, it was the same man," she says like I'm the absurd one.

I squeeze my eyes shut.

Not fair. Not fucking fair.

This event isn't even for him. It's for Mina, for crying out loud.

I try to think of a way out. Any way out. "Mom, I don't—"

"Anna."

One word. That's all it takes.

The warning in her voice is clear. She's not asking. She's *deciding*.

I grit my teeth, my entire body fighting against the inevitable.

"...Fine."

"Wonderful!" she chirps. "I'll let Joel know you're in."

I groan into my hands. "He already knows, doesn't he?"

Mom chuckles. "Of course he does. I talked to him an hour ago."

Oh my god.

I collapse back into my pillows as Mom *cheerfully* ends the call.

Then, I just lie there, staring at my ceiling.

One.

Two.

Three.

Then, I explode.

I *fling* my phone across the bed like it's infected with Joel Price's smug, insufferable aura.

I throw off my blankets and pull on a hoodie and sweatpants, then I march to the kitchen.

I make coffee like it has personally wronged me by not supporting me through that hellscape of a phone call.

Then, for the next ten minutes, I stand by the counter, gripping my mug, steam curling into my face, seething.

I *almost* text Tessa, because *why did she go along with this?*

> Me: Did you know about my mother's ridiculous plan to torture me?

I hesitate, then delete it.

No. It's not Tessa's fault. My mother is devious. I wouldn't go against her, either.

However...

I inhale. I exhale.

Then, I snatch my phone back up, fingers already flying over the screen.

> Me: ETHAN.

> Me: Did you KNOW ABOUT THIS??

Ethan: what?

> Me: Mom just told me I have to do music for Mina's party. WITH. JOEL.

Ethan: Lol yeah, she told me earlier

> Me: AND YOU DIDN'T WARN ME?

Ethan: well, for starters, didn't think you'd be awake yet. besides, figured it was safer to let you find out from her first. I don't have a death wish

Me: You are dead to me. 💀

Ethan: Harsh. But understandable. RIP me. 🪦

Ethan: Any chance you could make a playlist for my funeral?

Me: I hope your ghost is haunted by Nickelback and Baby Shark on loop.

Ethan: Damn. That's cold.

Ethan: What if I just had you and Joel—

Me: Finish that sentence and I'll kill you myself.

Ethan: Just saying, you could bond over my death.

Me: I'm blocking you.

Ethan: Love youuuu. 🫠

Ethan: Tell Joel hi for me.

I growl at his stupid text and open my calendar app.

Six days.

Six.

That's less than a week until I have to stand next to Joel Price and pretend like he doesn't ruin my life by merely existing. But it's also six fucking days of having to plan and practice with him.

Oh, and guess what?

Mom just made a group chat. *Swell.*

> Mom: Joel and Anna, you should start planning this week. Let me know if you need anything!

Joel's *already* responding, the traitorous bastard.

> Joel: Got it. Looking forward to it.

I hate him.

But it gets worse.

> Joel: Should we do a ballad, Ace? Maybe a heartfelt acoustic moment?

My entire body revolts.

> Me: I will walk into Lake Superior before that happens.

> Joel: Okay, okay. What about some EDM?

> Mom: I trust you both to be professional.

> Joel: Of course. I'm very professional.

I narrow my eyes at my screen.

> Me: Lies.

> Joel: You wound me, Ace.

> Joel: Guess I'll just have to prove myself when we rehearse.

I squint the last word, then slam my phone down on the counter. For good measure, I throw eye daggers in the direction of my spare room.

I am *so* not surviving this next week.

I thought the last one was bad. But this...

Even *more* forced proximity with him?

Fuck my actual life.

Yep, now's not the time to quit drinking. In fact, I'm going to need *more* wine. Stat.

And maybe a priest.

CHAPTER 20

Joel

Anna is avoiding me.

She's not even being *subtle* about it.

After the whole almost-kiss thing, she's been moving through the house like she's got a Joel-activated security system. Any time I enter a room? She's suddenly got somewhere else to be. If I start a conversation? She's giving me one-word answers and pretending she has emails to send.

It's adorable, really.

And maybe I'd be a good person and let her have her space.

But where's the fun in that?

Especially when we *have* to practice together for Mina's party, and she's dodging it like I suggested a séance to raise the ghosts of her bad decisions.

Monday, I texted her. *When do you want to practice?* She left me on read.

Tuesday, I asked her in person. She pretended she

didn't hear me and walked out of the kitchen with her entire plate of food.

Wednesday morning, I slid a note under her door.

We could always just perform an interpretive dance instead.

She crumpled it up and threw it at my head when she walked past me later.

We're making progress.

I'm still figuring out my next move when I step into the living room—

And *freeze.*

Because there, sitting pretty on the coffee table, is *her book.*

Taken by the Barbarian King.

Anna is nowhere to be found, but I am certain she didn't mean to leave it here.

And I am a man of opportunity.

I drop onto the couch, pick up the book, and flip it open to a random page—

Just as Anna walks into the room.

She *stops short.*

For a full two seconds, she just *stares.*

Then—

"What the fuck are you doing?"

I glance up, all innocence. "Oh, you mean *this?*" I hold up the book, grinning like a goddamn Cheshire Cat. "Just broadening my literary horizons."

Her *entire* face goes purple.

"Put. It. Down."

I turn a page leisurely. "You know, Ace, I gotta repeat —'barbarian king' wasn't really the vibe I expected from you." I skim a paragraph. "Although, I do see the appeal of a man who can lift a horse with one arm. Very practical."

Her nostrils flare. "*Joel.*"

"Or wait—" I flip to another page, pretending to be fascinated. "This might actually be my favorite part. The way he just *throws her over his shoulder* mid-battle? Incredible. Functional *and* romantic."

Then, I flip another page, lips parting as my brain *short-circuits*.

Oh.

Oh, *what the fuck*?

My eyebrows shoot up. My smugness *wobbles*.

Because *this* is—

Holy *shit*.

I wasn't expecting *that*.

Then, I reread the paragraph for good measure, because there's no fucking way I just read that correctly.

Oh. Nope. I did.

There are two men. And one woman. And a very enthusiastic use of—

I shut the book and reopen it, because my brain refuses to accept this as reality.

Holy shit.

My grip on the book tightens slightly as my brain processes the very *intense*—very *explicit*—arrangement of bodies currently described in vivid detail.

I can actually *feel* the heat creeping up my neck.

Anna is reading this?

My Anna. No—*Ethan's little sister.* The same girl who used to argue with me over the ethics of looting in video games and who once refused to read Harry Potter because "the magical system lacked logical consistency."

And yet, here she is, reading something that would make a Roman orgy look tame.

I don't know what's worse—the fact that I can never unsee this, or the fact that I... kinda get why she's into it.

And for the first time in my life, I have no idea what the fuck to say.

Anna lunges.

I barely dodge as she makes a grab for the book, her entire body radiating panic and murderous intent in equal measure.

"Drop it. Right the fuck now."

I clear my throat, recovering as quickly as possible, shaking off whatever the hell that just did to me.

"Hold on, hold on," I say, yanking the book just out of reach, forcing myself to smirk past the surprising mental imagery I just sustained. "I just need to—yep, okay, *confirmed*, that's some *very*... innovative swordplay."

Anna makes a sound like she's about to commit *violence.*

I drag a hand down my face and groan dramatically. "Ace, I think I need a *minute.*"

She lunges again, finally snatching the book from my hands.

She clutches it to her chest like a lifeline, her entire face on fire.

"Oh my god, you are *the worst—*"

"Is this, uhm, is it for research?" I ask, wanting to know but also kinda not wanting to know.

She lets out an *exasperated* groan and crosses her arms. "It's for *book club,* idiot."

I blink. "Book club?"

"Yes. *Book club.* I'm reading it for *educational purposes.*"

I stare at her.

She stares back. Arms crossed. Chin lifted. Doing *everything* in her power to look unaffected—except for the fact that her face is still red as hell.

I should let this go.

I should be a mature adult and move on.

But she left me alone with that scene for way too long.

I tilt my head. "What kind of book club exactly?"

Her expression doesn't even change. "A normal one."

I raise a brow. "A normal one?"

"Yes."

"Just some gals sitting around discussing plot structure?"

"Yes."

"And *thematic depth*?"

"Obviously."

"And, I assume, the historical accuracy of battlefield logistics? Because I'd definitely point out that lifting the horse thing."

Her nostrils flare. "Joel."

"Wait, wait—" I start laughing all over again, imagining her sitting with a bunch of women discussing sex scenes. "Do you guys have, like, meetings? Do you take minutes? I bet you do. Oh my god, please tell me you have ranking systems."

Anna drags her hands down her face, like she's regretting every decision that led her here. "We are not discussing the ranking system."

"Oh my god, yes—" I say, praising the god in the ceiling. "There's a ranking system. I bet it's chili peppers. It is, isn't it?"

She lets out a wounded sound. "I hate you so much."

"No, no—this is important. If you're a senior Dirty B, does that mean you've read the most filth?"

She pinches the bridge of her nose and purses her lips.

"Or is it, like, a merit-based thing? You unlock elite status after surviving a certain number of highly questionable plots?" I tap my chin. "What's the initiation process? Do you have to read a full book out loud while making intense eye contact?"

"For fucksake."

I press a hand to my heart. "You know, Ace, I have to say, I never pegged you for the type to analyze the finer points of—" I lower my voice, smirking, "—strategic sword placement. That's what you were talking about the other night, wasn't it?"

Her entire body locks up.

I grin.

That's it. That's *exactly* the reaction I was looking for. God, she's actually really sexy when she's all fired up.

Her glare could set fire to Lake Superior, but she doesn't take the bait. Instead, she exhales sharply, rolling her shoulders back, clearly *trying* to regain some control.

I watch her, curious, waiting for the inevitable excuse.

Finally, she says, "It's called the Dirty B's."

I blink.

I blink again.

And then I *lose my fucking mind*.

I throw my head back, laughing so hard I nearly slide off the couch.

She groans aggressively, muttering something that sounds like "I'm going to kill Tessa," but I'm *too busy losing oxygen* to fully process it.

"The Dirty B's?" I repeat, fucking delighted. "Like… that's what you actually call it?"

Anna glares. "Of course. It's short for 'Dirty Bitches.'"

I slap my thigh, still *dying*. "Oh, yeah, no, that really softens it."

Her eye twitches. "It's not supposed to."

I wipe a fake tear from my eye, grinning so hard my face hurts. "God, this is beautiful. I'm so proud of you."

She groans again, throwing herself onto the couch like she's *physically exhausted* by my presence.

Which only fuels me further, because she's sitting next to me. She's not running. Not hiding in her room. She's *here*.

"You know what?" I say, tapping my chin. "I think I need to start my own book club."

She lifts her head just enough to glare. "No."

I ignore her. "Yep. It's happening. A club that truly appreciates the literary merit of, uh..." I nod toward the book she's still clutching. "Highly creative battle techniques."

"*Joel.*"

I grin, slow and wicked. "I'm calling it The Dirty Bastards. Know any guys who might wanna join?"

Her head drops back against the couch as she whimpers in absolute suffering.

"*Why are you like this?*"

"Born this way, baby."

"Do not quote Gaga unless you can back it up." She throws a pillow at my face.

I catch it, laughing, because this is the most fun I've had in days.

Maybe weeks.

Hell, probably years.

She groans into her hands. "I *hate* you."

I lean closer, dropping my voice. "You sure about that?"

Her hands drop immediately, her glare back in full force, but I see it.

The slight twitch at the corner of her lips.

The way she almost—*almost*—smiles.

And I know, deep in my *very soul*, that I'm *winning*.

Anna stands up suddenly, as if that will fix this. "I—I need to check my email."

I smirk. "Do you?"

"Yep. Very important work stuff."

"Like what?"

She flounders for a second. "Uh. Corporate espionage. Hush-hush. Government secrets."

I grin wider. "Ah, yes. Your thriving spy career."

She glares at the coffee table like she can manifest an escape route. "You know, I should really start... cooking more."

I snort. "You *hate* cooking."

"Yeah, but, um, personal growth?" She gestures vaguely.

"Nice try," I say, stretching my arms behind my head, "we should pick songs for Mina's party."

Her face drops completely. I grin like the devil himself.

The whiplash is delicious.

"No."

I raise an eyebrow. "No?"

She scowls, but grabs her laptop from the coffee table, aggressively typing as she pulls up Spotify. "Fine. But we need kid-friendly music."

I nod solemnly. "Agreed. That's why we should open with Pony by Ginuwine."

Her eyes snap to me, horrified. "Joel."

"What? It's about horse riding."

She lets out a murderous sigh. "I am begging you to take this seriously."

I lean forward, bracing my elbows on my knees. "Okay, fine. No Ginuwine. But what about a nice, neutral option? You know. Something that works for all audiences."

Anna narrows her eyes. "Like what?"

I pause for dramatic effect.

Then I say, completely straight-faced, "*I Want Your Sex* by George Michael."

Anna stills.

For the first time in this entire conversation, she doesn't roll her eyes. She doesn't throw a pillow. She just looks at me.

And something in the air shifts.

It's subtle at first. Just the way her lips part slightly, like she wants to say something but *thinks better of it*. The way her shoulders go rigid—not in anger, not in exasperation, but in something else. Something that makes my pulse thud heavy in my ears.

She knows what I'm doing.

She knows I'm pushing it.

And she's deciding whether to push back.

I let the silence stretch between us, waiting, watching. My smirk is still there, but it's different now— heavier.

Her tongue darts out, wetting her lips, and I nearly forget how to fucking breathe.

I shouldn't be thinking about this. About her. About the fact that she reads *that* kind of book and how—deep down—I like knowing it.

I like knowing that under all that sharp, biting sarcasm, there's this *part of her* that gets lost in those kinds of stories.

That wants that kind of heat.

And fuck, now I'm imagining her like that—flushed, breathless, eyes hazy as she—

Nope.

No. Not going there.

I shift, suddenly feeling too warm, but I refuse to break first. Instead, I watch her watch me, neither of us moving. Neither of us daring to breathe too deep.

It's reckless.

It's stupid.

It's so fucking dangerous.

And I love it.

Then—

Anna blinks.

And just like that, the moment shatters.

She grabs another pillow and hurls it at my head, her voice sharper than before—like she's trying to convince herself this *didn't* just happen.

I dodge, laughing, and she groans into her hands. "I cannot believe I have to do this with you."

"Fine. We'll stick to The Wiggles," I say, forcing my voice to sound normal—steady, like I'm not still feeling the ghost of that moment hanging between us.

Like I'm not still feeling her eyes on me.

Like I didn't just cross into dangerous fucking territory and like it way too much.

I clear my throat, shifting where I sit, stretching out like I'm completely unaffected—but my body knows better.

Because that wasn't just teasing anymore.

That was something else.

Something sharp and tight and hot that curled low in my stomach, something that makes my fingers twitch like they want to test the tension instead of break it.

Anna exhales sharply beside me, her posture stiff, fingers gripping her laptop just a little too hard—like she felt it too.

Like she doesn't trust herself to look at me yet.

And maybe that should feel like a win.

But all it does is make my pulse pound harder.

I let out a slow breath, rolling my shoulders. "Right. So. Kid songs."

Anna doesn't look at me. Just clicks aggressively through her playlist, jaw tight, still forcing herself to act like nothing happened.

And maybe that's why I can't stop looking at her. Because for the second time since I've been here, she's not running.

The silence stretches for a second too long.

Then—

The most aggressively cheerful children's song I've ever heard fills the air.

I blink.

Anna finally risks a glance at me, lips pressing together like she's daring me to comment.

I stare at her. Stare at the ceiling. Stare at my goddamn life choices.

Then, exhaling hard, I lean forward, elbows on my knees, and scrub a hand over my face.

"Yeah, no. This is fine. This is all very, very fine."

She groans so hard I swear she's actively aging, but she doesn't move. "No, it's terrible, you moron."

"Oh, thank god." I practically sag with relief, looking over at her.

Part of me can't believe she's still here.

Still glaring. Still grumbling, sure. But still sitting right next to me, close enough that I can feel the warmth of her body beside mine.

Like she's forcing herself to stay put—as if leaving now would mean admitting something happened.

I lean back, exhaling slowly, letting the moment settle.

She clicks through her laptop, aggressively scrolling, eyes fixed on the screen like if she looks at me for too long, she might give something away.

I watch her fingers move over the trackpad, a little too tense, a little too deliberate.

She's rattled.

And fuck if I don't like it.

Not in the way I like winning an argument with her. Not in the way I like getting under her skin just to watch her snap at me.

No—this is different.

This is her not snapping at me. This is her staying when she could have walked away.

This is her not trusting herself to look at me, but not trusting herself to leave, either.

I clear my throat, shifting slightly, stretching out my legs like I'm completely fine. Like my pulse isn't still thudding from whatever the hell that just was.

Anna finally risks a glance at me, her mouth pressed into a thin, determinedly neutral line.

I smirk, just to see her eyes narrow.

She huffs, turning back to her laptop, clicking on the first song she sees.

Another bright, aggressively cheerful children's song blasts through the speakers.

I groan immediately, scrubbing a hand over my face. "Oh, for fuck's sake."

Anna finally smirks.

The tension still lingers. The air between us is still charged, like a wire humming just beneath the surface.

But when she looks at me now, it's different.

A little less guarded.

Less angry.

Like maybe—just maybe—she's starting to let me in again.

And for the first time in years, I start to think—

Maybe I have a chance.

CHAPTER 21

Anna

I am *not* okay.

I'm a complete mess. A full, walking disaster wrapped in a cardigan that's starting to feel too hot, sitting in the back of Dirty Books while my brain replays the worst possible highlight reel of my life.

Specifically—*Joel reading my book.*

And not just *reading* it. Oh, no. Of all the pages he could turn to, he had to read *that* part.

The sword crossing scene.

The scene that was so filthy, *I* had to put the book down to process. It was glorious. Until it wasn't.

The scene that, apparently, *broke* Joel's brain for a good thirty seconds before it rebooted.

I feel myself overheating just thinking about it. Clearly he hadn't Googled it. I don't know if I should pity him or be thankful for that fact.

"Okay, what's going on with you?" Vivian's voice

cuts through my spiral, dragging me back to the present like a snapped rubber band.

I blink at her, then at the rest of the Dirty B's, all of whom are now staring at me like I'm a new species of human. A *weird* species. One that doesn't usually malfunction in the presence of romance novels.

"What do you mean?" I ask, summoning every ounce of casual detachment I possess. I reach for a hint of boredom, but it doesn't sound right, even to me.

Lily narrows her eyes. "You haven't said a single thing about the book. Or rolled your eyes at Vivian's dramatics tonight."

"Or looked at her phone once," Carlie interjects, sipping her wine.

I blink at her, cringing slightly. *Shit.*

Tasia quirks an eyebrow and nods sagely. "Yeah, come to think of it, that's super odd."

"Are you kidding? It's not just odd. It's downright out of character," Quinn quips, giving me a once over.

"What are you talking about? I'm not *always* on my phone," I fire back, rolling my eyes.

The entire collective gasps.

Okay, so that's probably fair.

Quinn crosses his legs and peers at me skeptically.. "Oh, she *totally* has something going on."

I freeze, hoping that if I don't make any sudden movements, they'll all move on.

"I have to agree with Quinn. What's up, Anna?" Lily asks, always the first to try to help out when none is necessary.

Shit.

"Nothing," I say too quickly, reaching for my wine and taking a big gulp. Then I remember what I almost did last night and set it back down, shoving it away.

Vivian and Lily exchange a look. The kind of look that says *we're not letting this go.*

"Anna," Lily says, tilting her head. "Did something happen? Do you need to talk about it?"

I shake my head. "Nope. Right as rain over here."

"You're sure?" Vivian presses, smiling like a shark. "Because your whole energy is off. And that's saying something."

That's because it is.

I swallow hard, refusing to look at any of them. Everything is fucking off. My world is no longer tilting at the same axis.

Tasia leans in, eyes sparking with the kind of curiosity that could rival my mother's. "Is it work? Or—" She pauses, her eyes flashing with mischief. "Is it because of Joel?"

Oh god. Why did she have to say his name?

Carlie sits up straighter, suddenly invested. "Oh yeah. I forgot about all that. How has it been living with Joel?"

I feel the blood drain from my body and there's nothing I can do to stop it.

Vivian claps her hands together. "Oh my god. It *is* about Joel! I *knew* it. Spill."

"There is nothing to spill," I lie, reaching for the wine again because, *fuck it.*

Quinn sighs dramatically. "Anna. Doll, we are here to

support you. If you can't lean on us, who can you lean on?"

I glare at all of them as I take another sip, savoring in the taste of regret and bad decisions as it washes over my tongue. "There is *nothing* going on."

Tasia eyes me suspiciously. "Then why do you look like you want to sink into the floor?"

I open my mouth. Then close it. Then consider launching myself out the nearest window. But it's at the front of the store and that's too far away.

This is *fine*. Everything is *fine*.

Then—my phone buzzes.

"Oh, see? Me, being totally normal," I say, making a show of picking up my phone. I glance down, and immediately, I go back to wanting to die.

> Joel: Have fun at Dirty B's. Don't forget to ask if any of the men wanna band together to form Dirty Bastards.

I *hate* him.

I *really* hate him.

But... unfortunately, my traitorous mouth twitches. Just a little.

And *unfortunately, Vivian* sees it.

She gasps, slapping the armrest on her chair. "Oh my *god*."

I straighten. "What."

"Oh-ho-ho. *Oh*. That was a smile. Was the text from Joel? I want see," she says, untangling her legs and attempting to beeline my direction.

I school my face into neutrality and shove my phone under my thigh. "No, it wasn't. It was work. And I don't smile."

"It was *absolutely* a smile," Lily confirms, her eyes lighting up like she just cracked the case of the century. "I saw it."

I roll my eyes, but my heart is pounding in my ears so loud it might actually drown out this conversation if I let it.

"Prove it," Vivian says, leaning over me. "If it wasn't him, show me."

"Rude. No," I say, shoving her back as I press my leg down for good measure, You never know, she might make a grab for it. Honestly, I wouldn't put it past her.

"Come on, Anna. You *never* get weird about book club unless something's messing with your head." She pauses. "Or *someone*."

I shake my head aggressively. "Nope. Absolutely not."

Quinn smirks. "Oh, I bet it is."

Lily grins like a mad woman. "I second that."

"Oh my god, you don't know anything," I attempt. "You're all just—"

Vivian cuts me off. "Anna. Dear, sweet, Anna. You are *spiraling* over a man. And not just *any* man. *Joel Price*. The guy you swore you'd never speak to again. The guy you have *hated* for *years*."

Oh my god, she just used air quotes.

"I *still* hate him," I say automatically, my face deadpanning.

Vivian crosses her arms. "Do you?"

"Yes!"

She tilts her head, unconvinced. "Then why were you smiling?"

I scowl. "I wasn't."

"Oh, babe," Vivian says, her smirk growing wicked. "You *so* were."

"I *wasn't*," I repeat, doubling down because if I give even an inch, they will never let this go.

Carlie hums, studying me like I'm a live specimen under a microscope. "Let's just unpack this for a second."

"No, let's *not*—"

She leans forward, resting her chin on her palm. "Joel sent you a text that made you smile. *And* you're spiraling. So the real question here is..." Her lips quirk knowingly. "Why? What's changed? If I were writing this out, you'd be falling, enemies to lovers style."

I hate that my face burns hotter. I'm not the one who gets all weird about a boy. I'm not the one who *fucking spirals*. And I'm *definitely* not falling enemies to lovers style.

"I'm not spiraling," I insist, refusing to acknowledge the last part.

Vivian waves a hand. "Okay, fine. Then tell us why you're acting like you've had a full-blown *existential crisis* since you sat down."

"I *haven't*—"

Lily cuts in, her voice all faux-casual. "Is it the book?"

I go rigid.

Shit.

Quinn gasps dramatically. "Oh my god. *Is* it the book?"

"No—" I say too quickly, gripping my glass again like it's the only thing keeping me tethered to reality. "Why would it be the book?"

Vivian's eyes narrow, sharp as hell. How is it she can spot drama, but can't tell when it's okay to pass on a highway?

"Because, Anna, if I didn't know better, I'd say you look personally victimized by this week's pick," she taunts, a little too knowingly for my liking.

Why am I getting the impression I'm not going to win this?

Carlie tilts her head. "Which is weird, because *you* were the one who suggested it."

Vivian gasps, pretending to clutch at pearls around her neck. "You *did*."

Quinn lifts a brow. "Wait. Wait, wait, wait. That's *right*." He eyes me, then the book, then me again. "Oh-ho, this just got way more *interesting*."

"No, it didn't," I snap, but my voice is too defensive.

Quinn ignores me entirely, turning to Vivian. "What was that thing she said last week? About how this book was *super well-written*? Which, I must vouch for, by the way." He fans himself and sighs dramatically.

Vivian snaps her fingers. "Right! She was all, '*The tension is practically dripping off the page*'—"

"Oh *my god*." I cover my face with my hands. I did. I *did* say that.

Quinn grins triumphantly. "And now she can't even *look* at it. That's *so* fascinating."

I groan, dragging my hands down my face. "Fine. You really want to know what's wrong with me?"

Vivian gestures around dramatically. "Yes, that is literally what we've been trying to accomplish for the past twenty minutes."

I take a deep breath, mentally preparing for impact.

Then I drop the bomb.

"Joel found my book."

Silence.

Then—

Vivian gasps so hard, I'm actually worried she might pass out. She literally starts to shake in excitement as her brain starts to process.

Lily leans forward. "*Which* book?"

I glare, grabbing my copy from the table and waving it in the air. "Which one do you think?"

Carlie's lips twitch. "Oh no."

Quinn wiggles his eyebrows way too enthusiastically. "Oh, *yes*."

Tasia exhales deeply, shaking her head. "Oh, this is *so* much more entertaining than I expected."

I point at her. "You didn't expect anything, because I wasn't going to tell you."

She snickers in response. "Whatever you say."

Vivian's entire body is vibrating now. "Okay, okay, let me just—" She fans herself dramatically. "So. *Joel found your book.*" Her grin is *feral*. "And?"

I groan again. "And he *read it.*"

Lily's brows lift. "The whole thing?"

"No—" I shut my eyes, praying for strength. "Just a little."

Quinn practically squeals. "Oh my god, he read the sword-crossing scene, didn't he?"

I sink further into my seat. "He *read* the sword-crossing scene."

Chaos.

Absolute, pandemonium erupts.

Vivian is cackling. Tasia presses her hands to her cheeks like she's experiencing secondhand embarrassment or something. Quinn is just sitting back, sipping his wine like this is his Super Bowl. The *bastard*.

Carlie? She just smirks knowingly and mutters, "I'd totally put that in an enemies to lovers novel."

I point at her. "No. Do *not* even think about it."

She raises her hands in mock surrender.

Lily chuckles into her wine. "This is my *favorite* book club meeting ever."

Vivian leans in, gleeful. "Okay, but what did he say?"

I let out a miserable laugh. "Oh, he said *plenty*."

Quinn gasps. "Oh my god, did he ask questions? Please tell me he had loads of questions."

I make a strangled noise.

Lily hums, then giggles. "Should we have a moment of silence for his innocent brain?"

Vivian straight up guffaws. "I mean, was it innocent, though?"

Quinn points aggressively. "That's the real question. Inquiring minds must know."

"Oh my god, *stop*," I groan, pressing my palms to my eye sockets. "He made fun of it. He—he practically narrated it out loud with a goddamn dramatic reading voice. Okay? And I'm pretty sure it broke his brain."

Carlie laughs into her glass. "I'm actually *in love* with this."

I glare at her. She better not write about this.

Tasia bites the side of her lip. "Okay, but was he making fun of it? Or was he, like, *a little bit into it?*"

Vivian gasps, gripping Quinn's arm like he will somehow anchor her to the room. "YES. Did it turn him on?"

I choke violently. "WHAT? *No—*"

Quinn grins. "That's a *very strong* denial. I can say with certainty that if I weren't *already* gay, that scene alone would have me flipping to the poly team."

I gawk at him.

But in the back of my brain, now I'm actually wondering.

Did it—

I mean, he was flustered for a second. His face kinda flushed. I mean, I didn't look down or anything—not that I would. Dear god, what in the freeze-dried hell is this?

My phone vibrates again.

I glance down, praying for it to be literally anyone else.

Nope.

It's Joel.

> Joel: Come on, Ace. Have you asked
> them about the Dirty Bastards thing?
> Inquiring minds want to know.

I stare.

I stare *hard*.

I groan, loudly, tossing my phone onto the table.

"What now?" Vivian practically sings as she reaches for my phone.

I sigh dramatically. "He wants me to ask if any of the guys would be game for starting a Dirty *Bastards* book club. Yes, he knows I'm here and we maybe sorta talked about who else comes to the meetings."

Once again, for a single moment, *absolute silence.*

Vivian cackles. "You know what this means, right? If he read it, and he got flustered, there's no way he wasn't at least a *little* turned on. And now he wants to start his own book club? Come on. That's not a coincidence, that's a coping mechanism.'"

I blink. My brain stops.

Wait. No. That's not—

But—

Oh my god. What if it is?

I groan into my hands, but it's too late. The thought is already there.

And now I am never going to recover.

Quinn beams. "Turned on or not, I'm in, baby. Tell him he has his first recruit."

Carlie leans forward, intrigued. "Oh, this is *interesting*. I'll have to ask Adam."

Vivian grins. "This is *sexy*."

"Oh my god, I just realized—" Quinn clutches his heart. "This is my *calling*. I can be the gay liaison between the two factions of Dirty B's."

I glare at all of them. They're ridiculous.

Tasia snickers into her wine. "I can't believe you've manifested this."

I shoot her a look of betrayal. "I *did not* manifest this."

Lily hums. "Didn't you, though?"

Carlie taps a finger against her chin. "I mean, this is just a *logical progression*. If we have the Dirty Bitches, of course a Dirty Bastards had to form. The universe demands balance."

Quinn nods sagely. "Yin and yang. Equal but opposite forces. A *sacred* brotherhood to match our sacred sisterhood."

Vivian is full-on wheezing now. "Oh, I *love* this so fucking much."

I groan, dragging my hands down my face. "I *hate* this."

"I don't think you actually do." Lily smirks.

I open my mouth to argue, but—

BUZZ.

I freeze.

Every eye in the room locks onto me.

Tasia sets down her wine glass with a knowing glint in her eye. "It's him again, isn't it?"

I consider throwing my phone across the room to avoid checking. Instead, I glance at the screen.

Yep.

Joel. *Again.*

> Joel: So? What's the verdict? Is Quinn
> in? Did he already start drafting an
> initiation ritual?

I squeeze my eyes shut. *I am going to die in this bookstore. Right here. Right now.*

Vivian, still vibrating with excitement, leans in. "Well? What did he say?"

I take the longest breath of my life. Then I slowly look at them all. I shouldn't tell them. I really shouldn't.

"Joel wants to know if you've already started drafting an initiation ritual, Quinn."

Quinn practically levitates with glee.

"OH. MY. GOD." He slaps the table, thrilled beyond measure. "He *sees* my potential. He *knows* my worth. I feel so honored. "

"He doesn't *see* anything. He hasn't even met you in person yet," I slap back.

"*Yet*—" Quinn gasps, "You all heard that right? She said *yet*. There will be a meeting coming soon."

Vivian is actually wiping away tears of laughter.

Carlie just shakes her head, grinning. "Honestly, *this* I'd put in a book, too."

I groan loudly, hating everything. Absolutely everything.

My stupid phone buzzes again. Can't he take the hint? I haven't responded to any of these asinine texts.

"What now?" Vivian asks, rocking on her chair.

I glance down, and immediately want to die.

> Joel: Oh, also—already asked Ethan.
> He's in.

I choke on air.

"Oh no," Carlie gasps in what sounds like delight. "What did he say?"

I grab a napkin off the table and scream into it.

"Oh my god," Vivian claps her hands together, absolutely losing it. "WHAT. DID. HE. SAY?"

I lift my miserable gaze. "He asked my brother already. Apparently, he's in now, too."

"This is the absolute best day of my life," Quinn says, fanning himself.

Carlie's expression is one of awe. "Oh my god, Joel *moves fast.*"

Vivian leans in, grinning so wide it's terrifying. "So. Just to summarize. Joel, number one—keeps texting you. Number two—invented a *book club for men* to match yours. And number three—has immediately recruited Quinn and your brother."

"And apparently London," Lily says, holding up her phone.

"Holy shit. Someone kill me," I mutter under my breath.

Vivian bats her eyelashes. "But you still *hate* him, right?"

I groan, leaning back and resting my gaze on the ceiling. "I *hate* everything about this."

Lily pokes my arm. "Are you *sure?*"

I lift my head just enough to glare at her.

But then I make a fatal mistake.

I glance back down at the text thread. And there it is. Another new text.

> Joel: I think this makes us book club rivals. That means we need a tournament. What's the best way to prove superiority—dueling? Feats of strength? Reading comprehension?

And god help me—my stomach does a little flip and…

I smile.

I feel my face betray me in real time.

Before I can *stop it*. Before I can *correct it*. Before I can bury my feelings deep where they belong.

Vivian gasps.

Carlie gasps.

Lily gasps.

Tasia, quirks an eyebrow.

Quinn faints theatrically.

And just like that—

I am never living any of this down.

CHAPTER 22

Joel

Anna's hair keeps slipping from behind her ear, falling in loose waves around her face as she scrolls through our playlist for Mina's doljanchi. She doesn't tuck it back. Doesn't acknowledge it. Just keeps her eyes on her phone screen like it holds the secrets of the universe.

She's been doing that all week—pretending to be perfectly fine, acting like everything is totally normal, as if things on Sunday night didn't happen.

As if I didn't almost kiss her. As if *she* didn't almost kiss me.

And maybe that would be fine. If I wasn't still thinking about it. If my brain hadn't spent the past four and a half fucking days replaying every single detail—her lips parting, the way she leaned in, the heat of her breath against my skin before Ethan burst into the scene and ruined everything.

But I have been thinking about it. A *lot*.

And now? I kind of want to see if I can make it happen again.

I know I shouldn't. I was only here to make sure she forgave me. To clear the air and rid myself of this heavy weight on my chest. I guess I sorta managed that last part. The weight is gone, but it's been replaced by something else. Something way more feral and unpredictable.

I strum a few chords, letting the sound fill the space between us. She doesn't look up. But the corner of her mouth twitches—just the barest hint of a smile before she schools her expression back to neutral.

"Alright, so we've got a solid list for Mina's doljanchi," she says, still not looking at me. "I suppose we should run through it one more time to make sure we're set."

"You sound excited."

Her eyes flick up. "I sound *prepared*."

"Same thing." I shrug.

"Not remotely."

The corner of my lip curves up despite itself. "Come on, Ace. You have to admit, you're actually enjoying yourself. We make a great time. Always have."

She rolls her eyes, but there's no heat behind it. "I *enjoy* being competent."

"Yeah? So you're saying if I threw you a curveball right now, you wouldn't flinch?"

That gets her attention. Her fingers tighten around her phone, and she narrows her eyes. "Define curveball."

I lean forward, resting my forearms on the guitar. "Come to my show tonight."

She freezes. Just for a second. It's barely a breath, a hesitation so small someone else might miss it.

But I don't miss it.

Then she scoffs, shaking her head. "Absolutely not."

I let out a dramatic sigh, plucking at the strings. "That was fast. Didn't even think about it."

"I *did* think about it," she counters. "For half a second. And then I dismissed it. Because it's a terrible idea."

"Why?"

She blinks, like she wasn't expecting me to ask. "Because," she says after a beat. "Because I have other plans."

I arch a brow. "Yeah? What plans?"

"My own."

I grin. "That sounds fake."

She leans back into the couch cushions, dropping her gaze to her phone like she's bored. "It's not."

I strum a slow, lazy chord. "If you say so."

She actually snorts through her nose like a bull. "I do."

I nod, pretending to accept that, even though I know —*I know*—she's thinking about it now. The flicker of hesitation, the way she shifted her weight, the way she refused to meet my eyes for just a second too long.

I mean, she's not coming.

But she kinda *wants* to.

I tap my fingers against the body of my guitar, studying her. "We're good enough at this. I don't think we need to run through it again. Instead, you want to tell me why you're so against seeing me perform?"

She lets out a sharp laugh. "Oh my god, Joel."

"What?"

She throws her hands in the air. "Because—because it's weird, okay?"

Okay, wasn't expecting that.

I tilt my head. "Weird how?"

She opens her mouth. Closes it. Her hands hover for a second before she drops them back to her sides. "I'm not doing this with you."

I shoot her a half smile. "Sounds like you already are."

She groans, dragging a hand down her face. "You are so—"

"Charming? Persuasive?" I offer.

"Infuriating. Frustrating. *Obnoxious*."

"That too." I beam at her.

She exhales, long and slow. "Let's just focus on the music, please."

I bite back my grin and nod. "Whatever you say, Ace."

But as she turns her attention back to the setlist, shifting her focus with a little more force than necessary, I catch it—the faintest trace of a smile tugging at her lips.

God, if it doesn't make my heart flip a little bit.

We've planned out a few songs that I'll be playing solo. A few we'll do together—me on guitar, her on piano. And then a few favorites for Mina that there's no way in hell either of us are replicating. The straight-up soundtrack will have to do.

So far, I'm the only one singing, though, and I don't know how I feel about that.

I let the moment sit—let the quiet stretch between us. The air feels heavier than it should, charged with something neither of us is willing to acknowledge. I should probably let it go. Hell, I should probably just focus on Mina's music, like she clearly wants me to.

But I don't.

Instead, I shift the guitar on my lap and pluck out a familiar tune—the melody of a song we used to mess around with years ago, back before everything got complicated.

Anna's fingers tighten on her phone, her eyes flicking up for just a second before she quickly looks away. But I see it. That flicker of recognition.

I keep playing, slow and easy.

"You remember this one?" I ask, schooling my voice to remain casual.

She exhales through her nose again. "Of course, I remember it."

"Sing it with me."

She shakes her head. "We're not doing this, Joel."

I grin, nudging her with my elbow. "Oh, we absolutely are."

She doesn't argue, but she doesn't join in, either.

I slow the tempo, making the notes drag, waiting her out.

Finally, she rolls her eyes, muttering something under her breath before shifting forward in her seat. Then, in a voice quieter than I was expecting, she sings the opening line.

It's not perfect. It's hesitant, almost careful, but damn, it still hits me straight in the chest.

I ease into the harmony, our voices blending like they always have—effortless, natural. Like muscle memory kicking in between the two of us. Even after all these years—through voice changes and god knows what else. It's still there.

The magic.

The song fades to a close, and for a second, neither of us speaks. The only sound is the low hum of the city beyond the window, the distant buzz of traffic, the faintest sound of her steady breath.

She's looking at me now, something unreadable in her gaze. Her fingers tap against her knee—light, restless.

"You still sound good," I tell her.

She snorts, shaking her head. "You act like that's a surprise."

"Not a surprise," I admit. "Just nice to hear again."

Something flickers across her face, too quick for me to catch. She looks down, tracing the rim of her phone case with the tip of her finger.

"I should go," she says, but she doesn't make any move to leave. "I have a ton of work to do."

I set the guitar aside and lean back on my hands. "You know, I was thinking..."

Her gaze snaps up. "That's dangerous."

I smirk. "Debatable."

She waits, clearly wary.

I let the pause stretch just enough to make her squirm, then say, "What if we added a song?"

Her brow furrows. "What?"

"For Mina's party. What if we threw in a surprise?"

She eyes me. "Why do I feel like you already have something in mind?"

I shrug. "Maybe I do."

She crosses her arms. "Joel."

I press a hand to my chest, feigning offense. "What? You don't trust me?"

"No."

"Harsh."

She huffs. "What song?"

I pause, then say, "You know which one."

Her jaw hardens and her eyebrows tug in. "No."

I tilt my head, watching her reaction closely. The immediate no isn't what makes me pause—it's the way her fingers tighten around her phone, her shoulders going rigid for just a second too long.

There's something she's not telling me.

"You sure about that?" I ask, keeping my tone light. "Because you just made a face."

Her lips press into a thin line before she says, "I did not make a face."

I smirk. "You totally did. In fact, you're still doing it."

She exhales sharply, shifting in her seat, her gaze flicking anywhere but at me.

I let out a slow breath, dragging a hand through my hair. "I get why you don't want to sing it."

Anna doesn't move, her fingers still tight around her phone.

I shift the guitar on my lap, plucking at the strings absently. "You think I don't, but I do."

She exhales sharply, shaking her head. "Joel—"

"I took something from you," I say, voice quieter now. "Back then. With the song."

That stills her. Not a big reaction, just a flicker, the slightest hesitation. But it's there.

I exhale through my nose. "I told myself it was just about the music. That giving you credit after the fact made it okay." I swallow, glancing at her. "But it wasn't just the song, was it?"

Her breath catches. It's tiny, barely a sound, but I hear it.

I rub my thumb along the edge of my guitar. "It wasn't just music for me, either. *You* weren't just music for me."

She blinks, her fingers going still.

I don't say more. I don't need to. I just let it sit there, between us, in the heavy quiet. Besides, if I said it— *actually said it*—it would be real and I'm not sure I'm ready for that yet.

For a moment, I think she might say something. Her mouth parts, her expression flickering with something I can't name.

But then, she just shakes her head, like she's trying to push it all away.

I nod slowly, shifting back, forcing an easy breath. "Alright."

She exhales, looking down at her phone, tracing the edges of it with her thumb again.

And that's when I see it.

Her fingers twitch, gripping just a little tighter, and something clicks into place in my mind.

I tilt my head, watching her closely. "You opened it."

She stills.

Doesn't argue.

Doesn't deny it.

I exhale, my lips pressing together. I wasn't expecting that.

Anna sighs, setting her phone down beside her. "You're *so* annoying."

I let out a quiet chuckle, but it's softer this time. "Yeah," I say. "I know."

She doesn't look at me right away, just stares at the setlist between us. But something about her feels... unsteady. Like she's standing too close to an edge she didn't realize was there.

Her jaw tightens. Then, she shakes her head, her voice quieter now. "I can't do that song. Not now, not ever, Joel."

I frown, setting aside my guitar so I can turn to face her.

She swallows, her fingers gripping her phone like a lifeline. "It still hurts too much."

I don't move, barely breathe.

Anna Chang just admitted to me she has feelings. Feelings about the song. Feelings about us singing it. Hell, feelings in general.

Maybe even feelings about me.

She exhales sharply, pressing the heel of her hand against her forehead before dragging it through her hair. "Look, we have this... thing. A temporary ceasefire. We get through Mina's party, and then you can go back to being famous or whatever, and I can go back to my life."

I study her for a moment. I don't know what to say or how to make this better.

Maybe there isn't a way.

Maybe I already ruined it beyond repair and this little glimmer of civility—that's all it will ever be between us.

That thought feels like a punch to the gut.

She shakes her head, like she's trying to clear something away, then pushes off the couch, grabbing her phone. "I really do have work to do."

I nod, because what the hell else can I do?

She moves toward the door, but just as she reaches for the handle, her fingers hesitate on the knob.

It's small. Barely a pause. But again, I see it.

And that's the problem, isn't it?

I see all of it.

The way her breath stutters, just for a second, before she squares her shoulders. The way her knuckles tighten around her phone, like she needs something to hold onto. The way she won't look at me—not because she's indifferent, but because she *isn't.*

And then, just before she pulls the door open, she does it—she tucks her hair behind her ear.

I exhale, my grip tightening on the neck of my guitar.

For a second, it's like we're teenagers again.

Her leaving. Me watching her go.

Only this time, I'm not letting it happen.

Not like that.

I need to *do* something.

The envelope wasn't enough. A couple of songs won't be enough. I could play every damn track I've ever written and it still wouldn't be enough.

I don't just want her to *hear me.*

I need her to *see* me.

But how the hell do I do that when every time I get close, she bolts?

The door closes behind her with a soft click, leaving me alone in the quiet.

I run a hand down my face, mind already turning over ideas, searching for something, anything.

A grand gesture of sorts.

Something so unmistakably *us* that she won't be able to ignore it.

But what?

What the hell do I have left?

I pluck a single note, the sound ringing sharp in the silence.

Then another.

Then another.

And then—*I know.*

It's reckless. Maybe even stupid.

She'll absolutely hate it.

But for the first time in days, something in my chest eases.

If she won't come to me, then I'll make damn sure she can't look away.

CHAPTER 23

Anna

The university cafeteria is packed to the brim, every inch occupied by extended family members, friends, and people I'm fairly certain my mother just invited off the street.

Korean first birthdays are no joke, but this? This feels like a production. A three-ring circus complete with toddlers running wild, distant aunts fussing over me like I'm still in high school, and my mother orchestrating the entire thing like a general preparing for battle.

I adjust the sleeve of my hanbok, smoothing out the fabric like I've done at every major family event since the beginning of time. It's a deep green with delicate embroidery, familiar and comfortable, even if the layers are a bit warmer than I'd like. At least my mom didn't try to shove me into a *new* one.

Joel, however—

I press my lips together, trying so hard not to laugh.

He's standing near the dessert table, looking

thoroughly out of his element in his own hanbok, a deep blue number my mother definitely made sure fit him *perfectly*. The fabric drapes on him all wrong, like he has no idea how to exist in clothes that aren't ripped jeans and leather jackets. He keeps tugging at the collar, eyes darting around like someone is going to attack him with more layers.

I can't stop the snort that escapes me.

Joel catches the sound and narrows his eyes, pointing at me. "Say *one* word, and I swear I'm going to grab a mic and tell your entire family about the time you tried to dye your hair blue and it turned out green."

I grin. "Joke's on you, my mom *already* tells that story to anyone who'll listen."

He sighs dramatically, flicking at his sleeve. "This is a setup. I look like a Disney prince." Then he visibly shudders. "God, I can't believe I just said that out loud."

I stare at him, horrified, but also on the verge of laughing. That was actually pretty good. Not that I'll ever tell him that. In fact— "Yeah. What's *wrong* with you?"

He groans, shaking his head like he's trying to physically shake the words out of existence. "No. No, I take it back. That was disgusting."

"Fully unhinged," I agree.

He grins. "Absolutely vile."

"A moment of total insanity."

"A betrayal of everything I stand for."

We stare at each other for a beat, the full-body cringe

mutual, before I shake my head and chuckle despite myself. "I'm going to pretend I didn't hear it."

Joel nods solemnly. "Please do. I need to live in denial for at least twenty-four hours."

"Longer, honestly." I fold my arms, smirking. "Like, *forever*."

"Agreed." He tugs at the collar of his hanbok again, scowling. "This thing's bad enough. But adding *that* comparison? I feel like I need to burn this entire outfit after tonight just to rid myself of the association."

"Oh no, my mom would never let you," I say. "She'd probably track it down and get it dry-cleaned just in case you ever need to wear it again."

His expression turns even more horrified. "Your mom is terrifying."

I sigh. "Welcome to my life."

Before Joel can respond, a blur of pink and tulle barrels into my legs.

"Auntie Anna—" Mina shrieks, her tiny hands gripping my hanbok with impressive strength for a one-year-old. She's decked out in full doljanchi regalia, her pink and gold hanbok as pristine as it's ever going to be before the chaos begins.

I scoop her up automatically, bouncing her slightly as she babbles excitedly. "You ready for your big moment, kiddo?"

She smacks my cheek in response.

Joel snickers. "That's a yes."

"Shut up," I mutter, adjusting Mina in my arms. But then I notice the way he's watching her—fond, almost thoughtful, his usual teasing smirk softened around the edges. It's the same way he used to look at my little cousins when we were younger, like he actually enjoyed being around them.

The thought makes something in my chest tighten.

I shove it aside immediately.

Ethan appears from the other side of the room, already looking exhausted as he corrals two toddlers who have decided that now is the time to test their vertical limits via a buffet table. "Okay, we're about five minutes from doljabi time," he announces, barely dodging a flying cookie. "Anna, Mom wants you and Joel front and center."

I sigh. "Of course she does."

Mina wiggles in my arms, reaching for Ethan, who promptly hands off one of the squirming toddlers to Joel like a pro before taking her. Joel catches the kid on reflex, eyes widening in alarm as he suddenly finds himself holding a very sticky, very wiggly child.

I grin at his misery.

"Congrats," I say sweetly. "You're officially part of the family."

Joel groans, holding the child at arm's length like he's just been handed a ticking time bomb. "This is some kind of punishment, isn't it?"

I smirk, but before I can say anything in response, the toddler, either oblivious or completely entertained by Joel's suffering, giggles and wipes their hands—covered in something sticky and suspiciously red—right across the front of his hanbok.

Joel freezes. "Oh, come on. What even *is* this?"

Ethan slaps him on the back. "You don't ask questions. You just accept it."

Joel mutters something under his breath, shooting me a glare like I personally orchestrated this situation. Which, honestly, I *would* have if I'd thought of it first.

I'm still grinning when my mom appears, clapping her hands. "Alright, let's get started! Everyone, gather around!"

The chaos shifts as the crowd begins repositioning toward the doljabi table, where an elaborate display of symbolic items sits, ready for Mina to choose her fate. I slip into my designated front-and-center spot, setting my hands primly in my lap as if that will somehow stop the impending doom I can already feel brewing.

Joel plops down beside me with a sigh. "So what are we betting?" he asks, nodding toward the table as he tries to wipe away the red goo.

I glance over at Mina, who's already eyeing the objects in front of her like she's assessing battle strategy. "Mom's praying for doctor. Ethan's betting on judge. Dad's convinced she's going to be in business."

At that moment, Mina reaches forward, grabs the money first, then immediately yeets it over her shoulder.

The room bursts into laughter.

"She said *absolutely not* to capitalism," Joel murmurs, chuckling.

I shake my head. "She's my favorite person alive."

The laughter dies down as Mina makes her second attempt, zeroing in on the microphone.

The collective gasp from the room is immediate.

My mom practically vibrates in place. "She's just like you, Anna."

I groan. "God, let's not start that."

Joel leans in. "I don't know, Ace. Seems like fate."

I elbow him in the ribs. "Shut up."

He chuckles softly.

But I can't ignore the way my mother is looking between the two of us now, a glint in her eyes that makes me deeply uneasy.

And then she says the words I've been full-on *dreading*.

"Since our little star has chosen music, I think it's only right that Anna and Joel play something for us to celebrate."

I exhale slowly, schooling my face into something neutral as the room shifts. People murmur excitedly, already repositioning to get a better view, while my mother beams.

Joel leans in slightly. "No escape now, Ace."

I resist the urge to stick my tongue out. Instead, I stand, smoothing down my hanbok before picking my way through the crowd toward the makeshift performance area.

Joel follows with a little too much ease, like he's enjoying this way more than he should be.

Aunties and uncles clear a space around the small stage setup—just a keyboard, a mic stand, and enough room for Joel and me to not actively kill each other on stage.

As I settle onto the bench, I glance up, scanning the crowd. My mother is practically glowing. My father is nodding approvingly. And Ethan—

Ethan just winces slightly, like he's sorry for everything.

You should be, bro. You should be.

Joel finishes adjusting his guitar strap and gives me a quick nod. "Ready?"

I flex my fingers over the keys. I know this. We practiced this. We have a plan.

I nod back. "Let's go."

I take a breath, centering myself over the keys as Joel strums a quiet chord, testing the sound. The murmur in the room fades as people turn their attention toward us.

We know this setlist. We *planned* this setlist. This is *fine*.

I let the familiar melody settle into place under my fingertips, the opening notes smooth, practiced.

Joel's voice slides in effortlessly.

And just like that, the noise, the crowd, the chaos—it all falls away.

For the next half hour, it's just music.

Just us.

And it actually *feels* good.

The harmonies land, the rhythm stays perfectly in sync, and even though we haven't performed together in years, it still feels easy.

When we hit the last chorus of the final planned song, I feel it—*relief.*

I survived.

The last notes fade into silence, and then—thunderous applause.

I can feel my shoulders finally unclench as I lift my hands from the keys, already pushing back from the bench, ready to retreat.

And then—

"Actually..."

Joel's voice is smooth, too smooth, but I hear the shift underneath it. The quiet determination.

My stomach drops.

I whip my head toward him. *Oh, you absolute menace.*

He flashes me a knowing look, adjusting his guitar strap. "I've got one more. This one—" His voice lowers just a fraction, like the words are meant just for me. "This is for you, Ace."

The crowd erupts, completely oblivious to the fact that I am currently having a full-blown existential crisis. What in the hell is he *doing?*

I glance out into the crowd.

My mother is glowing.

My dad—he's just open and curious.

Ethan is narrowing his eyes in suspicion. *Yeah, smart.*

I turn back to face Joel, because running doesn't feel like an option at this point. My mother would kill me.

The first chords ring out, clear and full, vibrating straight through me like they can rearrange my DNA.

I know this song.

I knew it when it was just an idea. I knew it when we sat in my living room, working through the chords together.

But now?

Now, it feels whole—like it's found its voice.

The arrangement is fuller, the music layered, and for a split second, I don't breathe.

Because something is different.

The weight in the air shifts, pressing against my ribs, heavy and unrelenting.

The room has gone completely still.

People aren't just watching.

They're *waiting*.

I can feel my mother's excitement radiating from across the room, my father's quiet curiosity, and Ethan—

Ethan leans forward slightly, a subtle suspicion creeping onto his face.

Yeah. Smart.

Joel's voice breaks through the quiet, steady and sure, weaving through the space between us.

The lyrics hit like a slow, unfolding realization.

I feel them before I understand them.

Every single note, every word, feels like a confession.

Not just a song. Not *just* music. *Isn't that what he said last night?*

This is something else.

And suddenly, it's happening.

That awful, twisting tightness in my throat.

The sting behind my eyes.

I blink hard, once, twice, like I can push it back down —like I can stop whatever this is before it starts.

This is not the place.

But I *can't*.

The words keep coming, and my chest cracks open, too wide, too much, all at once.

I need to leave.

I need to get out before—

Before—

I turn sharply, shoving through the crowd, my breath coming too fast, my pulse hammering in my ears.

I hear Joel's voice behind me, but I don't stop.

I don't turn around.

I don't dare let myself see his face.

Because if I do—

If I see Joel looking at me—

If I see what I think might be in his eyes—

If he sees it mirrored in my own....

I'll never be able to pretend I don't know the truth.

I'll never be able to take it back.

So I keep moving.

I push through the doors, into the hallway, into the cold—into anywhere but here.

I don't let myself think.

I don't let myself name it.

Because if I do—

If I let the words form—

Then I can't undo them.

And I don't know who I am if I admit what this is.

CHAPTER 24

Joel

My heart is a jackhammer, pounding against my ribs as I strum the opening chords to *Always You*.

This isn't just a song. It's *the* song.

The one that's been sitting in my chest, waiting for the right moment to be heard. And maybe now's not the best time, but it's the right one. Hell, it might be the only chance I get where she's too bogged down by familial obligation to run.

God knows she won't come to my performance tonight to hear it.

This song, it carries every unsaid thing between me and Anna. She has to hear it. She has to know...

I need her to.

I find her in the crowd the second I start singing. She's still standing near the stage, arms crossed tight over her chest, chin up like she's daring me to make her feel something.

I start singing, letting the words carry this thing that feels to big.

I was too young to name it,
Too scared to let it grow.
So I called it nothing, buried it
    deep—
But love has roots I didn't know.

I glance over to her, locking my gaze on hers.
Her eyes—*fuck*, her eyes betray her.
She's listening.
I don't let myself look away. If she's going to pretend this means nothing, she's damn well going to do it knowing I see her doing it.
The words come easy now because they're real. They're *hers*. My voice is steady, but inside, I'm raw, exposed in a way I haven't been in years.

You were the song I never finished,
The note that lingered in my chest.
You were the fire I let burn down,
And the spark I never let rest.

I don't just sing this song. *I pour myself into it.*
My throat tightens, and I have to swallow hard.
I hit the next note, but my voice catches for a split second. A crack I can't hide.
And I know she catches it. I see it in her expression.

Every note, every lyric—it's not just a performance. It's a confession, a prayer.

A last chance.

I watch Anna like my life depends on it.

Because maybe it does.

It reminds me of that day—the one where I sang her song for the whole school. But really, it was for her. My last goodbye.

If only I had known...

Her face stays still, unreadable. Arms crossed, chin high. But I see it—the tightness in her throat, the way her fingers dig into her arms.

I push harder, my voice roughening.

> **Did you know?**
> **Did you see?**
> **That every almost—still led me back**
> **to you and me?**

Her breath catches.

And for a second—*just a flicker*—I let myself hope.

Maybe she won't run.

Maybe she'll stay.

Then her chin wobbles. Her eyes shine with unshed tears.

And I know.

Shit. She's gonna bolt.

I should've planned for it. Should've known better than to think she'd stay and let me bare my fucking soul in front of an entire room of her extended family.

But I was desperate. I thought—*hoped*—that maybe, just maybe, she'd hear the song and understand. That it would be enough to crack open whatever this is between us.

Stupid.

I see her shoulders tighten. See her shift on her feet. And then—she turns around and runs.

I drop my guitar onto the stand so fast the strings vibrate in protest. "Shit," I mutter, already moving.

I push through the crowd, ignoring the whispers— the way Mina reaches out for me as I rush past.

Someone murmurs, *Are they together?* and I hear Ethan's baffled, "What? Of course not—"

None of it matters.

Anna matters.

I lose sight of her for half a second, and my stomach clenches.

Not again.

I push forward, shoving past shoulders, ignoring the startled looks. The need to reach her is animalistic— instinctual.

I get into the hallway just in time to see her disappear around the corner, and I sprint. My legs are on fire and my heart is pounding in my ears.

By the time I reach her, she's at the end of the corridor, staring at the closed security gate blocking off the university's main wing for the weekend.

End of the line.

Her breath is shallow, like she's trying to pull herself together.

I slow my steps, but my voice is firm. "You weren't supposed to run."

She flinches, then straightens, whirling on me like a goddamn storm.

Good. Let her rage. I'm not leaving.

"What the hell was that, Joel?" Her voice is sharp, slicing through the air between us. "Was that supposed to be—what? A grand apology? A manipulation? That was my *whole family* in there. You think you can just sing some song and—"

"No," I cut in, quiet but certain. "I just wanted to tell you the truth."

She scoffs. "Oh, great. Because you've always been so good at that."

She wants me to bite. She wants me to fight her, to snap back, to play the game we've been playing since we were teenagers.

I don't.

I step forward, slow and sure, closing the space between us. Not enough to crowd her. Just enough that she feels it.

"I don't know what to do with this anymore, Anna." My voice is rough, barely above a whisper. "I don't know what to do with *you*. With this... ache." I rub my hand across my chest like it will somehow lessen what radiates from that space.

She blinks, caught off guard, but I keep going.

"I know I screwed up back then. I know I hurt you. But that's not what this is about. I didn't play that song because I wanted to fix something that's broken." I exhale, shaking my head. "I played it because I wanted you to hear me. To know that every time I look at you, my brain just—stops."

She swallows, her throat working around something unsaid, but I'm not done.

"I wanted you to know that it's not just guilt. It's not just regret." I let out a shaky breath. "God, you're so infuriating, Anna. But I love it. I love your fire, your wit, your goddamn stubbornness. Somehow, I'm even attracted to the way you make me crazy. And I don't—I don't know what it means. I don't know where to put it —what the hell to do with it. I just—"

Her hands are clenched into fists. She's vibrating with tension, and I expect her to shove me, to yell at me, to do something.

Instead, she whispers, "You don't get to say that."

"I do." I take another step. "And I mean it. *Fuck*, I mean every word of it."

She inhales sharply, eyes darting away like she's looking for a way out, but there isn't one. She's trapped here with me, just like I'm trapped with this thing between us.

Her breath is shaky when she finally speaks. "You're insane. Bonkers. Out of your fucking mind."

"Maybe." I nod, slow. Then, shrug. "Maybe not." I drop my voice even lower and confess, "But I know I want *you*."

There. It's out—and I can't take it back.

Her gaze snaps to mine. Her lips part like she's about to say something, but she doesn't. Maybe she can't.

For a moment, we just stand there.

The air between us is electric, buzzing with everything unspoken, everything denied.

Her breath is coming fast, but she refuses to look directly at me.

I step in closer—slow, deliberate. Close enough that I know she feels the heat between us, the pull that's always been there, even when we were too damn young to name it.

"You feel it too," I murmur. "I know you do."

She flinches, but her gaze flicks back to mine, burning with frustration. "No."

I shake my head, a hint of a smile slipping through. "Liar."

Her fingers twitch, like she's fighting the urge to do something—shove me, pull me closer, I don't even know.

Maybe she doesn't either.

I lower my voice, let it roughen around the edges. "You think I don't see the way you look at me? The way your breath catches when I get close? It's the same for you. I *know* it is."

She shakes her head, stubborn as ever, but she's shaken.

"Tell me I'm wrong," I press, stepping even closer.

She doesn't.

Her chest rises and falls too fast, her throat working around words she won't let herself say.

I lift my hand and trail my fingertips along the column of her neck, needing to feel her beneath them.

A sharp inhale. A full-body shudder.

She's breathing hard, her chest rising and falling too fast, like she's just run a mile.

The scent of vanilla and adrenaline clings to her skin, mixing with the lingering warmth of the crowded party.

She's so close now, just inches away, and I focus on the heat rolling off her body. It grounds me.

Her fingers flex at her sides, like she's fighting the urge to do something.

Fight me. Touch me.

Just don't run, Ace.

Stay.

"You're wrong," she finally whispers, but it's barely a breath.

"Liar," I repeat, tipping my head down, close enough that if she just leaned in—

She shoves me. Hard.

I barely stumble, but her hands stay fisted on the front of my hanbok. Her touch sparks my pulse to ratchet and now it's my breath that hitches.

"Why are you doing this?" Her voice is strained, almost desperate. "Why can't you just let this go?"

"Because I can't." The words are ragged, torn from somewhere deep. "I don't think you can, either."

She makes a sound—frustration, denial, something breaking. Her chest is heaving, her pulse a wild, stuttering thing against her throat. I want to run my tongue over it.

The silence stretches, thick and suffocating, like neither of us can breathe.

Her gaze flicks to my mouth.

And that's it. That's the moment.

I see it happening before it does, but I can't convince my brain that it's the truth—*not yet.*

Her fingers grip tighter to my hanbok and my pulse kicks like a gunshot, tempting other parts of me to awaken.

Her breath ghosts against my lips, one last moment of hesitation—

And then, she yanks me down—and suddenly, her mouth crashes into mine.

It's not soft. It's not careful. It's raw and messy and too much and not enough—everything all at once.

For a second, I don't move.

I just let myself feel it.

Anna Chang—stubborn, impossible, *infuriating* Anna—is kissing me.

After all these years. After all the pushing and pulling, the fighting, the pretending—she snapped first. Sort of.

She's kissing *me.*

My brain short-circuits. My entire world tilts on its damn axis.

Because this? This wasn't supposed to happen. Was it?

Was this what I was going for?

And then my body catches up.

Something deep in my chest ignites, roars awake. A primal, gut-wrenching *YES.*

Yes, *finally.*

Yes, we're doing this.

The realization slams through me, and suddenly, I can't just stand here like a fucking idiot. I have to kiss her back.

I tilt my head, deepening it, taking control now that I know she's giving in. My hands move—not to hold her back, but to hold her close. To *keep* her close. Because now that I have her, there's no fucking way I'm letting go.

I twist my fingers through her hair, pulling her flush against me.

Her body melts, then tenses, then melts again, like she doesn't know if she's supposed to fight it or let it devour her.

The second she gasps against my mouth, I take the opening—deepening, demanding, fucking losing myself in her.

She presses closer, her hands sliding up my chest, and I swear to God—I've never felt anything like this. Never like her.

If we weren't in the middle of a goddamn school—

She pulls me closer, like she doesn't know how to stop, either.

I tilt my head, deepening everything, tasting her frustration, her surrender, her fucking fire.

And when she whimpers against my mouth?

It wrecks me.

Because this isn't just anger or frustration or history combusting into a kiss.

This is relief.

It's inevitable.

It's every stolen glance, every late-night argument, every moment we spent trying to convince ourselves this didn't mean something.

And fuck, I'm gone. *So fucking gone.*

The hallway, the party, the years of pushing and pulling and pretending—all of it fades.

There's just this.

Me. *Her.*

And the truth we can't run from anymore.

When she finally pulls back, she doesn't move far. Not that I would let her.

Her lips are kiss-swollen, her breath uneven.

I don't let go.

Not yet.

Her hands are still clutching onto my hanbok, like she doesn't realize she hasn't let go.

My forehead drops to hers, both of us still breathing too hard, too uneven.

"So, that happened," I whisper, not even meaning to say it out loud.

Her eyes flick to mine, wide—like she's barely holding it together.

Like she can't believe what she just did.

Like she might do it again.

Like she might run.

But there's no way in hell I'm gonna let her.

I keep my hands on her waist, grounding her, grounding us.

Then, I drag my thumb across her lower lip, just once, testing—*was that real?*

Her eyes lock onto mine. Wide. Wild. Wrecked.

She's shaking. Or maybe I am. I can't tell anymore.

Then I murmur, voice still hoarse from kissing her—my body still vibrating with energy. "You kissed me."

She swallows hard, that beautiful smart mouth of hers somehow silenced.

"You kissed me *first*," I repeat, because it feels so fucking good to say it.

She blinks fast, like she's trying to make sense of it but it's not computing.

I let out a breath, grinning like an idiot. "Took you long enough, Ace."

Her jaw tightens as she comes to her senses. Just a little bit. "Don't start."

I chuckle. "I think I just did."

She groans, hiding her face in her hands.

And fuck, I think I'm in love with her.

Hell, I think maybe...

Maybe I always have been.

CHAPTER 25

Anna

I cannot breathe.

I mean, *technically*, I am breathing. My lungs are working. My heart is *definitely* still beating—too fast, too hard, too much.

But my brain? *Completely fried.*

Because I just kissed Joel Price.

And not *just* kissed him.

I grabbed him, pulled him in, melted against him like he was the only thing keeping me upright, and then—*then*—I let him take me apart, piece by piece, with his mouth, his hands, his words.

I want you.

The memory claws at me like my teenage dream come to life.

I feel it everywhere.

My lips are still tingling, my body still on fire, and I swear I can feel his hands on my waist even though he's not touching me anymore.

And that's a problem.

Because if I don't move, I might do it again.

I inhale—big, deep, calming breath. Then exhale.

It doesn't help.

Because every single nerve in my body is still vibrating, still clinging to the memory of his hands, his mouth—his stupid, *stupid* words.

I step back too quickly, too abruptly, like he's made of lava. My back slams into the gate, causing it to clang far too loudly for my liking.

Joel just watches me, eyes unreadable, chest still rising and falling too fast.

"You okay there, Ace?"

His voice is too soft, too careful.

Like he's trying not to scare me off.

I scowl. "I—yes. Fine. Totally fine. What? I'm great. Perfect, even."

He hums, studying me. "Really?"

"Really."

Joel tilts his head, green eyes searching mine.

And God, why does he always look at me like that?

Like I'm something he wants to figure out, wants to understand—wants to keep.

My stomach flips violently.

"Because you look like you just had a religious experience."

Oh my God.

"Get over yourself," I mutter, running a frantic hand through my hair.

Joel doesn't grin.

Not this time.

His lips part slightly, like he's about to say something else, something important, but I can't—I don't want to hear it.

Because what if he says something else I can't ignore?

What if he's right?

My lips are still tingling.

My fingers are still curled into fists, like I'm holding on to the last shred of my self-control.

And he sees it.

He *knows.*

I force myself to move. Take a small sidestep. Get space. Get distance. Get *sanity.*

"That was—" My voice does not sound normal. I clear my throat, try again. "That was… probably a mistake."

Joel's brows lift. "Probably?"

Abort. Abort.

"I mean—" I shake my head frantically. "*Definitely.* A mistake. Absolutely. Forget it ever happened."

Joel's expression tightens.

Like that was the wrong thing to say.

His throat bobs as he swallows, his gaze flickering over my face, as if trying to piece together what's happening in my head.

And I don't know why I feel guilty.

I don't know why it physically hurts to call it a mistake.

Because it wasn't.

It *so* wasn't.

But if I say that out loud, everything changes.

So I don't.

I don't say anything at all.

The silence between us stretches—thick, weighted, dangerous.

Joel is still watching me, but now there's something else in his expression. Something sharper. He's standing there, chest still rising and falling too fast, jaw tight, like he wants to call bullshit but doesn't know if he should.

Because he's waiting.

Waiting for me to take it back.

Waiting for me to say something real.

I can't let him see how shaken I actually am. How I can still taste him. Or how I still feel like I'm coming apart at the seams—like something big and terrifying and irreversible just happened, and I don't know how to put myself back together.

I swallow, the lie still bitter on my tongue.

His gaze flickers down—to my lips, to my fists clenched at my sides. He sees it.

He knows I'm lying.

And I hate that.

I hate that he's always been able to see through me.

I take another step.

His jaw tics, but he doesn't stop me.

Doesn't move at all.

It's like he's forcing himself to stay still. Like if he reaches for me now, he won't be able to stop.

I suck in another shaky breath, trying to steady myself, but my chest is too tight. I can still feel his hands on my waist. The way he held me there, like he needed me as much as I needed him.

And God, the way he kissed me—

I squeeze my eyes shut.

No.

No, I can't think about this now.

Because if I do, I'll fall apart completely.

I press my palm against the gate behind me, grounding myself.

Joel watches the movement. His lashes fluttering like he's barely holding himself back.

Like if I gave him even the smallest opening—he'd close the space between us again. A part of me actually wishes he would. Is that as wrong as it sounds?

I suck in a breath—about to say something, anything, just to cut through the tension.

And then, because the universe hates me—

"Anna? Joel?"

I freeze.

Joel's head snaps up, his whole body tensing.

Oh, no.

Oh, *no no no.*

I know that voice.

And from the way Joel suddenly looks like a deer caught in headlights, he's more than aware, too.

Slowly, like we're about to be caught committing a crime, we turn.

And there she is.

My mother.

Standing just a few feet away, eyebrows lifted, arms crossed over her chest.

She takes one long look at the two of us—me, still pink-faced, still breathless. Joel, stiff and suspiciously silent. The inches between us that feel like nothing at all.

And then she smiles.

Not just any smile, either.

A full, beaming, happy-mother smile.

I swear, I just about black out.

"Oh," she says, voice too damn soft, too damn pleased. *"Finally."*

I choke on air.

Joel visibly swallows as he turns to me with questioning eyes.

I step forward frantically, still spiraling.

"Mom—this isn't—" I wave my hands wildly between me and Joel. "It's not—"

She waves me off. "Oh, sweetheart."

She clutches her chest like I've just given her the best news of her life.

"Oh, sweetheart," she says again, shaking her head with so much emotion I think she might actually cry. "I hoped. I really, really hoped."

Oh my God.

Oh my *actual* God.

This can't be happening.

Joel shifts beside me, clears his throat, visibly trying

to figure out what the hell to say. But there's nothing to say and opting for—"I was just snogging your daughter" —probably not the best choice.

"Mrs. Ch—Liz," he corrects himself quickly, "I— um—"

Mom doesn't let him finish.

"Oh, honey," she says, walking over to me so she can grab both of my hands like we're in a freaking Hallmark movie. "I knew this would happen eventually. I just—I didn't know when. But after that day in your kitchen..."

I am still in shock, still vibrating from the kiss that just changed my entire molecular structure, and my mother is acting like I just got engaged.

I pull my hands back. Quick. Abrupt. Panicked. "Mom. Stop."

Joel looks like he wants to say something, but he's clearly still recovering from being caught in this Twilight Zone episode.

"I'm serious," she insists, grabbing my face like she used to when I was a kid. "This—this is what I wanted for you both." She smiles at Joel like he's my knight in shining armor.

I stare at her, horrified. "What?"

She cups my cheeks, beaming. "You two. Oh, Anna, I always knew."

I wrench away, face blazing, wheel in my head spinning out of control. "You always knew what?"

She nods like she absolutely did. "Since you were kids. Appa, too. We knew if you two could just get over whatever issues you had, you'd find a way back to each other."

I look at Joel.

Joel looks at me.

We both visibly malfunction.

Mom sighs, patting my cheek. "Oh, honey. You don't see it, do you?"

See what? The absolute disaster that is my life right now? The fact that my entire world just shifted off its axis, and I have no idea what to do with it?

And then, because the universe is on a mission to fully destroy me—

"Anna? Where—oh, what the hell is this?"

I turn slowly, like I'm being punked.

And there he is.

Ethan.

Holding Mina in his arms, my adorable, innocent one-year-old niece, while his wife, Tessa, stands behind him, brows raised.

I swear, my soul leaves my body.

Because Ethan is not stupid.

And he's *definitely* not blind. Or deaf. He heard that damn song.

His gaze sweeps over the scene. Me. Joel. Our mother —literally glowing with pride.

He blinks once. Twice. Then his expression shifts.

And then—*he knows.*

Ethan's jaw locks.

His entire body tenses.

He looks at me, then at Joel, then back at me, and I can actually see the moment it clicks.

"Oh, *hell no*," he mutters, passing Mina to Tessa without even looking away.

Joel immediately takes a step forward, palms up.

"Ethan," he says, cautious, but calm. "Listen, man—"

Ethan cuts him off. "What the actual is going on here?"

Mom sighs, so incredibly deeply, you'd think she was summoning all of the ancient gods to her aid.

Tessa, to her credit, doesn't look surprised at all.

I, however, am about to self-destruct. This all too much.

Ethan's gaze snaps to me.

"Anna?" His voice is way too sharp.

I make a strangled noise.

"Ethan, it's fine," Mom interjects, clearly exasperated. "This is wonderful news."

Ethan's eye twitches.

Joel tries again, his voice steady. "Look, I care about your sister—"

"You *care* about my sister?" Ethan repeats, indignation painting his tone.

Mom groans, rubbing her temples. "For heaven's sake."

Joel visibly steels himself. "Yeah. I do."

And just like that, Ethan looks like he's ready to commit murder.

"Are you kidding me?" Ethan gestures wildly between us. "How long? When the hell did this start?"

I gape at him. "I—what?"

"Don't *'what'* me. Was it before or after I suggested he stay with you, Anna?"

I shake my head frantically. "It's not like that. We're not—it's nothing!"

Joel's jaw tightens.

Something flickers in his expression.

Something that feels like disappointment.

My stomach plummets.

Ethan lets out a slow breath. Runs a hand through his hair. Then exhales, still looking like he's trying to wrap his head around this.

Same, bro. *Same.*

Ethan's voice is sharp, cutting, filled with something too tangled to name.

"Really, Joel?" He shakes his head, muttering a curse under his breath. "You pick now to do this? At Mina's party?"

Joel flinches.

My chest tightens.

Ethan's words cut too deep, and the worst part? I see it hit Joel.

I see it in the way his jaw locks. In the way his shoulders shift, how his fingers twitch at his sides—like he wants to fix this, but he doesn't know how.

And for some reason, that makes something snap inside me.

"That's not fair," I blurt before I can stop myself.

Joel's head whips toward me, startled.

Ethan's brows shoot up.

Oh.

Oh, *crap.*

I don't know why I said it.

I just know I had to.

Ethan narrows his eyes. "Since when do you defend him?"

Joel visibly stills.

And I feel it—the sudden shift in the air, the weight of what Ethan just said pressing into my chest.

Because he's right.

I don't defend Joel.

I never have.

So why am I doing it now?

I cross my arms, defensive. "I'm not—defending him, I'm just—"

Ethan lifts a brow. "You're just what?"

I clench my jaw. "This wasn't his fault."

Ethan lets out a sharp breath, shaking his head. "Jesus, Anna."

I tense. "What?"

His gaze flicks between me and Joel, like he's seeing something for the first time.

And I hate it.

I hate that look.

Because it's recognition.

It's *realization.*

And I'm not remotely prepared for it.

Ethan exhales slowly, pressing his fingers to his temples. "You know what? I should have known."

I swallow.

Joel doesn't say a word.

"I should have seen it," Ethan mutters, shaking his head again. "I mean, it was all right there. Wasn't it?"

Joel shifts, finally speaking. "Ethan, man, I swear—"

"Don't. Don't go into it." Ethan glares at him. "Because the second you say it out loud, I'll have to accept that it's happening and I'm not ready for that yet."

Joel presses his lips together.

And somehow, that makes it worse.

Because he respects Ethan too much to push it.

Ethan sighs. "Look, I don't know if I want to punch you or just walk away."

Mom, who has been watching all of this like it's the best movie she's ever seen, finally steps in.

"Enough," she says, firm but gentle.

Ethan huffs. "Mom—"

"Ethan." She rests a hand on his arm, her look far too knowing.

Ethan settles, the words he was about to say snuffed out before they even start.

Hell, even Tessa is beaming at us.

My chest tightens.

I can feel Joel's eyes on me.

Can feel the way Ethan is watching me, waiting.

And for the first time in my life, I don't know what to say.

Because if I say nothing, that means I'm not denying it.

And I can't lie to myself anymore.

Mom smiles, voice warm, filled with certainty. "Just be happy, sweetheart."

I glance over my shoulder at Joel, his soulful green eyes watching me like I'm the key to his own personal universe.

And for the first time in years, I wonder if I could let myself be.

CHAPTER 26

Joel

The door clicks shut behind us.

Anna moves like she's escaping a crime scene—which to be fair, wasn't far off.

Ethan made that pretty clear.

I want to talk—clear the air, but she heads straight to the kitchen sink to stare out the window that looks over her backyard.

She goes straight to pretending nothing *remotely* unusual happened today.

I follow her, heart still hammering, breath still uneven. We didn't speak in the car because this is something we need to talk about face to face. I need to see her eyes—her micro expressions. Her body language.

This day—*this entire fucking day*—has been too much. My skin feels too tight. My body to big. Something has to give.

And yet...

She's acting like that kiss didn't just flip our whole world upside down.

Not just hers—*ours*.

No.

I won't let her do this.

I won't let her shut it down and shut me out.

Not this time.

As I approach, she makes to leave, but I catch her wrist before she can put any more space between us.

She stiffens, her jaw setting, her eyes shifting back to her backyard through the small kitchen window like it's a portal to another world. One she can escape into if she glares at it long enough.

I don't pull her back, don't grip too hard. Just enough so she knows—I'm not letting this go.

"Anna," I say, voice low, rougher than I intend. "Talk to me."

She doesn't face me or turn around.

Her other hand is braced on the counter like she needs it to stay upright.

"Joel, don't." Her voice is quiet, laced with something I really hope isn't regret.

I step closer. "Don't what?"

She lets out a sharp breath, shaking her head. "Just... *don't.*"

That's not an answer. That's a deflection.

And I'm not letting her close herself off.

"Tell me what you're thinking," I press, softening my grip, but not letting go. "Because I know you're thinking something."

She laughs once, hollow. "Yeah. I'm thinking this is a fucking disaster."

I don't flinch, but—*fuck*.

It shouldn't hit this hard. I should have expected it—hell, *I did* expect it. Anna Chang has spent years perfecting the art of self-preservation. But hearing her say it out loud? Hearing her call *this* a mistake?

It burns.

Something tightens in my chest, coiling around my ribs like a slow, suffocating squeeze. My pulse hammers in my ears, drowning out the distant sounds of the neighborhood outside.

I need her to take it back.

I need her to tell me she didn't mean it.

I need—

I just need her to not look at me like that.

"Ace—"

She finally turns, finally meets my eyes, and I hate what I see there.

Not regret.

Not even anger.

Fear.

My stomach twists. Because I know I put that there.

Not today. But years ago.

When she was still full of life and believed in me.

When she still had faith that I wouldn't let her down.

"This whole day has been too much," she says, her voice tight. It's like she's inside my head. I literally thought the same thing. Just when I think she's going to close down, she whispers, "This—" She drags a hand through her hair. "I don't know how to do this."

I take a slow breath, choosing my next words carefully. "I'm not asking you to have it figured out right now. I know I sure as hell don't."

She exhales sharply, frustrated. "Then what are you asking from me?"

I hesitate, then say the only thing that really matters. "For you to not shut me out."

Her lips part like she's going to argue, but she doesn't.

Because she knows.

That's exactly what she was about to do.

She shakes her head, muttering a curse, then pulls her wrist from my grasp. I let her.

"I just... I need a minute, okay?" Her voice is low and almost cracks.

I nod, even though everything in me wants to tell her to stop running from this. From *me*.

That I won't hurt her again. *Never*—I'll never do it again.

She takes a deep breath, like she's trying to get her emotions under control.

And then, before I can think better of it, I say— "Come to the show tonight."

She freezes.

I don't say it to pressure her.

I just need to know where I stand.

"Joel," she says, already shaking her head.

I take another step toward her, slow, careful.

"Anna. Just—come. Please," I say, feeling like a lovesick fool who knows the love of his life is slipping through his fingers.

Her lips press into a thin line. "I can't."

I study her face. She means it.

But this time, I can tell—it's not because she hates me.

It's not because she doesn't want to see me play anymore.

It's because she's terrified.

Not of me.

Not of the crowd.

Of what *this* means.

I let out a slow breath, rubbing the back of my neck. "Look, I get it. I do. But I meant what I said, Ace. I don't want to shut this down before we even figure out what it is."

She doesn't move, doesn't look away.

And that's when it hits me.

Tonight is supposed to be my last show at Nocté.

After that, I don't know what happens next.

Does she expect me to pack up and move on, like I was supposed to?

Do I stick around and see if she'll let me stay?

Does she even want me here?

The thoughts tumble at me so fast that I almost ask her.

But I don't.

Because if she tells me to go, I don't think I can handle it right now.

So instead, I try one last time.

"You don't have to have all the answers tonight," I say. "But don't let fear be the thing that makes the choice for you."

She blinks fast.

I swear, for a second, I see something break in her expression.

But then—she looks away. "Have a good show, Joel."

It's not a no.

But it's definitely not a yes.

And as much as it kills me to walk away from this conversation unfinished, I do.

Because pushing her right now won't help.

And tomorrow?

I don't know if I'll still be here.

I pause in the doorway, hand gripping the frame. I don't turn around—if I do, I won't leave—but I wait. Just for a second. Just to see if she says something.

A long breath. A shift of weight. The quiet sound of her exhale.

But she doesn't move.

She doesn't call me back.

And that?

That fucking kills me.

𝄞

The club is already packed when I step inside, the bass vibrating through the floors, the smell of whiskey and sweat thick in the air.

I should be getting in the zone.

Last show.

Last night at Nocté.

Last reason to stay.

But my head is still back in Anna's kitchen.

With the way she wouldn't look at me when she said she couldn't come tonight.

With the way she didn't tell me to leave, either.

With the way she's scared shitless of what happens next.

I exhale sharply, dragging a hand through my hair as I head toward the bar.

Myles is behind it, pouring a drink from a cocktail shaker into a glass with the same smooth precision she always has.

She clocks me the second I step up, eyes narrowing.

"Jesus, Price," she says, setting the glass down. "You look like you just got hit by a truck."

I grunt, twisting the cap off the water bottle she slides my direction. "Rough day."

Myles lifts a brow, wiping her hands on a rag. "Yeah? That have anything to do with Mina's party?"

I pause mid-sip.

"I was there." Myles smirks. "Tessa's my friend, remember?"

My breath catches in my throat.

Shit.

What the hell did all of that look like to the people who were there for Mina? Did they notice the tension? Did they know what happened after?

"Wanna tell me about it?" She asks, her face sliding into a smirk that says she already knows way too much.

"You know, don't you?" I mutter, taking another sip of water.

She nods sagely. "Tessa told me."

I groan. "Of course she did."

"Tessa told everyone, Joel. By the time you two left, the entire damn party knew about that kiss. I mean, to anyone paying attention, that song alone was enough to make it obvious. But what do I know?"

I mutter a curse under my breath, rubbing my hand over my jaw.

Maybe it really wasn't my smartest move ever. No wonder Anna can't even look at me.

Myles leans in slightly, studying me. "So... what's the deal? You kissed Ethan's little sister at a baby's birthday party and now you're brooding into a bottle of Aquafina?"

I glare. "I'm not brooding."

Myles tilts her head. "You are literally glaring at hydration."

I exhale sharply. "It's my last show and—" I roll my shoulders, trying to shake off the weight pressing into my ribs. "She's not coming tonight."

Myles' expression softens a little. "That sucks."

I nod. Yeah. It fucking does.

Before I can say anything else, a voice cuts through the noise.

"Price."

I turn to see London approaching, all business, as always.

"Got a minute?"

I push off the bar, glancing back at Myles, who just gives me a knowing look before turning back to her customers.

I follow London toward the back hallway near the greenroom. "What's up?"

London folds his arms across his chest and a lazy smile floats to his face. "Got an offer for you."

I brace myself, wondering what the hell that could be. "Yeah?"

"Noah, the club owner, wants you back next weekend. Encore shows. Friday and Saturday. You up for it?"

I blink.

Another weekend.

My stomach twists, but before I can answer, my phone buzzes in my pocket.

I pull it out.

Matt.

My manager.

London lifts a brow. "Everything okay?"

I hesitate. "Yeah, just my manager."

I swipe to answer. "Hey, man. What's up?"

"Hey, Joel. Ready for the last show?"

"Yeah, feeling good," I lie, my gaze flitting to London.

"Good, good." Matt pauses for a second. Longer than normal. *Too long.*

That's my first clue.

"Joel," he says finally, his tone measured. Testing. Like he's not sure how I'm gonna react to whatever he's about to say.

I frown, shifting my grip on the phone. "Yeah?"

Matt exhales. "Listen, before I say anything, just know I wouldn't bring this to you unless it was serious."

I straighten, feeling my heart plummet into my stomach. Is he about to let me go or something? "What the hell does that mean?"

Another beat of silence.

Then, carefully—"I've secured the tour, man."

My stomach dips. We've been working on this tour potential for the past six and half months and I honestly didn't think it would ever happen. They were just too flighty.

Matt keeps talking, voice even. "I got the call today. They want you."

I exhale through my nose. "For what, exactly? How long?"

Matt draws it out. "Opening act. Europe. Two months."

The words should light me up.

A European tour.

The kind of break I've been waiting for. This could really open things up.

But instead of excitement, all I feel is panic.

It starts in my gut—a slow, twisting knot of dread, coiling tighter and tighter. My fingers grip the phone, but they don't feel like mine. My chest is too tight, my breath coming too fast. The room feels like it's pressing in around me.

This is what I wanted.

Isn't it?

Matt's still talking, his voice tinny through the receiver, but I can't make out the words. All I can hear is Anna. The way she whispered *I don't know how to do this.* The way she looked at me before I left, like she was afraid of what happens next.

If I take this tour, I *know* what happens next.

I leave.

And something tells me, if I go now...

I won't get another chance with her.

Matt must hear something off in my silence because he adds, "This is it, Joel. Everything we've been working toward."

Everything I've been working toward.

Everything I *thought* I wanted.

I don't respond right away.

Because my head isn't here. It's still back in Anna's kitchen. Still stuck in that moment where she couldn't even bring herself to talk about the kiss.

London watches me, arms still crossed, reading every single shift in my body language.

"You still there?" Matt asks, his tone dipping slightly into concern.

I blink, running a hand over my face. "Yeah. I'm here."

But I don't know where I'm supposed to go.

Matt exhales. "Look, I know it's fast. I know you

thought you had more time. But, Joel—this is huge. You say yes, and we lock it in. Your career goes exactly where it's supposed to. But we need an answer soon. They have two other bands waiting to get the offer if you say no."

I rub my thumb against my temple. "How soon do they need an answer?"

London lets out a breath through his nose. Like he knows something big is coming.

Matt doesn't hesitate. "Tonight."

"*Tonight?*" The word feels foreign in my mouth. My mouth goes dry and my stomach drops.

The walls of the greenroom feel thinner than usual. Beyond them, the pulse of the club is a living thing—bass rattling through the floor, the distant hum of the crowd, the sharp burst of laughter from someone near the bar.

This is what I wanted.

This is what I built my life around.

A year ago—hell, even six months ago—I would've given anything for a tour like this. A chance to finally break out of the indie circuit. To play for thousands instead of a couple hundred.

I close my eyes.

The crowd outside is still waiting for me.

I stare at the wall, my pulse hammering.

Two choices.

One where I leave—God only knows how soon.

One where I stay—and get more time with Anna. More time to figure out what this is between us..

Matt is still talking, something about how "they won't hold the slot forever," but I barely hear him.

Because all I can hear is Anna's voice.

This whole day has been too much.

I swallow hard.

"Joel?" Matt presses. "What do you say?"

For a split second, I imagine it—packing up, flying out, stepping onto a new stage every night in a different city.

The adrenaline. The crowds. The kind of high that only music can bring.

And then I see it—

A hotel room across the world.

A phone that doesn't light up with her name.

A life without her in it.

The thought is so sharp, so sudden, that I swear I feel my chest cave in.

I don't even realize my grip on the phone has tightened.

Because I have no fucking idea what to do.

For the past thirteen years, I've been working toward this. I thought I knew what I wanted—where I was going.

But now?

I'm not even sure if want it anymore.

CHAPTER 27

Anna

I don't know what the hell I'm doing.

My hands are clammy, my stomach's in knots, and my pulse has been racing since the second Joel and I stepped into my apartment. I didn't know what to expect when we got here, but I'll tell you one thing I really didn't anticipate—this weird buzzing that's settled under my skin.

He left an hour ago and I keep pacing, trying to breathe through it, but nothing is fucking helping.

Because I can still feel him.

On my lips.

In my chest.

Somewhere deep in my ribs where he doesn't belong.

The kiss was crazy. It should've settled things. Hell, it should've given me clarity to move on. Instead, it's cracked something open—something I don't know how to name and it's slowly expanding through my system like a slow moving poison. And there's only one antidote.

Shit.

I need to move.

I need to *do* something.

I go to the fridge. Open it. Stare inside like the meaning of life is buried somewhere between the leftover takeout and a half-empty bottle of oat milk.

I shut it.

Then, spinning on my heels, I drop onto my couch and turn on the TV. For a few minutes, I scroll through Netflix, not really paying attention to any of it. I know for a fact that I scroll past ten different K-dramas I *swore* I was going to watch earlier this week.

I shut it off, flipping the remote to the other side of the coach with a groan.

I pick up my phone. Drop it. Pick it up again.

I stare at the blank screen, wondering how this is my life.

Pocketing it, I start cleaning. A feverish, unhinged sort of cleaning—like if I scrub hard enough, I can erase the memory of Joel's lips on mine. I wipe down the counters. I rearrange the spice rack. I stare at my couch, half convinced I can still smell him in the fabric.

I need him out of my system.

Except—

I don't want him out of my system.

And that? *That's* the fucking problem.

I rake my hands through my hair, but it doesn't help.

I sit at my dining room table, but my leg won't stop bouncing. I should shower—wash him off of me, scrub away the feeling of his hands on my skin, his lips against mine—but I know it won't work. It's under my skin now. Deep in my chest, pressing against my ribs like a live wire. I groan, dragging a hand down my face. I need a distraction. A sedative. A goddamn exorcism.

Besides, I'd probably just end up thinking about him in the shower, anyway. The sound of his...

Before I can stop myself, I pull my phone from my pocket and tap out a fevered message.

> Hey. Want to hit Nocté with me?

The second I press send, I freeze.

What the *fuck* am I doing?

I stare at my phone like it just betrayed me. Like it sprouted hands and personally hit send *against my will.*

Did I jump timelines? Black out? Have I finally lost my last shred of self-preservation? Because it feels like it.

I consider throwing my phone across the room, but knowing my luck, Lily would still manage to respond. Probably with some feral screaming.

No, no. This is fine.

I can just... take it back. Say it was a joke. A typo. *A hostage situation.*

I said I wouldn't go. I told him flat out. Besides, I don't do spontaneous. I don't—

My phone buzzes.

Lily: Wait. Wait. You WANT to go???

Lily: Like… willingly???

Lily: Not at gunpoint???

Lily: Anna, blink twice if you're in
danger.

I groan, my head thudding back against the couch.

Do you want to go or not?

Lily: OH HELL YES.

I exhale, something unraveling inside me, but not in the way I want. I feel shaky, restless. Like if I stop moving, I'll start thinking.

And thinking right now is *definitely* dangerous.

Before I can spiral, my phone buzzes again.

Lily: I'm coming to get you. Be there
in 10.

Then—

Lily: Okay, maybe 5

I shoot up from the couch like my ass is on fire. *Shit. Shit. Shit.*

Five minutes? Five minutes is no time at all. That's barely enough time to reapply lip balm, much less emotionally prepare for whatever the *fuck* I'm doing.

I start pacing. Then I stop. Then I sit. Then I stand again because sitting feels *wrong*.

I could still bail. I *should* bail. Lily would get over it.

Yeah, I could text her back. Tell her I have food poisoning. Or an emergency. Or that I spontaneously combusted.

But before I can think up a solid excuse, I hear a car horn outside.

Shiiiiiiiit.

What am I *doing*?

I don't chase.

I don't put my heart on the line.

I don't let myself hope for things that aren't guaranteed.

And yet, I'm currently sprinting around my apartment like a gremlin trying to get ready for battle.

What does one even wear to a moment of self-inflicted emotional ruin? Something hot? No, that's trying too hard. Something casual? No, that's *not* trying hard enough. Something mysterious and aloof?

Oh my god, what does that even mean?

I throw on a top. Take it off. Throw on another one. Repeat the process three more times until my bed looks like a crime scene of indecision.

Lily honks outside again.

Oh god. *Oh god, this is happening.*

I grab my jacket. Forget my jacket. Go back for my jacket. Nearly trip over my own feet.

Jesus Christ, pull it together, Anna.

By the time I finally make it outside, my pulse is

pounding in my ears, and I'm gripping my phone like it might save me from impending doom. Maybe I should have written a will before this. Or at least made a power-of-attorney decision.

I yank open the car door, throwing myself into the passenger seat like I'm evading enemy fire.

"No comments. No analyzing," I say the second I close the door.

Lily barely holds back a *shit-eating* grin. "No promises."

I give her a *look*.

She holds up her hands like she's been falsely accused. "What? I didn't *say* anything."

"You're thinking it really loudly," I huff.

"That's not my fault. *You* just did the most out-of-character thing I've ever witnessed, and I once saw you voluntarily order a decaf."

I shoot her a glare, but my fingers are gripping my jeans, twisting the fabric between them. She notices. *Of course* she does.

Her smirk softens. "You okay?"

I shake my head. I don't know what I am.

Nuts, probably,

Lily puts the car in drive. "Then let's just go. No expectations. No pressure."

I let out a slow breath, nodding.

Sure, no pressure. Okay, Lily. Joke's on you.

I should turn back. Should stay in my apartment where it's safe.

But safe hasn't gotten me anywhere.

In fact, it's just led me right back here.

She glances at me. "So just to clarify, you don't want me to point out that you are, in fact, voluntarily going to a club to see Joel. Right?"

"Correct," I say, refusing to look at her while my knees continue to bounce.

"And you also don't want me to bring up the fact that you have not stopped fidgeting since you got in the car?"

"Also correct."

Lily hums, way too pleased with herself. "Cool, cool. No comments. No analyzing. No judgment."

She taps her car's dash radio, and a second later, the speakers fill with slow, familiar chords.

His chords—then, his voice.

I whip around. "Lily."

She feigns innocence. "Oh, weird. I guess my Spotify shuffle just *knows* things."

"Turn it off," I spit out.

"Wow. You're reacting really strongly to a *totally random* song choice."

I reach for the volume knob. She smacks my hand away and does it herself.

"Admit it," she grins. "You have a massive, ridiculous, *all-consuming* thing for him."

I grit my teeth. "Lily."

She cackles.

I drag my hands down my face. "I should have texted Ethan instead. He would have hated it, but he would have sat in the driver's seat and fumed—silently."

She gasps, clutching her chest. "How dare you, Chang."

"I mean it," I say, smirking at her.

"That is *literally* the most offensive thing you have ever said to me."

"Oh, please. You once forced me to go on a blind date with a guy who brought a PowerPoint presentation about his personal brand." I deadpan.

"What? I thought you'd like that about him," she says with a shrug.

I press my lips tight and my eyebrows nearly form a single line.

"And yet, here you are, trusting me again." She beams back.

I mutter a curse under my breath.

Lily smirks. "It's okay, babe. You're in safe hands."

"I literally feel like I'm about to die."

"Yeah, that's love."

My stomach flips. That thought—that one right there, makes me feel like I'm about to hurl.

But then Lily is parking and my blood pressure is ratcheting up on a mission to the moon. Weirdly, the second she shifts into park, she slaps the lock button like she thinks I'll dive out of the car and bolt.

I glare. "Really?"

She shrugs. "I've seen you sprint when startled and we need to have a chat."

"That was *one* time."

She shoots me a knowing look but doesn't say anything.

Okay, fair.

And for the first time in a long time…

I don't want to feel safe.

I just want *him*.

God, this must be what going crazy feels like.

Lily shifts in her seat, turning to face me fully. "Okay. Before we go in, I need you to hear me." I sigh, rubbing my hands over my thighs. "Oh god."

"I know you, Anna." She ignores my dramatics. "You're about two seconds away from overthinking this to death. From coming up with some bullshit excuse about why you shouldn't be here, why you shouldn't want this, and why going to see Joel is a terrible idea."

I scowl. "I mean… have you met me?"

She points. "See? That right there. That's the voice of a woman about to sabotage the *hell* out of herself."

I groan, tilting my head back against the seat. "Lily—"

"Nope." She cuts me off, holding up a hand. "Listen to me. Do you like him? Be honest."

My stomach does a *whole-ass gymnastics routine.* "Lily."

"Answer the question."

I swallow hard. My hands are still gripping my jeans. My chest feels tight. My pulse won't slow down.

And all I can see—*all I can feel*—is him.

The way he looked at me before he left. The way he *kissed* me like he meant it. Like he wanted it just as much as I did.

Lily softens. "It's okay to say yes, you know."

My throat is dry. I manage, barely above a whisper, "I don't know what to do with it."

She nods, like she was expecting that. "That's fine. You don't have to *do* anything yet. But you *do* have to let yourself *feel* it."

I stare at her, something sharp catching in my ribs.

She keeps going, relentless in that way she always is when she's fighting for me. "You've spent *years* convincing yourself that Joel was this off-limits, self-centered asshole, but guess what? *You're here.* You are literally about to walk into this club because you *want* to. That's growth, Anna."

I swallow hard.

Lily reaches for my hand, squeezing it tight. "Don't run from it, babe. Just... let yourself have this moment. Let yourself *want* him. See where it leads. At least then you'll know."

I let out a slow, shuddering breath.

And for once—*for once*—I don't argue.

I just nod.

Lily beams. "Good girl. Now, let's go be hot and mysterious."

I snort a laugh and she unlocks the doors.

Nocté is packed.

The second we step inside, the heat, the bass, the press of bodies—it all slams into me at once.

The air is thick with sweat and cheap beer, sticky and

humid in a way that should make me want to bolt. But I barely notice because the energy in the room shifts.

I can't explain it, but suddenly, everything feels heavier—like the air itself is thick with something I can't quite place. My chest tightens, my breath catches, and then—

I hear him.

His voice filters through the speakers, low and rough and so painfully familiar that I feel it in my *bones*.

Lily stops walking. "Oh, *shit*."

I don't move. I don't breathe. I just *stand there.*

And then—

The second I see him, my breath goes *nowhere*.

He's lost in it. Completely, utterly lost. His hair is a mess, his black T-shirt clings to his frame, the sleeves tight around his tattooed biceps as he grips his guitar like it's the only thing keeping him tethered.

He's always been beautiful.

But this—

This is *something else.*

He's got the whole crowd in the palm of his hand, his voice weaving through the space like a slow, steady fire, wrapping around the room—around *me*.

I forgot what this feels like.

I forgot what *he* feels like when he's in his full glory.

Even from across the room, he's under my skin. In my veins.

Lily leans into my ear. "Holy *shit*."

I don't answer.

I can't.

Because Joel doesn't know I'm here.

And I don't know what happens when he finally sees me.

But I'm not running.

Not this time.

For some idiotic reason, I'm seeing this through.

CHAPTER 28

Joel

The crowd is alive, buzzing, pressing in from all sides. The heat, the sweat, the restless anticipation —it should be grounding me.

But it's not.

I stand just offstage, fingers flexing and unflexing around the neck of my guitar. The house lights are low, shadows stretching across the dance floor, and the bass from the overhead speakers thrums in my chest like a second heartbeat.

I should be amped. Should be itching to step onto that stage and do the only thing that has ever made sense to me.

Instead, my skin feels too tight.

My chest is a fucking battlefield—my lungs refusing to settle, my ribs stretched like a wire pulled taut.

Because all I can think about is *her*.

What would she think about the tour? Would she care or tell me to get lost?

What if I stayed? Played some more shows at Nocté? Would it piss her off that I'm staying longer?

Shit, I told myself I wouldn't let her invade my head tonight. That I'd get on stage, go through the set, finish the show, and move the fuck on if that's what she wants.

But my head won't shut up.

Did I push too hard? What if she just needs more time? Should I have told her—

No.

I shake it off, adjusting the strap over my shoulder. *Focus*, Price.

The setlist is burned into my brain. My fingers know what to do. My voice will follow.

Music is what I do.

Even when nothing else makes sense, music does.

It'll pull me back. It always has.

Mark gives me the nod to head on stage.

I roll my shoulders, shake out my hands.

I've done this a thousand times. Stepped onto a stage, let the music take over, let it strip me down, pull me into something bigger than myself.

But tonight?

Tonight, I can't get out of my fucking head.

The weight in my chest is pressing down, pressing in, pressing too goddamn much.

I adjust my guitar strap, but my fingers won't stay steady.

My throat is already dry.

The crowd is chanting, their energy electric, but I feel like a live wire ready to snap.

I take a deep breath, try to force it down, force it away.

But something about tonight feels final.

And I don't know if I'm ready for that.

I step forward.

The lights slam into me.

As expected, the first song is muscle memory.

I sing. I play. I move.

But something's off.

The words come out too tight.

The rhythm is there, but it's shaky.

I adjust the mic, try to loosen my grip, but my hands are too stiff, too tense, too goddamn tight.

Somehow, the crowd still loves it—the front row dancing and singing along.

I let the music take over, let it drown out the noise in my head, let it bury every thought that isn't a chord progression or a lyric slipping past my lips.

The songs should pull me under, bury me in the rhythm, drag me away from my own thoughts. That's how it works.

That's how it's always worked.

But tonight?

Tonight, the music isn't enough.

I wait for the music to calm me.

It doesn't.

The second song starts, darker, heavier.

I play it too hard.

My fingers slam into the chords with more force than necessary.

The band follows, picking up on my energy, shifting with me. Thank fuck for that.

To the crowd, I'm sure it just sounds like I'm feeling it.

They don't know I'm trying to escape.

That I'm pushing too hard, too fast, trying to outrun my own goddamn thoughts.

It doesn't work.

The lyrics leave my mouth, but they don't feel real.

They're phantom words about feelings I don't want to feel.

I grit my teeth.

Sing harder.

Nothing.

I grip my guitar, pressing my fingers into the strings until they bite back. The band is tight, the sound is clean, the crowd is losing their minds—but I feel fucking hollow. This is nothing like the first show. This is deeper. Heavier somehow.

I thought after that kiss, after the way she grabbed me like she needed me, like she wanted more— it would be different.

But it wasn't.

And now, I don't know what to do with that.

I sing, I play, I pretend.

But nothing reaches me.

The lyrics leave my mouth, but they don't feel real. They're phantom words about feelings I'd rather not feel.

I keep my eyes forward, focused on the sea of moving bodies. I wish I could be that fucking carefree. Floating on a reality where the only thing that matters is booze and the thump of the bass.

Don't look for her. There's no point.

Because she's not here.

I saw the way she hesitated in the kitchen. The total fear in her eyes. The way she couldn't say what we both knew was the truth.

She's not ready for this. Not for me.

So I play like this is just another show.

Like this is just another night and not the end of something.

Lie to yourself, Joel. Pretend it doesn't hurt.

The weight in my chest shifts, pressing harder, dragging lower. I pour everything into it—frustration, regret, every fucking unspoken word.

And still, it's not enough.

The crowd moves, sways, continues to sing back to me. But it all feels far away.

Like I'm here, but not really.

Like I'm playing into the void.

Like I could scream into this mic, put every ounce of my soul into this stage, and it still wouldn't fix this ache under my ribs.

I don't even realize I'm looking toward the back of the room until—

There.

A flicker of black hair being flung over a shoulder.

A shadow beside the bar.

My pulse jolts, hard and fast.

I blink, forcing my eyes to snap forward.

I won't do this to myself again.

I've imagined her in places she's never been before. Convinced myself I saw her when she was miles away.

That's all this is.

Another trick.

Another moment of wishful thinking.

It's not her. It's *not*.

Just someone who moves like her.

Someone who stands like her.

Someone who—

My breath cuts short.

Because now I see Lily.

And London.

And then—

No. No *fucking way*.

My stomach free-falls.

Because it's her.

Here.

Watching me.

The chord in my fingers goes sharp, ringing out wrong, exposing me.

I recover—barely.

Too late.

The band keeps playing, keeps covering—but I'm gone.

Everything tilts.

The lights are too bright, the air too thick, the heat crushing down on me like a tidal wave.

She wasn't supposed to come.

She said she wouldn't.

So why—

Why is she here?

I rip my gaze away, but it's too fucking late.

She's here.

And now, everything is different.

The song nearly derails because I forgot how to breathe.

I rip my gaze away. I try to shake it off, to pretend I didn't just see the one person I was certain would never show up.

But it's too late.

For some insane reason, she *came*. And I don't know what it means.

The next song is hers.

Hell, they're all hers.

The crowd doesn't exist. The club doesn't exist. The lights, the heat, the bass shaking the floor—none of it matters.

Because she's watching me.

She's hearing everything.

Every lyric I wrote about her—even before I realized I was doing it.

Every moment I've spent aching for her.

Every second I've waited for her to see me the way I see her.

And she's still standing there.

Why hasn't she left?

She should have stormed out the second she realized what this was—what this has always been.

But she doesn't.

I don't know what that *means*.

I don't know what the hell to do with it.

The final song is coming.

I know it.

The band knows it.

The crowd sure as hell knows it.

And they start chanting for it.

"Do You See Me."

The song that put me on the map.

The song that made me a fucking name in this industry.

But they don't know.

They don't know who it really belongs to.

And I can't play it.

Won't.

Not without her.

Not when I gave it back.

The crowd is relentless.

I hesitate for a full heartbeat too long.

Mark gives me a look. The crowd gets louder, shouting for it.

I lick my lips, my breath unsteady.

I grip the mic like it's the only thing holding me up.

And I say, voice wrecked, heart ruined— "This last one... is about love."

The second the first chord of *Always You* rings out, something in me tilts. It's subtle at first, like a thread being tugged loose inside my chest, unraveling something I didn't realize I'd tied so goddamn tight.

I search her out—locking eyes with her. I need her

to listen, to feel this song as I fucking break for her. She ran before, but maybe... maybe this time she'll hear me out.

I should be focusing on the song. On the lyrics I've nailed down for her. On the way my fingers move over the strings, steady, deliberate.

But I'm not.

Because all I see is her.

And for the first time since she walked back into my life, I don't know what the hell I'm looking at.

Anna is still.

Not frozen. Not locked up in tension, but *still*.

Her hands aren't clenched. Her shoulders aren't tight. She's just... standing there. Watching me with such an open expression it damn near shatters me.

Because I don't know what that means.

I don't know if I can trust what I'm seeing.

She's not running.

But is she staying?

I push into the first verse, and my voice wavers just slightly, my throat raw from the weight of this moment. From all the moments before it.

And I watch her. I can't not.

I watch the slow rise and fall of her chest.

The way her lips part, like she's forgetting how to breathe, too.

The way her fingers twitch at her sides, like she wants to grab onto something—like maybe she's holding herself back from reaching for me.

Or maybe that's just what I want to believe.

I blink hard, keep singing, but fuck, my mind is playing tug-of-war with itself.

Is she just listening?

Or is this something more?

Does she feel me—*this*?

Does she... *want* this?

My pulse kicks, hard and fast.

I push into the next verse, and I swear to God, I see something shift in her.

Her shoulders drop the smallest fraction. Her fingers relax.

And fuck—her eyes.

They've never looked like this before.

Or maybe they have, and I was too stupid to notice.

Because there's no fear there.

No barriers.

No walls between us.

Is this real?

I swallow hard, fingers tightening around the guitar. It doesn't make sense.

Anna doesn't let go this easily. She doesn't let herself be seen.

But she's standing here, in this room filled with people, with music, with me—

And for the first time, she's not hiding from it.

I don't understand.

But I want to.

God, do I want to.

I push through the chorus, let the weight of my own words sit heavy on my tongue.

And then—she exhales.

A long, slow breath, her chest rising and falling like she's matching the rhythm of the song.

Like she's letting herself feel it.

Like she's letting herself truly be here.

I nearly miss the next chord.

Because fuck.

This isn't the same Anna who walked away from me in that kitchen.

She's still guarded—of course she is. But something's different.

Something is so goddamn different I don't know what to do with it.

My heart slams against my ribs.

Does she feel this too?

Does she know what this means to me?

She doesn't move.

Doesn't look away.

Just keeps standing there, breathing, and I feel it like a shock to my system.

I push through the next verse, my throat tight, my voice rough, and she doesn't waver.

For the first time, I let myself believe it.

She's here.

Really here.

And fuck, maybe—maybe she's staying.

The final chorus comes, and I don't know what the hell's going to happen when this song ends.

But for the first time since I stepped on this stage, I don't feel so goddamn heavy anymore.

And maybe—*just maybe*—neither does she.

345

CHAPTER 29

Anna

I *t's always been you.*

The words don't just cling to me—they sink in, take root, fuse with every shattered piece of me that I never let heal.

My chest tightens. My hands feel unsteady at my sides.

I blink, but the club is a blur. The faces, the lights, the sounds—none of it feels real.

Only the weight of his voice, still reverberating inside me.

Still *wrecking* me.

It was worse this time around. Worse hearing it in its completion and knowing what he's been trying to tell me.

I should be furious.

Hell, I should be anything other than this—standing here, caught in a moment that feels bigger than I know how to handle.

But I don't move.

I can't.

Because his song is a confession.

Every lyric, every note, a breadcrumb leading back to me.

I was too young to name it,
too scared to let it grow.
So I called it nothing, buried it deep,
but love has roots I didn't know.

I exhale sharply, but it barely cuts through the tightness in my ribs.

Love has roots.

So does pain.

And for years, I thought I had dug him out. Thought I had torn every last piece of him from me.

But now—now I feel them.

The roots. Still there.

Still growing beneath the surface.

And no matter how much I tried to convince myself otherwise, they never really left.

The crowd is roaring, but it's nothing more than static behind the sound of his voice still echoing in my head. I should move. I should breathe. I should *do something.*

But I don't.

Because I *can't.*

I'm stuck in this moment, in his voice, in the truth I

spent years trying to ignore and for some ungodly reason, I can't anymore.

This is what he was trying to tell me earlier. It's what shattered me at the party. I couldn't listen—couldn't hear it because I knew it would destroy me.

It's always been me?

Even when he left? Even when he picked someone else? Even when he took my song and let me think it was nothing to him? That *I* was nothing to him.

I should be so goddamn wary of this—of him—of everything he's just confessed in front of a packed club like it was the easiest thing in the world.

But I'm not.

Because I feel every single word of that song like a live wire running through my veins. They feel like a pulse just under my skin—like something I've been waiting for but never let myself name.

They circle my brain again.

Did you know?

Could you tell?

That I looked for you in everyone else?

I even helped him with the chord progression for this song—I don't know why this is hitting different now.

Maybe because he only hummed the song then.

Maybe because I'm standing still for once.

Maybe because there's nowhere left to hide.

Probably because, for the first time, I'm letting myself actually *hear* him.

You were the song I never finished,
the note that lingered in my chest.

My throat tightens.

Because shit—that's exactly what he was to me too.

A song with no ending.

A half-written melody I've been singing for years, pretending I didn't know the words.

But I did.

I always did.

Did you know?

Did you see?

That every almost

still led me back to you and me?

A shiver races down my spine.

Because yes.

I knew. Deep down.

Even when I didn't want to.

Even when I tried to convince myself I was over it. *Over him.*

Every almost-love, every half-hearted relationship, every guy who made me laugh but never quite felt like home—it was always there. It's why no one else ever felt right.

There was always a weight in my chest I refused to acknowledge.

A ghost in the background.

A lyric I never stopped hearing.

"Okay, Anna," Lily's voice cuts through the noise, low and urgent. "Get ready."

I blink, my pulse thrashing in my ears. "What?"

Lily tilts her chin toward the stage, and I follow her gaze.

Straight to him.

To Joel.

Who drops his guitar and is heading directly for me.

Oh, *shit.*

Joel barely acknowledges the people reaching for him —the girl in the front row who tries to grab his arm, the guys who clap him on the back, the fans calling his name.

Another girl reaches for him, fingers skimming his chest. He doesn't slow.

His focus doesn't break.

And with every inch that closes between us, something inside me coils tighter.

A slow, suffocating pull low in my stomach.

My pulse stumbles, a rapid, uneven thrash in my throat.

I can't breathe.

Or maybe I'm breathing too much, too fast, too hard.

But I don't look away.

His eyes are locked on one thing.

Me.

And holy fuck.

"Oh, girl. He's got *the look,*" Myles mutters, sounding equal parts impressed and entertained from the other side of the bar.

London nods sagely. "That's definitely the *I've-made-up-my-goddamn-mind-and-nothing-is-stopping-me* look."

My pulse stutters.

Is it? Is that what this is?

Myles slides a shot glass in front of me with some sort of bartender-level wisdom.

"Babe," she says, tone serious, "you look like you might need this."

I stare at it. I stare at them. I can't possibly even think about that right now.

Instead, I turn to stare at Joel, still closing the distance between us, still looking like nothing else in the world exists.

Something shifts.

Not in the club. Not in the crowd.

In *me*.

Joel moves through the bodies like a force field surrounds him, still brushing off hands that reach for him, barely acknowledging the people calling his name.

Every step pulls him closer, and my pulse kicks up in response—faster, harder, like my body already knows something I don't.

Heat crawls over my skin, my breath catches, but I don't look away.

My feet stay planted.

My body leans forward before I can stop it, like I'm being pulled by something outside myself.

Because this moment?

It's what I wanted. Isn't it?

What I've been waiting for. Why I'm here now.

It's what I didn't even realize I was hoping for.

When he reaches me, his chest rises and falls, his breath just slightly uneven, like he hasn't come down from the song yet.

There's sweat at his temple, at the hollow of his throat.

And his eyes—*fuck*.

His green eyes that I always thought were just that—green.

But now?

Now I see the brown flecks and just how deep they go.

And then—he moves.

His hands slide into my hair, fingers threading through the strands, cupping the back of my head.

Warm. Sure.

Steady.

I expect him to call me out. To say something. But he doesn't.

He just holds my gaze and my head in his hands. I don't know if he's holding me still or holding me closer. Maybe both. Maybe neither. Hell, maybe he just needs to touch me as much as I need to be touched.

A breath hitches in my throat and soft growl escapes from his.

I barely have time to register the heat of his palms against my skin, the way his grip tightens like I might slip through his fingers—and then, his lips are on mine.

Soft at first.

Not hesitant—just controlled. *Measured.*

A press, a pull, a slow unraveling.

Like he's testing the weight of this.

Like he's making sure I feel every single second.

And I do. God, I really, *really* do.

I feel it in my chest, in my stomach, in the way my knees threaten to buckle.

My fingers tighten in his shirt, gripping, anchoring, holding on.

Because I need this.

I need *him*.

And God help me, I don't want him to stop.

Then, everything tilts.

Not just the room. Not just my breath.

Me.

He doesn't rush us.

This kiss isn't careful.

It's deep. Steady. *Certain.*

A claiming of sorts. And it's *everything*.

It's like it's a truth that's been waiting for me to stop fighting it.

And now, it's a slow burn that I feel everywhere.

I pull him closer, pressing myself to him.

His hands slide deeper into my hair, his grip tightening, but not to hold me still—to bring me in.

My chest is too tight, too full, too much.

My knees feel unsteady, but his body is right there, solid, sure.

Everything around us fades. It's just us and my head is swimming in it.

He kisses me like he's learning me.

Like he wants to burn this moment into his memory.

Like he doesn't want to forget.

And I don't want to either.

Heat unfurls inside me, curling into something dangerous, something I can't name.

I press closer.

And that's all he needs.

He makes a low sound, a quiet rumble in his chest, vibrating against my lips. His fingers curl against my scalp, and a full-body shiver rolls through me.

My stomach flips, my pulse is a wreck, my entire world is shrinking down to this moment.

This kiss.

Him.

This is nothing like before.

Not a reckless decision. Not a reaction. Not a mistake.

I was such an idiot for calling it that.

Because this?

This is undeniable.

I sink into it.

Let myself feel it.

Every shift of his lips. Every press of his hands. Every quiet, unspoken thing that lingers between us.

There are cat calls, and whoops around us. People telling us to get a room—but I don't give a shit.

I feel the shift in his breath, the weight of his chest pressing just slightly against mine. The deep, rhythmic slide of his tongue over mine—not demanding, not rushed.

Just right.

Somewhere in the distance I hear Lily's giggle of approval, but even that barely registers.

Heat licks up my spine, settling in the hollow beneath my ribs, something spreading through me that I don't have a name for but desperately want to express.

My lips part on a soft, unsteady gasp.

He takes it.

Swallows it like it belongs to him.

Like it's *always* belonged to him.

The kiss deepens, his hands sliding from my face, fingers pushing deeper into my hair. A quiet possession, a silent question.

I don't answer with words.

I press closer.

And that's all he needs.

A sound rumbles low in his throat, vibrating against my lips. His grip tightens just enough to send a shiver cascading through me.

My heart is racing.

Every nerve feels alive.

I don't know how long we stand here, tangled in each other, drowning in something too big, too much, too fucking inevitable. It could be minutes, it could be seconds. It feels like eternity.

He takes up all of my senses.

His lips, his hands, the way he kisses me like he's certain of this—whatever *this* is.

Like he knows I'm finally certain too.

He pulls back just enough to rest his forehead against mine, his hands still cradling my face, his breath mixing with mine.

His voice is a hushed mess. Rough, frayed, barely

above the noise. Like he doesn't trust it to hold steady. *"Come upstairs with me."*

My pulse stumbles.

I blink, still feeling the kiss on my lips, still trying to pull myself back into my body. The club is loud around us—people still cheering, music from the DJ now humming in the background—but all of it feels muted, distant, like I've stepped into some other reality where only Joel exists.

Upstairs.

I don't fully know what that means, but I can tell it's not about the place. It's a *choice*.

A next step.

A turning point.

My fingers are curled into his shirt, still holding on like I might fall if I let go.

And maybe I will.

Maybe I already have.

Because this isn't just about tonight.

This isn't just about a kiss, or the heat still curling in my stomach, or the way his breath is mixing with mine.

This is about finally choosing him.

Choosing *us*.

Choosing to stop running.

And the weight of that realization presses into my ribs.

I force out a breath, my heart thumping in a frantic, uneven rhythm.

I don't know what's waiting for me up there.

But for the first time—I don't need to.

I swallow hard, my grip tightening on his shirt, ready to say it.

Before I can say anything, before my brain can fully process what's happening, Lily jumps in.

Too fast. Too bright. Too much.

"Oh, Anna," she says, her voice climbing an octave. "You'll love the after party. It's going to be *amazing*. Just —so much fun. *So* much fun."

I turn my head slightly, blinking at her, but Joel doesn't move.

His hands stay firm, his thumbs still brushing along my cheekbones, keeping me locked in place.

London, standing beside Lily, crosses his arms and clears his throat.

"Yeah," he says smoothly, his tone way too even. "Lily's worked *really* hard on it. You should definitely check it out."

Lily nods. Too much.

"Yep. Worked *really* hard. So hard. Weeks of planning, really."

London full-on side-eyes her. "Lily—"

She steamrolls right over him. "There's a playlist of all of Joel's best hits and—uh—drinks. And I think snacks? Right, London?"

London shakes his head—just the tiniest fraction— but Lily *keeps going*.

"Anyway... Super exclusive. *VIP only.*" She finger guns at me. "Like, *if you know, you know.*"

Joel doesn't acknowledge any of this.

He stays exactly where he is, forehead still resting

against mine, gaze locked on me like he's waiting for something.

A decision.

A sign.

A *yes*.

I blink again.

Something about Lily and London feels... *off*.

Not in a bad way.

Not in a way that makes me second-guess Joel or this moment.

But enough that my instincts hum with awareness.

They're covering.

For what, I have no idea.

But right now?

I can't focus on anything except Joel.

I swallow hard, my hands still tangled in his shirt, my breath still unsteady.

Upstairs.

The word echoes in my head, but not in the way it should. This isn't about a party, about going somewhere to celebrate. This is about something else entirely.

And I don't know what's waiting for me up there.

But for the first time, I don't need to.

I trust him.

Not in the way I used to—when trust felt like a fragile, dangerous thing. Something that could be given too easily and taken away just as fast.

No, this trust is different. It's heavier, more real.

My stomach flips again, not from fear or doubt, but

from something that feels dangerously close to anticipation.

Joel's fingers flex slightly, his grip tightening for the briefest second—like he can feel the moment tipping, like he knows I'm on the edge of something big.

And maybe I am.

Maybe this is the moment I stop running.

Maybe this is the moment I finally, *finally* let myself believe this could be real.

For a split second, I think about what happens next.

Not just tonight. Not just upstairs.

Everything.

Because this isn't just about saying yes to Joel.

It's about saying yes to us.

To the version of me that's wanted this all along.

To the roots that never stopped growing.

To the idea that maybe, just maybe, love has been waiting for me to stop running.

My breath hitches.

I meet his gaze, let myself get lost in it. Let myself fall.

And I nod.

I keep hold of her hand as we step through the entrance of the Upper Tier, past the bouncer who barely glances at me before lifting the rope. The bass from below still pulses through the floors, but up here, the sound is muffled, the air heavier.

She doesn't hesitate, doesn't pull back, but I feel the awareness in her grip. She's taking in the dim lighting, the sleek black booths, the small private rooms tucked into the back. She doesn't know what this place is.

But I do.

I know exactly what kind of things happen up here. I could feel it that first night.

It's not just a VIP section. It's where people disappear into booths and private rooms, where the drinks are stronger, the lights are lower, and inhibitions blur into nothing. It's where people come when they don't want to be seen—or when they want to be *watched.*

There are assumptions about what happens up here.

I also know that's not why I brought her. She means too much for that.

Anna's fingers twitch slightly against mine, but she doesn't ask about the vibe, doesn't pull her hand away. She just keeps looking. Taking it all in.

I don't give her time to second-guess.

Instead, I tighten my hold and lead her toward a corner booth, away from the noise, the press of bodies, the expectation hanging in the air.

She slides into the seat, and I take the spot beside her instead of across from her, close enough that my knee brushes against hers.

Her eyes meet mine, dark and unreadable.

I search her face, looking for something—hesitation, regret, the instinct to run—but it's not there. She watches me, quiet but steady, her eyes flicking over my face like she's trying to piece something together.

Neither of us speaks.

And maybe we don't need to.

Because this is real. It *has* to be.

But I need to make sure.

I reach for her, brushing the backs of my fingers against her cheek, then crook my index finger to tilt her chin up. Her breath catches, her lips part just slightly, and then she moves toward me, meeting me halfway.

The kiss isn't rushed.

It's slow, deep—*a confirmation* that rolls through every fiber of my being.

Her fingers find my shirt again, twisting in the fabric

like she's grounding herself. Like she's grounding *us*. However, it sparks my body, causing blood to rush everywhere all at once.

I shift, pressing in, swallowing the little sigh she exhales against my mouth. Her lips are soft, warm, and she tastes like the drinks from earlier, like something I could get drunk on.

She doesn't pull away.

Doesn't *stop me*.

And that? That's what kills me the most.

Because I think she *wants* this just as much as I do.

When she finally does break away, her forehead stays close, brushing against mine. She exhales, something soft, something real.

"What the hell is this?" she whispers.

I don't have an answer for that.

I only know what it *feels* like.

Like something I'm not willing to lose again.

So I tell her the only thing I know to be true. "It's us."

She pulls back just enough to look at me, tilting her head. "That's not an answer, Price."

I smirk. "Sure it is."

She rolls her eyes but doesn't move away or tell me to fuck off.

And that? That's the biggest win of my fucking life.

She leans back against the booth, her body still angled toward me, like she's not willing to put more distance between us. I keep my arm stretched along the back of the seat, not touching, not pushing, just *being here with her.*

Honestly, I don't feel like I have to push for something more.

Because she's *here.*

And she's *not running.* And I can work with that.

Anna lets out a slow breath, studying me again, her gaze softer now, still searching. "You brought me up here to talk?"

I huff out a small laugh. "You sound surprised."

"I am." The most adorable half-smile graces her lips and I think I might have just died until she says, "I thought this was your sneaky way of getting me alone."

I grin. "I don't *need* to be sneaky, Ace. When I want you alone, you'll be begging me for it."

Her cheeks flush, but she covers it well, rolling her eyes again as she looks away, shaking her head.

"I mean, we might have to work up to sword-crossing, but I could be convinced to try anything once," I tease, loving the color that blooms across her cheeks. It's my new favorite pastime.

"Jesus Christ," she mutters, pressing her palms over her face.

It's easy between us now.

It shouldn't be.

After everything, after years of distance and fights and denying this thing between us—it shouldn't be *this easy.*

But it is.

And I don't want to let it go.

I exhale, running a hand over my jaw. "I do actually need to tell you something."

That pulls her back, her amusement and embarrassment fading just slightly.

I sit forward, resting my elbows on the table, fingers threading together.

"The tour," I say, watching her closely. I hold my breath, hoping...

Her brow furrows slightly, head tilting. "What tour?"

I drag a hand through my hair. "The one I just got offered."

She stills.

I *feel* the shift in her.

The way she locks her expression down, her fingers pressing together.

"You got offered a tour? Where? When? You just found out?" She says her words in a rush, as her lashes flutter against her cheeks.

"I just found out. Tonight. Right before the set. I wanted you to know before—before this goes any further."

Her lips part slightly. "Joel."

I let out a slow breath. "It's a big deal, Ace. Europe. Two months. It's the biggest gig I've ever been offered. It could lead to more."

She swallows, nods slowly.

But I don't stop there.

"London offered me something else."

That gets her attention.

Her gaze sharpens, her body going still. "What?"

I lean forward, holding her eyes. "A few more shows at Nocté. If I want it."

She exhales slowly, absorbing it. "So you have two choices."

I nod. "Yeah."

She watches me, searching my face. "And what? You can't make a decision?"

I shake my head. "Not without you."

She breathes in, and I *feel* the weight of it, the weight of *us,* the weight of everything that has led us to this moment.

But then—she surprises me.

She lifts her chin, meeting my eyes, and says, "You have to go."

I blink, caught off guard. "What?"

She shrugs one shoulder, the tiniest smile playing at her lips. "You have to go, Joel. It's *two months.* We've waited this long, haven't we?"

Something stirs in my chest, something sharp and unexpected. "So you're not worried?"

Her smile lingers. "Oh, I'm *definitely* worried." She leans in slightly. "I've seen you without supervision. You're a menace."

I laugh, shaking my head. "That's *bullshit.*"

She smirks. "Is it, though?"

I shake my head again, but my chest feels *lighter* than it has in days. Weeks. Maybe *years.*

And then—fuck it.

I shift closer, dropping my voice, watching her closely. "You could come with me."

Anna blinks, her expression unreadable at first.

I *watch* it register.

The way her breath catches. The way her fingers curl slightly against the table.

She doesn't answer right away.

For a half-second, my stomach free-falls.

Fuck. What if she says no? What if I just laid it all out there, and she doesn't want it?

What if I just proved I want more, and she's not ready?

She swallows, then whispers, "What?"

I hold her gaze, steady and sure. "You can work on the road, right? I've seen you, you could practically run your whole business from your phone. But you have that badass laptop and if you wanted, you could even join me. Be a part of the music again. Anna, you've gotta miss the music."

She blinks, opens her mouth, then closes it again.

And I realize—she *didn't* see this coming.

All this time, all these moments, *she didn't think I'd ask her to come with me.*

Like she thought she wasn't part of the equation.

Like she thought she was something I'd have to leave behind.

Fuck that.

"Please come with me, Ace," I say again, softer this time. "Stay as long as you want. As long as you *can*. I need time with you."

I watch her face, the flicker of emotions playing

across her features—*shock, hesitation, something unreadable, something softer.*

And then—

She kisses me.

Not out of heat.

Not out of desperation.

Not to distract from what we're saying.

But because she *knows.*

Because she *believes me.*

Because maybe she *wants* this as much as I do.

She pulls back just enough to whisper against my lips. "Come home with me."

I swallow, pulse hammering behind my ribs because her words mean everything. "You mean to *our* place?"

She groans, pushing at my chest, but I catch her hand, linking my fingers through hers.

"Shut up get us an Uber," she mutters, but she's smiling.

She doesn't rush to fill the silence.

Neither do I.

It stretches between us, thick with everything we're still learning how to say.

Her fingers are still tangled in my shirt, her breath still a little uneven. She's watching me the way she did downstairs, like she's trying to figure out if this is real—if *we're* real.

I'm still trying to figure it out myself.

Beyond our booth, people drift toward the back rooms, slipping past heavy curtains and disappearing without a second glance. Some barely make it that far, lost in whispered conversations, in hands that wander too easily, in promises that won't make it past the night.

She notices, but doesn't ask the questions lingering in her eyes. Anna's smart. I'm sure she'll come to the same conclusion I did about this place.

Her fingers still curled into my shirt, her lips still pink from kissing me, her body still angled toward mine like she doesn't want to pull away.

I brush my thumb over her knuckles, just once, just enough to feel her warmth. "So?"

She tilts her head. "So?"

I smirk. "Are you coming with me?"

Her breath catches.

I watch her lips part, watch the way her chest rises and falls too fast, watch her *consider it*.

She exhales, pressing her tongue to the inside of her cheek, gaze flicking down for just a second before she looks back at me.

And then, she grins.

Not wide.

Not big.

Just *enough*.

"I said come home with me, didn't I?" she murmurs, voice soft but teasing.

My stomach fucking flips.

I lean in, brushing my lips against hers, speaking against her mouth. "Yeah, but I'm greedy, Ace."

She rolls her eyes, but she's still smiling, still here, still *choosing me*.

I tighten my grip on her fingers, lacing them with mine.

Her voice dips lower, teasing but threaded with something more. "I'll think on it."

I arch a brow. "On what?"

Her smirk deepens as she leans in, just close enough that her breath brushes my lips. "On how fast you can get that Uber and get me undressed."

Fuck.

That's what she meant about going home? Wait, what?

Home = undressing = TONIGHT?

Am I dead?

Did I die? I didn't didn't I? She murdered me and this is my brain trying to create a better memory before I give in to oblivion.

I grin, my pulse pounding against my ribcage as her palm skims my thigh, driving the point straight to my brain—and everywhere else.

Okay, I don't care if I'm dead. RIP Joel Price. He died a happy man.

Enough talking. We're doing this.

"Challenge accepted," I blurt out, needing to be out of this booth and away from this club.

And I don't waste another second.

CHAPTER 31

Anna

The door barely clicks shut before Joel's mouth is on mine.

I don't overthink. I don't analyze or hesitate. I just let go and give in.

Everything crashes down—the years, the distance, the stupid fucking pride that kept me from this. From *him*.

God, we could have been doing this all along. Why weren't we doing this all along?

His hands are everywhere, gripping, mapping, learning. Mine do the same, tracing the contours of his arms, his chest, and abs. I yank him closer, because I need him right now.

I need him like air because I'm done suffocating without him.

He groans into my mouth as we stumble backward, bumping into walls, kicking off shoes, desperate and uncoordinated in a way that makes me laugh. We're like two love-sick teens who are desperate for our next fix.

Only, it's our *first* fix.

The first of many, I have a feeling.

Joel pulls back just enough to look at me, his eyes dark, his breath unsteady. "What's funny, Ace?"

I shake my head, lips still tingling—body absolutely humming. "You."

He smirks, but it's softer this time, like he's seeing something new in me. "Yeah?"

"Yeah."

And then I raise my palms to his cheeks and kiss him again. Because I can.

His hands find my hips, sliding under my shirt, dragging me against him. God his hands feel so good. It's like he knows exactly how to light my body up.

I feel every inch of him, and fuck—this isn't just heat. It's *something else*. Something bigger. Something so, *so* much bigger.

Something inside my chest cracks and I let out an almost sob. Not because I don't want this—but because I can't believe I actually *do*. Because we're really here and I can't even remember why I didn't want this.

He must sense it because the moment shifts. Slows.

I feel it in the way his lips soften against mine, in the way his fingertips trace lazy circles along my spine. This isn't just about want or lust or sex for either of us.

It's the weight of every *almost*. Every unspoken word. Every moment we spent pretending this didn't exist between us.

Joel stills, his forehead pressing against mine, his fingers threading into my hair.

For a second, we just breathe.

"You sure?" His voice is rough, frayed at the edges as he strokes the side of my cheek with the back of his hand.

He'd stop if I asked. He'd *wait*. Hell, I know he would. He already *has*.

He'd rip himself apart if I changed my mind.

I lift my chin, meeting his eyes, my fingers combing through his hair. "I've never been more sure of anything."

He inhales sharply, like the words that just passed my lips are words he never thought I'd ever say. His nose brushing against my cheek, and for a second, he just breathes me in.

"Jesus, Anna," he murmurs. His fingers flex at my waist, like he's grounding himself. "You have no idea how long I've wanted this—wanted to hear you say that."

I swallow hard, my fingers threading through his hair, pulling him back just enough to meet his eyes. They're such a deep green, practically burning, but there's something else there too—something that makes my chest ache.

I stroke my thumb across his lower lip. "Then stop waiting."

Something in him *snaps*.

Suddenly, he's moving. He carries me through the dim light of my apartment like I'm something weightless, something precious. But then—he pauses.

"Joel," I murmur, tightening my legs around his waist.

He smirks against my skin, his lips trailing along my

jaw, lazy and infuriating. "Mmm, I don't know, Ace," he murmurs. "You sure you're ready for me?"

I huff. "Are you seriously—"

His teeth graze my pulse point, and I *whimper.* Goddamn him.

"Say it," he murmurs, nipping at my collarbone, dragging this *out*, his hands gripping my thighs hard enough to bruise. "Say you *need* me."

My nails dig into his shoulders. "I *hate* you."

His laugh is dark, delicious. "Liar."

He nudges my bedroom door open with his foot, stepping inside with the kind of certainty that steals my breath. His grip tightens, and I feel his heart hammering through his ribs, matching mine—wild and unsteady. His breath is uneven against my cheek, and I realize— he's feeling this as much as I am.

He lowers me onto the bed, hovering over me, eyes locked on mine.

I reach for him before he can think too hard about what happens next. I pull him down, claiming his mouth with mine, desperate to close whatever space still lingers between us. It needs to be erased—eradicated.

Joel groans into me, his weight pressing me into the mattress, his body fitting against mine like we were carved from the same stone. I feel how turned on he is as he grinds his hips against me—and it just stokes the embers of my own fire. His hands slide over the skin of my stomach, slow but deliberate, and it sends a cascade of goosebumps throughout my body.

I arch into him, tugging at his shirt, needing more,

needing *to feel him*. He lets me strip him down, lets me map the lines of his chest, lets me feel every muscle, every inch of him under my fingertips.

I can't stop touching him.

I don't think I ever will.

Or staring—the tattoos on his arms and back are things I want to understand. To learn and embed into my mind.

He pulls back just long enough to lift my shirt over my head, tossing it somewhere behind him before his hands are on me again, spanning my ribs, my waist, his thumbs sweeping over my skin like he wants every inch of me to vibrate with pleasure. It's so damn close.

"You're so fucking beautiful," he rasps, raking his lower lip through his teeth. "I swear to God, Ace..."

I don't let him finish.

I crash my mouth to his, swallowing whatever words he was about to say.

He groans, sinking against me again, his body pressing me into the mattress, his weight settling exactly where I want it—where I *need* it. But there are still too many clothes in the way. My legs wrap around him, my fingers scraping down his back, and fuck—he shudders.

"Jesus Christ," he groans. "You're gonna kill me."

"Then die happy," I tease.

He drops his head against my shoulder, sucking in a sharp breath.

I laugh, but it cuts off into a moan as he presses a hot, open-mouthed kiss to the hollow of my throat.

"I'm trying to *survive* over here, Ace," he mutters, voice rough. "But you're making it really fucking hard."

I bite my lip, smug despite how wrecked I already feel. "Poor baby."

"Baby?" He raises a brow, like I just issued a challenge. "Oh, you're gonna regret that."

I *should*. But when his mouth trails lower, when his tongue flicks over the peak of my breast through my bra, when his teeth scrape just enough to send heat spiraling through me—I can't regret *anything*.

I can't even think.

I whimper, and his chuckle is low, smug, vibrating against my skin.

I slide my hand down, stroking him in my palm. He feels so good—just enough girth and length to make me quiver with anticipation.

His head snaps up, his eyes blazing. The groan that follows lights up every nerve in my body.

"*Fuck*, Anna." His hips twitch into my hand, a shudder rolling through his whole body. "You really *are* trying to kill me, aren't you you?"

I smirk, tightening my grip just to torture him. "Thought you could handle me, rockstar?"

His eyes darken.

"Oh, *I can handle you*." He grabs my wrist, stopping me. "But if you keep doing that, you're not getting what you really want."

My stomach clenches.

He smirks. "That's what I thought."

I arch up, meeting him, desperate for more.

His laughter is short, almost strained, but his lips are on my throat before I can say anything else. His teeth scrape just enough to send a full-body shiver rolling through me.

I don't know how long we stay like this, tangled together, exploring, discovering. The world outside this room doesn't exist. The years apart don't exist. The walls I spent so long building have already crumbled, and I *let them.*

I'm so ready to let him have every piece of me.

Because he's always had them anyway.

Joel stills above me, his forehead resting against mine for a beat, his breath uneven.

For the first time since we crashed through the door, neither of us moves.

It's the *weight* of it.

The knowing.

That when this happens—when *we* happen—there's no going back.

His fingers tangle with mine, threading together, pressing my hands into the mattress just above my head.

I watch his throat bob as he swallows hard, his lashes fluttering against his cheek. "This is real, isn't it? Please tell me it's real."

My chest tightens.

I can only nod.

A slow, almost disbelieving laugh escapes him. His nose skims against mine, soft, reverent.

"We were so fucking stupid," he murmurs.

I exhale a shaky breath, brushing my lips against his. "Speak for yourself."

Joel pulls back just enough to look at me, blinking like he misheard me.

His lips part. Then he huffs a laugh, shaking his head. "Are you kidding me right now?"

I grin, tilting my hips just enough to make him suck in another sharp breath. "Hey, I'm just saying, *one* of us had to be right eventually."

Joel groans, dropping his forehead to my clavicle. "Unbelievable."

A lazy grin spreads across my lips. "You knew what you signed up for."

"So true," he mutters, tracing his tongue up my collarbone to the column of my neck—and that has my smugness evaporating *real* fast. "Keep talking, Ace. See what happens."

I *would*, but then he's kissing me again—deeper, slower.

Somewhere in the middle of it, the remnants of my clothes find a way to the floor. The same happens to his bottoms, but we stay there, hands exploring each other while our mouths remain locked together. It's like we can't breathe without each other now.

Skin to skin, my brain wants to marvel at the way he feels in my hand, against my body, but processing beyond how good it feels is impossible. It's like I live for the sounds he makes and the ones he draws out of me.

And when he finally pushes into me, when our bodies fully, *finally* come together, I feel it deep in my soul. A knowing. A truth. Something ancient and *undeniable.*

We were never meant to be anything but this. It's why it hurt so deep then. Why I couldn't forgive him—or myself.

This was *always* our truth.

Joel shudders—hard. His lips drop to mine, his hands tightening at my waist like he's holding on for dear life.

"Jesus *fuck*. You feel—*fuck,*" he rasps, his voice nothing but gravel.

I gasp, my nails digging into his back, as a moan floats past my lips. "Oh, my God, Joel."

I can't even speak. Can't breathe.

His thumb skates along my jaw, his breath ragged. "Say my name again."

"Don't stop, Joel," I practically pant, keeping my eyes on his—holding his gaze like an embrace.

He stills above me, his breath uneven, ragged. His hands thread through mine, fingers tangling, pinning them above my head.

"Anna, I—" he murmurs, his voice breaking.

I kiss him.

He releases my hands and I hold him, digging my fingertips into his back.

And then we move.

Slow and deep.

Every thrust, every whispered name, every shuddering gasp and curse—it's a confession. A prayer. A breaking apart and a putting back together.

There's no turning back because I want this—*God, do I want this.*

So, I *let go.*

I give him everything.

And he gives it right back.

Joel moves, slow at first, like he's still absorbing the fact that we're finally here. That this is happening. That *we're* happening.

He's everywhere—his hands, his mouth, the heat of his body pressing into mine like he can't get close enough. Like there will never be enough of this, of us.

I feel him start to tremble.

A deep, ragged moan rumbles from his chest as I arch beneath him, my name slipping past his lips in something close to worship.

I hold onto him like he's the only thing anchoring me to this moment. Because maybe he is.

Maybe he always was.

It's too much, and yet—I want more.

Every thrust, every pull, every whisper against my skin sends me higher. Until I can't breathe, can't think— can only *feel.* Feel him.

He flips me over, guiding me to ride him, his breath warm and unsteady. "Anna," he rasps, voice breaking as he reaches up, his hands warm and playful on my breasts.

I bend forward, fisting my hands in his hair, needing to feel him deeper. "I know," I whisper back.

And then—I break.

The world slips away, pleasure ripping through me so fast and sharp, I almost forget how to breathe. But he's here—he's right here—watching me fall apart, following me over the edge, losing himself in me.

His body shakes with the force of it, his grip on me unrelenting, his mouth almost biting down at the space where my neck meets my shoulder like he can somehow keep this moment between us forever.

I don't even realize I'm still holding onto him.

"Holy shit," I mumble against his shoulder, my limbs still shaking.

He lets out a breathless laugh. "Ace, you just made me see *God.*"

I grin, half-delirious. "Hope you said something nice."

He lifts his head, grinning like the cockiest bastard alive. "Oh, I did. I said, *thank you, sir, may I have another?*"

I groan, shoving his face away. "You're the worst."

"And yet, you're still on top of me." He tips his hips up slightly, reminding me just how deeply embedded he is.

Then, he shifts just enough to look at me, his palm cupping the side of my face, his thumb brushing along my cheekbone.

I expect him to smirk, to tease, to say something else cocky.

He doesn't.

He just *watches me* with those soulful green eyes.

Like he *knew*, like he *always knew*, but having me here, *like this*, still knocks the breath from his lungs. I know the feeling.

His fingers skate down my side, tracing the curve of my waist, the dip of my hip.

"You okay?" he whispers. There's a hint of insecurity there, and I know I put that there. But I also know I'll be the one to remove it.

I don't even realize I'm smiling until I hear my own voice. "*More* than okay."

His exhale is shaky, like he's been holding something in for too damn long. "Good."

And then, finally, he pulls me against his chest, pressing a lingering kiss to my temple.

By the time we fall apart, by the time we're nothing but tangled limbs and desperate, uneven breaths, I know —*I know.*

There's no running from this.

No undoing it.

No pretending I don't want everything he's offering.

Joel shifts beside me, pulling me against his chest, his lips brushing my temple, his fingers tracing lazy patterns over my spine.

"Okay," I whisper into his neck as I plant more kisses there.

His whole body stills.

Then—slowly, deliberately—he turns his head, tipping my chin up so I have to look him in the eye.

There's something wild in his expression. Something wrecked and whole at the same time. Like he's still bracing for me to change my mind or maybe he's terrified of believing it.

His fingers tighten at my waist, his voice barely a breath.

"Okay?" His voice is quiet, rough at the edges.

I nod, pressing a kiss to his chin, letting myself believe it. "I'll go with you."

He exhales sharply, like the words knock something loose inside him. His hands slide up my spine, cradling me close.

And then, he whispers, "Say it again."

His chest rises sharply.

And I realize—this is the moment he's been waiting for. Not the sex. Not the tour. Not the second chance.

This.

Me staying.

Me *choosing him.*

Maybe because he never thought I would. Not after everything. Maybe he didn't think he'd ever deserve it.

I cup his face, smoothing my thumb over his cheek, anchoring myself to him. "I'll go with you, Joel."

And then—*he's kissing me.*

It's not desperate. Not rough.

It's slow. Deep.

A promise.

A thank you.

And when I whisper the words *one more time*, his grip tightens, and his lips find mine again. It's a slow, lingering kiss.

"You know this means your gonna be my groupie, right?"

I roll my eyes, shoving at his chest, but he just laughs, catching my hand, and threading our fingers together.

I huff against his shoulder. "Great. Stuck on a tour bus with you and a bunch of smelly men. My actual nightmare."

Joel lifts his head, eyes narrowing with mock offense. "Excuse me? *Stuck* with me?" He scoffs. "I give it a week before you're wearing a 'Mrs. Joel Price' shirt and fighting fangirls in the crowd with your evil death glare."

I snort. "I would rather choke on a guitar pick."

His grin turns downright wicked. "Oh, Ace. That's not the only thing you're gonna be choking on."

I freeze. My mouth drops open. "You did not just—"

Joel just smirks, smug and unrepentant.

"Oh my God," I groan, covering my face. "We're breaking up."

He tugs my hands away from my face, shaking his head like I'm the one who's ridiculous. "Too late, Ace. No take-backs. You signed up for this."

I narrow my eyes. "Did I?"

His smirk softens, something warm slipping into the edges. "Yeah." Then, he presses his lips to mine, lingering just long enough to steal my breath. "You did."

I sigh dramatically. "I really need to start reading the fine print."

Joel grins against my skin, lips brushing my jaw. "Too late. No refunds. No exchanges. I've branded myself to you now."

"Oh, I'm exchanging you *immediately* for store credit," I tease, tickling him along his side.

His laughter rumbles through his chest. "Ace, I am *custom-made* for you—you're never getting a deal this good again."

I roll my eyes, but I'm smiling. "Unbelievable."

He tilts his head, feigning deep thought. "Well, I guess there's one guy you could trade me in for."

I arch a brow. "Yeah?"

Joel nods solemnly. "Quinn. But, uh, from what you've told me, he's rooting for the other team."

I snort. "Accurate. Besides, I'd have to listen to all of his *deeply* unhinged Taylor Swift theories."

Joel grins. "Yeah, no offense, Ace, but you wouldn't survive that."

I groan. "You're right. I'd rather suffer."

Joel smirks, smug. "That's my girl."

My heart full-on beams at that sentence. God, I'm so toast.

I shove at his chest, but he just laughs, catching my hand, threading our fingers together.

And—damn it. He's right.

I really *did* sign up for this.

First, when I was a dumb, love-sick teenager. And now—when I actually know what I'm saying yes to.

And I've never been so sure of anything in my life.

Two months on the road, and I swear to God, I'm more in love with this woman than ever.

Which is annoying.

Because I was already at the maximum legally allowed amount of *in love,* and now she's just out here being all hot and brilliant and making me question everything I thought I knew about limits.

Honestly, I figured there was some kind of *cap* on it —like, there *has* to be limit before my heart just gives the fuck out. Right?

But no. Apparently, loving Anna is like a never-ending encore—just when I think I've hit the peak, another wave of *holy shit, she's everything* knocks me sideways.

Funny thing—I don't think she has any idea.

She doesn't see how every little thing she does wrecks me. Like the way she scrunches her nose when she's focused. The way she teases me like it's her life's mission to *humble* me. The way she pulls me into her space like she forgot she's been keeping me at arm's length for years.

She's been with me the whole tour and it feels fucking amazing.

Every night, I step onto a new stage, hear a new crowd screaming my name, and feel that rush of energy vibrating through my bones.

It's what I live for.

But nothing—and I mean *nothing*—compares to waking up next to Anna every morning.

She's in every piece of my life now. My hotel room, my dressing room, my damn *guitar cases* because she's always leaving her stuff in them. *("It was just one time,"* she argued. *No, it wasn't.*)

I love it. I love *her*.

And the scariest part?

It feels *easy*.

Like this was always meant to be our life.

And the more I watch her, the more I see it—the music still lives inside her.

I see it in the way her fingers drum against her thigh during soundcheck, like she's itching to pick up a guitar or settle onto the piano bench. In the way she hums under her breath when she thinks I'm not paying attention.

But she's *always* been music.

She might think she's all code and logic now, but that's not her. At least, not *all* of her. Not the full, complete picture.

I remember what it felt like to watch her play all those years ago—to see her lose herself in the sound, in the moment. She *lit up* on stage, and now?

Now, she pretends she's fine staying in the shadows. That she's just here to support me.

Bullshit.

She was *made* for this. And I want to watch her step back into the light more than I want my next fucking breath.

Still, she won't sing.

But I'm *so* close to getting her to.

Right now, though, she's tucked against my side in our hotel room in the middle of Paris while we FaceTime with her Dirty B's for her weekly bookclub meeting.

I gotta admit, it's fun. It's just us, drinks in hand, talking shit and books with our people.

Our people. When did that happen?

Because, *wow*, they really are.

It should be illegal to be this comfortable. This *domesticated*. But it's also so, *so* good.

Three months ago, no one would have been able to convince me this would be my life.

Honestly? If someone had told me back in LA that I'd be *here*—on a European tour, waking up next to Anna every morning, watching her steal my hoodies like they belong to her now (they do), falling asleep to the weight of her tucked against me—I would've laughed them out of the room.

Because this? This was the impossible dream.

Not the tour. Not the music. Not the crowds screaming my name.

Her.

Anna Chang, in my bed. In my life. Choosing *me* every damn day.

And fuck, I want to keep her here forever.

She fits into my world so seamlessly, like she was always meant to be in it. She rolls her eyes when I get mobbed by fans but then grips my hand tighter. She steals my fries like she's entitled to them by law.

And the way she looks at me when I play? Like she *feels* it in her chest, like she *gets* it.

I know it's only a matter of time before she's up there with me.

And holy *shit*, I can't wait for that moment.

"So, Anna," Vivian drawls over the phone, smirking. "Are you excited to be in Paris? I mean, I heard Joel was invited to more shows at Nocté, but what's that compared to Paris?"

Lily hums, too casual to be innocent. "Yeah, but turns out they didn't need it."

Anna slowly turns her head to look at me, then back to the screen, suspicion rising.

"...Wait. What?"

And then, *I* get it. Before Anna. And it's beautiful.

Joel Price, *notorious chaos gremlin, lover of one-upmanship, professional menace,* is fucking faster on the uptake for once.

I shove up from the bed, nearly knocking over my beer. "Oh, my God. You meddled."

Lily has the audacity to look unbothered. "Meddled is such a strong word."

Anna's *still* processing. "Hold on. You're telling me *you* convinced London to ask Joel to stay? He said it was the owner or something."

Lily grins, smug as hell. "Does it matter?"

"Yes, it matters," Anna says.

I throw my hands up, unable to contain my absolute *delight* at being proven right. "This means it was *fate*. One way or another, we were bound to be together."

Anna groans, covering her face with both hands. "Oh my God. You are so ridiculous."

Quinn sips his drink with a sage nod. "Divine intervention."

I point aggressively at the screen. "I adore your friends."

"You are the absolute worst," Anna claps back, reaching for her old fashioned—a new favorite.

I spin to Anna, grinning so hard my *face* hurts. "Say it."

She narrows her eyes. "Say *what*?"

"That you *believe* now. That fate, *Joel Price*, and *my raw, unmatched sexual magnetism* made this happen. We were always destined, my little feather plum."

Anna throws a pillow at my face.

I catch it. *Like a goddamn rockstar.*

Anna stares at me like she's debating whether she should kiss me or kill me. Probably both.

Lily snorts. "Honestly? He's got a point. I think there was definitely a dash of fate in there."

Quinn sighs dramatically. "I *love* that he has a point. And I'll voice for the sexual magnetism, too."

"Thanks, Quinn," I beam back.

He blows me a kiss.

Carlie, with an evil grin on her face steeples her finger under her chin and says, "God, I could so write this. Rockstar romance—brother's best friend. Fated to come back together. I mean, it has all the right tropes."

Anna glares. "Carlie. *No.*"

Carlie's already typing into her phone. "Too late. It's *plot bunnying.*"

"Christ." Anna pinches the bridge of her nose.

Vivian hums. "I mean, technically, *we* made fate happen. *We* meddled."

"Hey," Lily gasps, pointing at herself.

Quinn gasps. "Wait. Are *we* the main characters, then?"

"I mean, at some point, right?" Vivian's right shoulder shrugs.

Anna groans, shoving at my chest. "See what you've done?"

I grin. "What I've done is *win.*"

And speaking of winning...

I clear my throat and lean in, serious as hell. "Since I officially survived two months of book club exposure—"

Anna snorts into her drink. "Barely."

"—and have now read more *romance novels* than any one man should—"

Carlie perks up. "Oh, are you admitting you loved them?"

I point aggressively. "That's not the point."

Quinn grins. "That's a total *yes*."

I ignore him. For now.

I sit up straighter, adjusting my nonexistent tie. "As I was saying... it's finally time."

Anna frowns, the crease between her eyebrows the most adorable thing ever. "Time for what?"

I flash my most dangerous grin. "The Dirty Bastards book club."

Vivian claps like a school girl. "Oh my God, it's happening?"

Quinn chokes on his drink. "Yessss, finally! I didn't want to ask. I knew you were so busy with the tour."

I nod. "Well, it's happening. Be ready, Quinn. The first official Dirty Bastards meeting is going down as soon as we're back. Notify the boys."

Silence.

Then—

Quinn slowly leans in toward the camera, expression blank. "Oh, it's on. Welcome to the war, ladies. The Gents have entered the chat."

I squint. "What? No. I want a book club."

Quinn doesn't blink. "You want a war."

Anna hums, shaking her head knowingly. "Just roll with it."

I cross my arms. "You don't even know what we're reading."

Quinn presses his fingertips to his chest, smiling like the fucking diva he is. "Oh, it doesn't matter what we'll be reading, Price. As long as we have tournaments. What do we judge? Hottest annotations?"

Anna gasps, delighted. Then, she turns to me, her eyes turning absolutely devilish. "Oh, my God, yes."

Why does that look like I'm doomed?

"What—" I spit out.

Quinn holds up a fistful of pink glitter gel pens. "I've been waiting for this moment my entire life."

Carlie, practically vibrating with excitement. "Oh, I'm coming to that meeting."

Tasia nods. "Same."

Lily grins. "Oh, I wouldn't miss it for the world."

I blink. "Wait. Why are the Dirty Bitches are coming?"

Anna pats my thigh. "Because we all want to watch you suffer."

I gape at her. "Babe."

She just shrugs, smirking. "I go where the power is."

Quinn winks. "And the power is mine now."

And that's when I realize.

I may have made a mistake.

Anna giggles and tackles me onto the bed.

The last thing the OG Dirty B's see before the call cuts is me *cackling* while Anna puts me in a headlock—then makes me pay in all the *best* ways.

Two days later, we're at the venue, and I'm feeling *extra* reckless.

I have been trying to get Anna on stage for *weeks*.

I have literally tried *everything*.

Bribery. Teasing. *Sexual favors.* (Those were my favorite, by the way.)

Nothing has worked, though, and we're running out of time.

Seriously, I've pulled *every trick* in the book.

I tried the old *"just test the mic for me, Ace."* She walked away.

I suggested a "casual backstage duet." She *laughed in my face.*

I even hit her with the *"but what if the band gets food poisoning, Ace? What then?"* She told me to learn piano.

But tonight?

Tonight I have one last move.

One last shot to get her on this stage.

And I'm about to play dirty.

This is the Hail Mary of "get my girlfriend to stop *cowarding out* of her own fucking talent."

And yeah, I said cowarding out. I love this woman, but she's a *damn stubborn menace.*

I tighten the tuning peg on my guitar, casting a glance at the side-stage. Anna's there, arms crossed, *watching me.* She thinks I don't notice, but I do. I always do.

And the best part?

I see it.

The *want.*

The *almost.*

She's so damn close.

I step up to the mic. The crowd is electric tonight, the buzz in the air thick enough to feel in my veins.

She's gonna kill me, but here goes.

"This next song," I say, voice rough from hours of singing, "means a lot to me. It's the song that changed everything. It's been a while since I sang it, though. And —" I pause, my lips twitching as I find Anna side-stage. Arms crossed. Brow raised. Fully aware of *exactly* where this is going.

She shakes her head. *Don't you dare.*

Oh, I *dare.*

"And tonight, I wanna sing it the way it was always *meant* to be sung."

The crowd erupts, some already anticipating what's coming. It's been a long time and they've been changing for it.

Anna's eyes *narrow* like she's about to lunge for me, but I hold out my hand, challenging her.

"Come sing it with me, Ace—because yes, *I see you.* I've always seen you."

It's her song. Her question to a stupid teenage boy who was too scared to answer her back.

She wrote it when she thought I didn't see her. When she thought I never would.

Her lips part. She *blinks.*

Before she can overthink it, before she can take it back—Anna *steps* onto the stage. She's stepping into the spotlight she was always meant to have, and I get to stand beside her this time.

And holy shit, I've never seen anything more beautiful in my life.

The crowd's screaming is *deafening*, but all I can hear is the *thunder* in my chest.

She takes a slow step forward, then another.

Oh, fuck me, she's really doing it.

I actually forget how to *breathe*.

I *definitely* forget how to hold my guitar.

The entire stadium could explode, and I wouldn't notice.

Because all I see is her.

Walking toward me.

Joining me.

And my heart?

Absolutely fucking gone.

And I swear to God, time *fucking stops*.

Every nerve in my body *electrocutes*.

She's coming to me.

She's doing this.

That's my girl.

My fingers tighten on my guitar. I have performed in stadiums, I have faced down angry producers, I have survived the Dirty Bitches, but nothing—nothing—has ever terrified me more than the idea of fucking this moment up for her.

When she reaches me, her eyes sparkle with emotion, but she shakes her head. "God, you're so dramatic."

"And you wouldn't have it any other way." I grin back.

And when she takes my hand, when she turns toward me, when she gives me *that look*—

It feels like fate all over again.

The End. 

&

Loving *The One Night Stand Club*? YAY!

Then get ready to witness absolute *chaos* because *Dirty Games* is coming!

Quinn and Nico's rivalry-to-lovers romance is about to bring you:

- Explosive chemistry (and we mean *explosive* —Quinn is a menace)
- Book club battles (because Quinn will not let Nico win)
- Unfinished business (aka, that *one* time they hooked up, and Nico ghosted)
- So. Much. Banter.

Quinn has always been the biggest personality in the room. Loud. Chaotic. Impossible to ignore.

And now?

Nico is taking up space—his space—in the new *Dirty Bastards* book club.

And worse?

The bastard **refuses** to acknowledge the sparks still burning between them.

But Quinn? Oh, he's playing to win.

See ya soon, Dirty B! The games are just getting started.

About the Author

Carissa Knight writes steamy, emotional romcoms where second chances get messy, feelings get avoided (until they don't), and unresolved tension simmers for pages. Her books are built on tropes she loves deeply—especially second chances, forced proximity, and the occasional enemies-to-lovers situation that gets *way too personal*.

Though her romcom debut is recent, Carissa's no newbie to storytelling. Writing since 2010 as **Carissa Andrews**, she's an **international bestselling** and **award-winning author** of paranormal and urban fantasy. Now, under her romcom pen name, she's leaning into the chaos of love, heartbreak, and hot dumbasses who absolutely *do not* have their lives together.

Based in Minnesota, she writes for the readers who crave big emotions, found family, and characters who take way too long to admit they're in love.

Learn more at: romcomcarissa.com

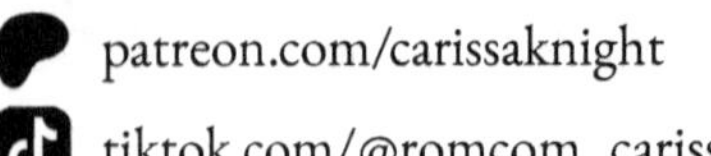

patreon.com/carissaknight

tiktok.com/@romcom_carissa